December 1976.

ON HUMAN FINERY

Fashions for 1883

ON HUMAN FINERY

Quentin Bell

New edition revised and enlarged

1976
THE HOGARTH PRESS
LONDON

Published by
The Hogarth Press Ltd
40 William IV Street
London WC2N 4DF

Clarke, Irwin & Co. Ltd
Toronto

ISBN 0 7012 0411 7

Design and production in association with
Book Production Consultants, Cambridge

Printed in Great Britain by
Butler & Tanner Ltd, Frome and London

Contents

Illustrations

Colour Plates

Between pages 152 and 153

Foreword

This is not a work of erudition but of theory; the reader who seeks erudition will find an abundance in other works of which those mentioned below form but a small sample. Works of a purely theoretical nature are less common, but many scholars have given us their conclusions together with their observations.

It will be found that I have made a decided attack upon the theoretical construction of several writers and, amongst others, those scholars to whom I am most profoundly indebted. I must confess, though it can but aggravate the charge of ingratitude, that in many cases my debt has been not only of that kind which arises from the necessities of ignorance, but also of a direct nature: an author may stimulate or instruct even when he fails to convince.

The following works have been consulted:

Binder, P., *The Peacock's Tail*. London, Harrap, 1958.

Boehn, Max von, *Modes and Manners*, tr. J. Joshua. London, Harrap, 1932. *Modes and Manners in the 19th Century*, tr. M. Edwardes. London, Dent, 1909.

Boucher, François, *Twenty Thousand Years of Fashion*. New York, Abrams, 1966.

Buck, Anne M., *Victorian Costume and Costume Accessories*. London, Jenkins, 1961; New York, Nelson.

Cunnington, C. Willett, *English Women's Clothing in the 19th Century*. London, Faber, 1937; New York, Yoseloff. *English Women's Clothing in the Present Century*. London, Faber, 1952; New York, Yoseloff.

Cunnington, C. Willett and Phillis, *Handbooks of Mediaeval Costume*. London, Faber, 1952. *Handbooks of English Costume in the 16th, 17th, 18th, and 19th Centuries*. London, Faber, 1954, 1955, 1957, 1959.

Flugel, J. C., *The Psychology of Clothes*. London, Hogarth Press, 1930; New York, Int. Univ. Press.

Gernsheim, Alison, *Fashion and Reality 1840–1914*. Faber, 1974.

Gibbs-Smith, Charles, *The Fashionable Lady in the 19th Century*. H.M.S.O., 1960.

Holland, Vyvyan, *Fashion Plates 1770–1899*. London, Batsford, 1955.

Konig, Rene, *The Restless Image, a sociology of Fashion*, tr. T. Bradley. London, Allen & Unwin, 1973.

Langley Moore, Doris, *The Woman in Fashion*. London, Batsford, 1949. *Fashion Through Fashion Plates, 1771–1970*. London, Ward Lock, 1971. *The Child in Fashion*. London, Batsford, 1953.

Laver, James, *Taste and Fashion* (revised). London, Harrap, 1948. *A Concise History of Costume*. London, Thames & Hudson, 1969; New York, Abrams.

Nystrom, Paul, *The Economics of Fashion*. New York, Ronald Press, 1928.

Poiret, Paul, *En Habillant l'Epoque*. Paris, Grasset, 1930.

Price, Julius M., *Dame Fashion*. London, Low Marston, 1913.

Roach, M. E. and Eicher, J. B., *Dress, Adornment and the Social Order*. New York, Wiley, 1965; Chichester, Wiley, 1970. *The Visible Self*. New Jersey, Prentice-Hall, 1973.

Rudofsky, Bernard, *The Unfashionable Human Body*. London, Hart-Davis, 1972; New York, Doubleday, 1974.

Webb, W. M., *The Heritage of Dress*. London, Richards, 1907.

White, Palmer, *Poiret*. Studio Vista, 1973.

(In footnotes it is generally assumed that works have been published in London.)

Grateful mention should also be made of Willett Cunnington's theoretical work, *Why Women Wear Clothes* (London, Faber, 1941), of Mr Gerald Heard's *Narcissus, an Anatomy of Clothes* (London, Kegan Paul, 1938), and above all of Thorstein Veblen's *The Theory of the Leisure Class*, all quotations from which are taken from the 1949 edition published by George Allen & Unwin.

I have the greatest pleasure in acknowledging the assistance that I have received in obtaining illustrations from the British Museum, the National Gallery, the National Portrait Gallery, *The Times*, the proprietors of *Punch* and of *Vogue*, the Ronald Press Co. of New York, Flammarion of Paris, and am particularly beholden to Messrs Harrods who have been most kind, also to my sister Mrs David Garnett who has allowed me to make use of her large collection of fashion plates.

Preface to the Second Edition

This book was written in 1945 and was published two years later. My publishers have offered me a second chance to present my views on dress to the public and, better still, will allow me many more illustrations which, in a work devoted to one of the visual arts, is a decided advantage. At the same time I have an opportunity to make certain additions and corrections and to reform a prose style which, I am shocked to find, stands in great need of amendment.

This is in fact a rather different book from that which I first wrote. It is a good deal longer, much better illustrated and, I hope, better written than its predecessor.

To some extent the first edition was a polemic. I advanced my own theory concerning clothes and fashion, and in so doing attempted to demolish, every other book on the subject that I had read with the exception of Veblen's *Theory of the Leisure Class*. Nor was I ready to accept Veblen without a good many substantial modifications. Now when an author produces a second edition of a controversial work, and when that edition contains a fair number of additions and corrections, the reader may fairly suspect that the writer has shifted his ground, that he finds certain positions untenable and certain generalisations invalid. Can such an accusation be made in this case?

It can. I am not a scholar; my arguments are based upon the researches of other people and, during the past thirty years, the literature of fashion has presented me with facts which have made me reconsider some of my former statements; at the same time fashion itself has developed in a number of surprising ways and some of the developments have obliged me to modify certain generalisations.

The reader who compares the first with the second edition will discover that I now have a rather better understanding of the role of Puritan dress in the English Civil War. He will find that I have had to revise my views a little in considering the development of costume during the first forty years of the present century, that I have had to take into account the history of fashion in the period 1945–1970, and that this, in turn, has led me to a completely new speculation as to the probable development of fashion in the future. He may notice that an inaccurate statement concerning the dress of children has been corrected, and may guess that this results from a reading of Mrs Langley Moore's book on this subject. He will see also that I have recast and in a large measure corrected my previous remarks on the relationship of fashion to the fine arts. My observations on this subject, because they lead me rather far from the subject of human finery, are put into an appendix. I have created another appendix which is in effect a short conspectus of the fashions of the past six hundred years; this appendix is not intended for scholars but for those who may not have a very clear picture of the development of European clothes during this period, a development to which I allude constantly in my text. Two other appendices have been removed, one because I am assured that it is based upon misinformation, the other because the substance of what I say is included in an earlier chapter.

But none of these alterations affects my main argument. The fact that I am now preparing this new edition is in itself a proof that I believe that I have a valid case. Indeed it seems to me that the weight of recent scholarship and of recent events shows very clearly that we can only understand the history of dress by an application of Veblen's theories, and that fashion can only be understood if we admit the capital importance of the class structure.

Many new works dealing with the theory of fashion will be found listed in a brief and by no means exhaustive bibliography; but I would like to express my indebtedness to a few which have appeared within the last thirty years and have had a large effect upon this volume. I cannot deny myself the pleasure of mentioning *The Woman in Fashion* by Mrs Langley Moore which was published in 1949. In this beautifully written and beautifully illustrated book the authoress, armed with an erudition to which I cannot aspire, and informed by an attitude to fashion which is almost completely opposed to mine, arrived quite independently at a theoretical position very close to my own, and leaves me with the comfortable conviction that the big battalions of learning are on my side. I would like also to mention, but for a rather different reason, a work from the same hand, *Fashion through Fashion Plates*, and with it Alison Gernsheim's *Fashion and Reality*; both these works, excellent in themselves, confront us with the main problem in this field of study, the problem of evidence.

Clothes wear out; they are cut up and altered, and we have very few specimens that are more than two hundred years old. Even when we do have good specimens they are likely to be, not the clothes that ordinary people wore every day, but particularly fine dresses, as for instance wedding dresses or some particularly smart evening dress (which is usually supposed to have been worn at the Waterloo Ball). In other words we have that which is not typical. We have therefore to reply upon the image; but images are misleading. To suppose, for instance, that Lely's portraits of the ladies of the court of Charles II, or David's pictures of the leaders of fashion at the end of the eighteenth century, give a fair notion of what the passer-by would probably have seen in the streets of London or Paris would, almost certainly, be a mistake. Such pictures are useful to the historian as a caricature is useful; it is evidence from which we may make intelligent deductions but is not, in itself, reliable.

The fashion plate, although designed to give its purchaser an idea of what is being or soon will be worn, does not give us a picture of reality; as Mrs Langley Moore points out, it belongs to a fictitious world, prettier than life, and again this is the kind of evidence that has to be used with discretion. Alison Gernsheim's very useful work does take us a step nearer to reality; but photographs can be as misleading as pictures. The posed photograph of 120 years ago was the equivalent of the painted portrait. The sitter dressed in his or her best, sat, or rather was propped into a becoming attitude and the image was carefully touched up. It is only with the advent of the snapshot that we find something like a reliable document.

What one would like would be a window through which we could look into the past and there see men and women of all ages and all classes working, shopping, and amusing themselves. Thus we might learn not only what clothes were worn but, and this is something of capital importance, how they were worn; in what manner clothes affected posture and what habits of movement and carriage they dictated to their wearers. No evidence could be more enlightening or more fascinating, if only such a thing were possible.

And of course it is perfectly possible. The window into the past is there waiting for someone to draw the curtains. There are, in various archives, thousands and tens of thousands of miles of film, news films, films of fashion parades, documentaries, dramas of contemporary life and so on. For three-quarters of a century the material for a really authoritative survey of fashion has been accumulating, and the material for the past fifty years must be abundant. The editorial problem would arise not from any lack of material but from an embarrassment of riches. The technical problems of reproducing old film are by no means insurmountable, and all that is needed is a little energy, a little drive, and a not very large sum of money. Alas I am deficient in all these qualities. I have tried indeed, but tried in vain to enlist the aid of students and the capital of industrialists. But one day such a film will be made and it will be a major contribution to the study of costume.

A quite different aspect of the search for evidence is presented by those who, looking to the present rather than to the past, have considered the subject of costume as a branch of sociology or anthropology. Here the major contribution has come from the United States and it has been a valuable and important aid to our understanding of the subject. I have been particularly impressed by *The Visible Self* and by the extremely useful compilation of articles dealing with the sociology of fashion published under the title *Dress Adornment and the Social Order*; both works result from the very fruitful collaboration of Professor Mary Ellen Roach of the University of Wisconsin and Professor Joanne B. Eicher of Michigan State University.

I would like to thank these authors for being so informative and so stimulating; in the preparation of this second edition they have helped me to sharpen my ideas and, on occasion, to correct them. I would like also to renew the thanks which I expressed in my first volume to individuals, and museums, who again have been most kind.

1
Sartorial Morality

'No one finds difficulty in assenting to the commonplace that the greater part of the expenditure incurred by all classes for apparel is incurred for the sake of respectable appearance rather than for the protection of the person. And probably at no other point is the sense of shabbiness so keenly felt as it is if we fall short of the standard set by social usage in this matter of dress. It is true of dress in even a higher degree than of most other items of consumption, that people will undergo a very considerable degree of privation in the comforts or the necessaries of life in order to afford what is considered a decent amount of wasteful consumption; so that it is by no means an uncommon occurrence, in an inclement climate, for people to go ill clad in order to appear well dressed. And the commercial value of the goods used for clothing in any modern community is made up to a much larger extent of the fashionableness, the reputability of the goods than of the mechanical service which they render in clothing the person of the wearer. The need of dress is eminently a "higher" or spiritual need.'

THORSTEIN VEBLEN,
The Theory of the Leisure Class

Although *The Theory of the Leisure Class* is undoubtedly the most valuable contribution yet made to the philosophy of clothes, Veblen has been strangely neglected by our writers on dress; his works contain a challenge which, in England at all events, has been ignored. In this book I want to use Veblen as I think he ought to be used and, with this end in view, I have not hesitated to restate much that will be familiar to his readers. To them it will be obvious that, although I have attempted to develop and at some points to contradict this great man, his teachings provide my point of departure and inform all my arguments. I have found it convenient to expose his ideas as though they were my own and to reserve for a final chapter a discussion of those points at which there is a sensible divergence of views between us. It must however be said at once that, although Veblen is capable of talking nonsense, and difficult nonsense at that, and although some of his generalisations have been falsified by later events, still, no student of costume can possibly afford not to read him.

The economists, who have realised something of the greatness of Veblen, tend, I think, to neglect his theory of dress and indeed any theory of dress, and to see in the subject little save a vain peering into bonnet shops and museum cases, a vent for the interminable vapourings of Carlyle's Teufelsdröckh. Indeed the study of dress does not quite lie within their province; it belongs rather to sociology. And yet even the sociologists, in Britain, seem to leave it to the historians who seem indifferent to sociology or, in the United States, to sociologists who do not bother about history. But the study of clothes is of capital importance in any consideration of human behaviour (whether sociological or historical) and it is one of Veblen's great virtues that he saw, as Ruskin had seen before him, the importance of what he calls the 'higher or spiritual needs' and the inadequacy, in any complete account of social conduct, of the concept of 'economic man'.

That concept, or perhaps one ought to say the popular version of that concept, is in part true, in that we can point to a great many human transactions in which men respond to economic pressures with predictable regularity, so that it is possible to calculate quite exactly the manner in which a market will react to circumstances, and it will be found that there are situations in which men function almost as money-making machines. And yet, at the same time it is obviously true that the criteria of economic gain will often be dismissed or forgotten. This must always have been obvious to anyone with the slightest knowledge of history (it was very clear to Carlyle), and it will be generally allowed not only that the hero and the saint can be indifferent to the appetites which regulate the market place, but also that in moments of deep communal emotion the heroic or saintly emotions will be shared by a majority, perhaps even by an entire nation. But because this sort of thing happens only in moments of great national or sectarian enthusiasm, it tends to be separated from the general run of day-to-day history and in some sort discounted. When the ideological ferment is over, humanity returns to the familiar business of money-making and money-taking, and the old economic laws reassert themselves.

But when we consider the question of whether a black tie should be worn with a dinner jacket, or whether heels should be high or low, we are a good long way from the passion of the hero or the ecstasies of the saint; indeed we are well within the area of everyday life. The seeming triviality of such questions, the virtual impossibility of linking our sartorial decisions with the grand spiritual passions of mankind, make clothes not less but more important to those who seek to understand their fellow men (and themselves). We are dealing here not with abnormal, but with normal behaviour, and when we begin to reflect upon it we discover that our normal behaviour is crazy. Veblen was the first to show just how insane, from a rational economic point of view, are the decisions that men have taken and continue to take in this department of life. The study of clothes, as he saw, is a study of monstrosities and absurdities. It is, as I have said, a borderline science, important to the historian in that it exhibits in a pure form the pursuit of status, and particularly interesting to the art historian in that here, if anywhere, we can trace a direct relationship between aesthetic and social feelings.

To this we may add that a major part of the study of clothes is concerned with those variations of aesthetic sentiment which we call 'fashion'. Here the charm of the subject lies precisely in its ephemeral nature; in sociological studies fashion plays the role which has been allotted to *Drosophila*, the fruit fly, in the science of genetics. Here at a glance we can perceive phenomena so mobile in their response to varying stimuli, so rapid in their mutation, that the deceptive force of inertia, which overlays and obscures most other manifestations of human activity, is reduced to a minimum.

The evidence is moreover abundant, not only without but within. We have all known the pleasure and the pains of attire. When Veblen describes the needs of dress as 'higher' or 'spiritual' we can verify his assertion from our own experiences. Who does not appreciate the expense, the inconvenience, perhaps even the discomfort of that which they feel themselves compelled to wear?

> 'But you can't wear those shoes to go to the Browns' party.'
> 'My other shoes hurt me.'
> 'I'm sorry about that but you can't possibly wear *those* shoes.'
> 'Why?'
> 'People would look at you.'
> 'Oh, very well.'

No doubt there is a valiant minority which does wear those shoes, which is not afraid to be 'looked at', but in the great majority of cases, and cases of this kind have been occurring for hundreds of years, the uncomfortable shoes are worn and the decencies are observed even at the price of a severe blister.

In obeying custom we undergo distresses which are, from a strictly economic point of view, needless and futile. We do so for the sake of something that transcends our own immediate interests. That which we may call our 'baser nature' may protest against the tyranny of tailors and dressmakers; but their commands are continually urged upon us by our sense of propriety. There are some who can rejoice in fashion, others may detest it or regard it as a more or less harmless nuisance; but as any photograph or reasonably faithful image of any gathering of human beings will show, there will be very few who are ready positively to defy the laws of custom.

> Dress [says Lord Chesterfield] is a very foolish thing; and yet it is a very foolish thing for a man not to be well dressed, according to his rank and way of life; and it is so far from being a disparagement to any man's understanding, that it is rather a proof of it, to be as well dressed as those whom he lives with: the difference in this case, between a man of sense and a fop, is, that the fop values himself upon his dress; and the man of sense laughs at it, at the same time that he knows that he must not neglect it; there are a thousand foolish customs of this kind, which, not being criminal, must be complied with, and even cheerfully, by men of sense. Diogenes the Cynic was a wise man for despising them, but a fool for showing it.*

This very nicely expresses the attitude of what one might call the sceptical conformist, of him who laughs at conventions and yet obeys them. Where a convention is established it is usually wise to accept it. An ill-dressed man is in many situations disadvantaged; girls will slight him, he will find it hard to obtain credit, there are strong prudential reasons for dressing well enough, at all events, to avoid adverse notice. There are also moral considerations which have the same effect; often it is the friends, the companions, the wife of the badly dressed man who suffer most from his shortcomings. And so it is possible to imagine a person whose own appearance was a matter of complete indifference to himself but who nevertheless dressed well enough to silence ordinary criticism simply and entirely on a calculation of the advantages that such a course of action could bring to him and to his friends. It is possible but it is not easy, for is there anyone who feels no emotion at all, no scintilla of reassurance and self-satisfaction when he knows that his appearance is so *comme il faut* as to defy criticism? There are few, I think, and fewer still who can without a qualm confront a giggling public which considers his appearance wholly ridiculous, even though he well knows that it is the public, not he, which is being absurd.

We are concerned here with a number of feelings, prudential, ethical and aesthetic, and with the workings of what one might call a sartorial

* To his son, November 19, 1745

conscience. There is indeed a whole system of morality attached to clothes and more especially to fashion, a system different from and, as we shall see, frequently at variance with that contained in our laws and our religion. To go to the theatre with five days' beard, to attend a ball in faultless evening dress (mark the adjective) but with your braces outside, instead of within your white waistcoat, to scatter ink on your spats, to reverse your tie, these things are not incompatible with moral or theological teaching, the law takes no cognizance of such acts. Nevertheless such behaviour will excite the strongest censure in 'good society'. Nor, such is the perversity of social arrangements, will the impeccable *tenue* which is (or used to be) demanded of a gentleman at a hunt ball produce at all a favourable reaction at those deafening celebrations of pop music which delight the young. In 'good society' it is not however sheer lunatic eccentricity such as the absence of trousers or a wig worn back to front which excites the strongest censure; far worse are those subtler forms of incorrect attire: the 'wrong' tie, the 'bad' hat, the 'loud' skirt, the 'cheap' scent, or the flamboyant checks of the overdressed vulgarian. Here the censure excited is almost exactly comparable to that occasioned by dishonourable conduct.

And, let me repeat, it is not simply the judgment of society which acts upon the individual. Our confusion when, having sat for two hours on the platform of a public meeting, we discover that we have been wearing odd socks, our still worse confusion when we find that our flies have been undone (even though nothing of any consequence has been revealed) has something of the quality of guilt. Indeed, I think it may frequently happen here, as in other moral situations, that the offender may be not simply the worst but in fact the only sufferer. A rebellious collar stud, a minute hole in a stocking may ruin an evening without ever being observed by the company at large. Our clothes are too much a part of us for most of us ever to be entirely indifferent to their condition: it is as though the fabric were indeed a natural extension of the body, or even of the soul. 'A sense of being perfectly well dressed', a lady is reported as saying to Emerson, 'gives a feeling of inward tranquillity which religion is powerless to bestow.' In the same way Nietzsche has said that a pretty woman, conscious of looking her best, never caught a cold however scanty her gown; the saying is poetically if not literally true. We know that female prisoners, isolated from mankind, sustain their morale by the use of cosmetics, much as empire builders used to dine in boiled shirts although separated by two thousand leagues of desert from the next black tie; in the same way a uniform is known to exert a powerful effect upon conduct, and its careful upkeep is accounted a most important part of the duty of a soldier.

So strong is the impulse of sartorial morality that it is difficult, in praising clothes, not to use adjectives such as 'right', 'good', 'correct', 'unimpeachable' or 'faultless', which belong properly to the discussion of conduct while, in discussing moral shortcomings, we tend very naturally to fall into the language of dress and speak of a person's behaviour as being 'shabby', 'shoddy', 'threadbare', 'down at heel', 'botched' or 'slipshod'.

It is pertinent, therefore, to ask to what extent the standards of sartorial morality conform to the other accepted standards of society such as utility and beauty. There can be no doubt that clothes can and sometimes do meet a certain number of strictly utilitarian needs. In colder climates they control the temperature of the body and in most climates they have, through use, become indispensable for this purpose. In the same way, when once they have been established, they become necessary to modesty (an ambiguous concept to which I shall presently return). They may also be considered as an aid to beauty (another ambiguous term) but the statement holds good whether we are thinking of the manner in which a sculptor uses drapery in order to describe form or to suggest movement, or whether we have in mind the glittering decorations and revelations of the show girl – either way clothes can be used to intensify emotion. Finally, clothes have industrial uses, they not only shield us from dirt and danger, they also provide a vehicle in which we carry our belongings. Ideally it would be possible to design clothes which were not only beautiful, but comfortable and useful. But in the history of clothes it will usually be found that 'beauty' is considered more or less incompatible with efficiency. We do not wear fine clothes for industrial purposes, and when we do 'dress up' the chances are that we shall sacrifice both comfort and convenience. Indeed in certain epochs the words 'rational' and 'sensible' have almost come to be words of abuse where dress is concerned.

There is one characteristic of the dress of almost every society in almost every age which must always prevent it from being perfectly useful or entirely becoming. The purpose of custom is not to distinguish, but to classify. In almost any society clothes tell us the sex of the wearer and usually classify men and women into adults and children; further distinctions of class, occupation, faith and rank are common to most cultures. All these categories are established by the character of the dress which, in addition, may be obliged to conform to a general aesthetic pattern by being 'in fashion'. In so far as costume is a matter of custom it is of its very nature opposed to any kind of eccentricity, which is by definition a breach of custom. Although there are circumstances in which some individuals may take an initiative, it will be found that such innovations are themselves governed by a larger pattern; clothes are imposed on a class or nation without reference to the needs of the individual. Whether those needs be governed by the desire to look as beautiful as possible or to have clothes which will be wholly convenient, they will be subordinated to the demands of custom or of fashion. Uniformity must be incompatible with functional form inasmuch as the needs of any given individual will be different from those of any other individual; but in fact, so far from approaching a condition in which they can be adapted to suit everyone, sartorial standards do not provide even a generalised level of beauty or utility. It is not that some individuals are required to sacrifice something of their personal comfort or personal beauty in order that a generalised standard may be imposed upon all, but (in most historical situations) everybody without exception is expected to undergo certain kinds of discomfort and disadvantage, and this not for anyone's practical advantage but, as one may say, for the advantage of an ideal. Clothes hurt us in a pecuniary, a physical, an aesthetic and frequently a moral sense; they are (very often) expensive, unhealthy, ugly and immodest.

It will be seen therefore that a conflict must exist between the practical needs of the individual and what we can call the 'futile'* demands of sartorial morality.

The grievances of the individual usually arise from the fact that being well dressed is always an expensive business. It does not usually occur to the consumer that much of his expenditure is, strictly speaking, unnecessary; that is to say that it is incurred for wholly spiritual reasons, for what is called 'respectability'. But society, through its censors, is more various, more persistent and more violent in its strictures.

> Moreover the Lord saith, Because the daughters of Zion are haughty, and walk with stretched forth necks and wanton eyes, walking and mincing as they go, and making a tinkling with their feet: Therefore the Lord will smite with a scab the crown of the head of the daughters of Zion, and the Lord will discover their secret parts. In that day the Lord will take away the bravery of their tinkling ornaments about their feet, and their cauls, and their round tires like the moon, the chains, and the bracelets, and the mufflers, the bonnets, and the ornaments of the legs, and the headbands, and the tablets, and the earrings, the rings, and nose jewels, the changeable suits of apparel, and the mantles, and the wimples, and the crisping pins, the glasses, and the fine linen, and the hoods, and the vails. And it shall

* Futile only in the sense of being non-utilitarian and from an economic point of view wasteful.

> come to pass, that instead of sweet smell there shall be stink; and instead of a girdle a rent; and instead of well set hair baldness; and instead of a stomacher a girding of sackcloth; and burning instead of beauty.*

There is no reason to suppose that Isaiah was the first moralist to attack human finery. He had many imitators particularly amongst the Christian teachers. The Church of Rome (despite the fact that she has herself shown remarkable talents as a modiste) was a persistent critic throughout the Middle Ages and already, in the sixth century, St Gregory of Tours was loud in his complaints.†

The pagan philosophers were only a little less violent than the doctors of the Church; sumptuary laws are as old as Solon, and the indecent extravagance and luxury of the Roman Society forms a constant theme of republican critics. As a rule the critics of dress have been men and their criticisms have been directed against women; but not always. The French defeat at Crécy was ascribed by contemporary moralists to the indecency and extravagance of the costume of the French nobility.‡ In the same way Puritan criticism of fashionable dress has been as much concerned with men as with women.

Second in time, but not in vehemence, have been the medical critics who saw in dress a danger to the body no less great than that which had appeared to menace the soul. Ambroise Paré (1517–90) was one of the first to exclaim at the practice of mortifying the flesh with corsets of steel; there may easily have been others, for corsets have been a fashion and an affliction of both sexes since the time of Petrarch.§ The very dangerous effects produced by any mechanism which distorts the shape of the abdomen and compresses the thorax have been a constant subject of medical criticism in the West, as the effects of footbinding have been in the East. Very décolleté blouses have been condemned as an invitation to pneumonia, and in the late nineteenth and early twentieth centuries long trains were denounced as being unhygienic. Indeed at this period the volume of medical criticism was so great that positive efforts at reform were attempted.

Dress has ever been the despair of the political economist and the administrator. Fashions are condemned because of their extravagances because they create industries only to destroy them, because they are worn by the wrong people and proper distinctions of rank are obliterated. But, since the Middle Ages the usual complaint, and that which recurs again

---

*Isaiah, iii, 16–24. †See von Boehn, I, 182. ‡von Boehn, I, 218.

§*Ibid.*, 192. See Stella Mary Newton, *Health Art and Reason*, 1974; also Rudofsky, *The Unfashionable Human Body*, New York, 1974.

and again, is that fashion does not favour home industries. It is on this ground that legislators have usually sought to direct its course. Many laws have also been passed which had as their object the maintenance of clear distinctions in dress as between different classes.

It is not until the nineteenth century that we find aesthetic critics of dress. Until then, or at least until the middle of the eighteenth century, artists seem to have accepted the prevailing fashion, whatever it might be, with ease and indeed with enthusiasm. It was in England that the Pre-Raphaelites and G. F. Watts began not only to criticise but to propose reforms, and it is here that we find the fashions of the age condemned, for the first time, as ugly. Again it was in England and the United States that the first protests were made by those who found the fashions of the age absurdly unpractical, and these were later to be joined by humanitarians who objected to the use of certain kinds of plumage and fur.

Finally it may be said that fashion has always been the butt of the humorist; its extravagances provoke his powers of caricature, his sense of fun, his indignation, his prurience. Every mode has been laughed at and abused in its time.

Need one add that the sermons and the censures, the protest and the ridicule of the centuries have produced negligible results. The critics have frequently been persons of distinction armed with the eloquence of indignation, and with all the force that is given to those who can invoke the powers of religion, morality and patriotism, and with all the weight that is supplied by good feeling and good sense. Yet, nearly always, they have been worsted. At best they can win temporary victories, holding actions; fashion always triumphs in the end. Nor has the style of dress changed in response to the opposition; we repeatedly find the satirist attacking a nascent mode which continues unaffected to its apogee, undeterred (perhaps even assisted) by the clamour that it has provoked.

It may be said that these are but the trivial victories of an essentially trivial conflict, with no bones broken and no one vitally affected. No doubt this has often been the case particularly in the history of fashion during the past two hundred years. But until the emergence of modern capitalism every civilised country has enacted sumptuary laws for the preservation of class distinctions, morality, thrift and industry. In Europe, since the beginning of the Middle Ages the number of these regulations has been prodigious. Attempts were made, first to restrain the consumer, and later, when that proved ineffectual, to regulate production and importation. The penalties were severe, adequate provision was made for enforcing the laws, which were frequently voted by large majorities in the corporate institutions of the age. Nothing was spared in the effort to curb fashion, but the history of sumptuary laws is a history of dead letters. All that remains today of the formidable body of legislation that was enacted by mediaeval Parliaments is a kind legal ghost: the regulations which still govern the dress of peers and peeresses when the Sovereign is being crowned.

The history of dress in Europe is the history of a serious and almost invincible social force which is frequently in conflict with the law of the land. The conflict is one between two inimical sentiments which exist, not only within the same societies but within the same persons, for we shall often find that the legislators were the first to break their own sumptuary laws. Nor should we too easily dismiss as prudes, or cranks, or killjoys, the enemies of fashion. We may not sympathise with Tolstoy who found in the tight jerseys of the 1880s an intolerably exciting invitation to lust, nevertheless there is an ambiguity, a moral equivocation about those societies which, while assenting in theory to the idea of feminine purity, encourage girls of marriageable age publicly to exhibit and indeed dishonestly to advertise their charms. Nor can we simply dismiss those who claimed that women were condemned by social pressure to wear clothes which were dangerous, unhealthy, and in the opinion of many artists, very ugly. Still less can we deny the importance of the observation of those feminists who perceived that while women were constricted, hampered and hobbled by their finery they were effectively enchained, all the more so in that they were taught by society to rejoice in their fashionable fetters. The case against the fashion is always a strong one; why is it then that it never results in an effective verdict? Why is it that both public opinion and formal regulations are invariably set at nought while sartorial custom, which consists in laws that are imposed without formal sanctions, is obeyed with wonderful docility and this despite the fact that its laws are unreasonable, arbitrary and not infrequently cruel?

I hope to provide some kind of an answer to these questions in subsequent chapters. But first I must attempt to describe the nature, enactment and enforcement of these laws.

2
Sumptuosity

> 'Il y a, dans les décisions de la mode et des femmes, une sorte de provocation au bon sens qui est charmante et qui ne peut fâcher que les esprits chagrins.'
>
> PAUL POIRET

A morality of dress implies a set of values which enable us to perceive whether a garment be 'right' or 'wrong'. But here a confusion may arise for, although any given article of clothing may be good in isolation, when displayed for instance upon the shelves of a museum, the same garment may lose its virtue when placed in an unsuitable context. A smart head-dress such as that illustrated in Plate I is in itself an admirable confection, and it remains admirable within the context of fashions for the year 1785, but if worn with a bathing dress of the year 1974 it would strike the wrong note, as it would also if it had been worn twenty years after the time when it was first seen. Indeed the whole dress is designed for one kind of occasion and for a particular epoch; removed from its historical or occasional context a dress may still be admired but it may also appear out of place, absurd or out of fashion. It will be found that specialisation, both in the sense of a dress only being permissible within a given period and also in the sense of there being a multitude of contemporary styles for different social occasions, has become more and more a characteristic of European costume during the past five hundred years, and it is these two forms of context which will concern us when we come to study fashion. Here, however, I want to examine the merit of clothes in so far as it can be perceived in isolation, the virtue, that is to say, which resides in all fine clothes. In order to do this I require a word which will enable me to make it clear that I am not talking about fashionable dress. This is not so easy to find, for our notions of excellence in clothes have become very strongly associated with the idea of novelty, of the latest, the most up-to-date thing, so that we hardly have a term with which to describe the garments of all well-dressed people, fashionable or un-fashionable. 'Unfashionable' is in itself an unhelpful word for it suggests a failure to be in fashion, whereas it is often the case that fashion has not been the dressmaker's object. To call the toga or the mandarin's gown

PLATE I

Conspicuous Leisure

'chic' is to suggest a process of change which barely existed in ancient Rome or China; the clothes of the beefeater or the samurai are eminently respectable, precisely because they are not up to date; the tarboosh was never 'all the go' for it has never gone.

So many writers have failed to make this distinction and so have been led into uttering highly misleading statements that I, at the risk of being tedious, am going to labour the point.

Imagine then a ceremony for the conferment of degrees at the University of Coketown. It is a gay scene; here we have doctors in scarlet, the Chancellor, the Vice Chancellor and the pro-Vice Chancellor all gorgeous in green, gold and silver lace. The Mayor of Coketown is splendid in ermine and is adorned with official chains elaborately worked in precious metals suggestive of antiquity, by his side a furry personage bears a mace of great splendour. All these are sumptuous figures and so too, despite his relative sobriety of aspect, is the chief of police, all sparkling and neat in silver buttons and snow-white gloves.

Not one of these ornamental figures is fashionable; by this I mean that they are intensely conservative in their dress, they are bound by an immutable custom and quite unable to change their appearance. If the Vice Chancellor were to sport a large green feather upon his gold tasselled mortar board, or if any member of faculty were to improve his appearance with a yard of tulle or a cluster of pearls, the result might, from a purely aesthetic point of view, be exquisite – in every other way it would be deplorable. Indeed if but one in the chief constable's constellation of buttons were to be omitted, or if it were to be replaced by some confection of blue glass or silver filigree, one would feel that law and order were overthrown.

But now look at the wives; Mrs Professor Hagfish, or the Vice-Chancellor's lady, or the proud mothers who come to see their offspring graduate (of the student body itself more shall be said later); look even at the neat pin-striped, well-waistcoated fathers, these too are sumptuous. The ladies in fact are very grand; they wear wreaths of roses upon their heads, their hair is – or at least was in the days when I attended such functions – rinsed to a becoming shade of blue, they sport pearls and gold, silks, satins, furs and high-class tweeds, their shoes are tight, their hats are high and their husbands (such as have not joined the academic procession), while less obviously gorgeous, are highly presentable. In fact these too are sumptuous. But their way of being sumptuous is a fashionable way. A green feather or a yard of tulle more or less on the blue rinse will cause no offence. The husbands are relatively free to vary the colours of their ties, and although there will be a certain degree of uniformity inasmuch as you are unlikely to see a green rinse amongst ladies or wellington boots amongst the gentlemen, still, if you go year after year to see successive generations graduate, you will notice that the ladies' skirts climb up and down, waists are attempted or abandoned, and even the gentlemen seem a shade less drab than they did thirty years ago. In short, while the academic element in the gathering is merely sumptuous the lay element is both sumptuous and fashionable.

Nor is the reason far to seek. The town (as opposed to the gown) is not a hierarchical body, indeed it is drawn from all walks of life and united only by a desire to rise worthily to the occasion. The University is hierarchical, it confers different kinds of degrees, it is served by different kinds of officers, and for each class in the academic establishment there is an appropriate form of dress. Coketown, it may be, is a relatively new foundation; nevertheless in its sartorial regulations it looks back to a mediaeval past, and one feels that it will cling to its symbolic decorations until they do indeed embody the tradition of centuries. But even if the academic dress were changed, as indeed the costume of the chief of police has been changed, still that alteration would not constitute fashionable change as I use the term. Fashion develops continuously as the result of a continuous public appetite for change; the producer offers novelties knowing that the consumer will probably accept them. When the uniform of the police changes it may be because policemen feel that they want to wear something rather more in line with current fashions, but the alteration will be made as the result of an administrative decision. And whereas a fashion never stops developing, but runs constantly towards extremes, a uniform, whether it be military, civilian or academic, remains for long periods unaltered.

Thus, at a degree ceremony, we find two different kinds of sumptuosity: the fashionable and the static. And yet (so hard it is ever to tell the exact truth about anything) there is an anomaly. A close scrutiny of Professor Hagfish will reveal the fact that his cap, his gown, his hood are static, in fact exactly like the regalia (if that be the word) worn by his grandfather at a degree ceremony in 1902. But the rest of Professor Hagfish is mobile. For observe: his socks, his shoes, his tie, his pullover, his jacket belong only to the present, his grandfather was a blacker, bleaker, more sober fellow. In fact the Professor exists at two levels; the outer shell is timeless, but the lower depths are fashionable.

The point that I have so laboriously been making is that all fashionable dress is in some degree sumptuous but there is a great deal of sumptuous dress which is not fashionable. I am here concerned with sumptuosity, whether fashionable or unfashionable, and by sumptuosity I mean those qualities in dress which in one way or another have provoked the respect and the admiration of mankind. It is as well to note in passing that I am speaking entirely of the clothes, not of those who wear them, for it will often happen that fine clothes are worn by one person in honour of another person. It is not the footman but his master whom we applaud when the livery is handsome. It will be seen therefore that sumptuous clothes, although they usually are worn by those who belong to a privileged class and perform no menial tasks, can also be worn by persons who, without belonging to a privileged class, lead an ornamental, as distinct from an industrial existence, usually, though not always, as the ministers of some wealthy employer. In this latter class we find flunkeys and other expensive menials, soldiers, priests and uniformed officials. In modern society many persons change their role from time to time and are sumptuously dressed only on special occasions. This is true even of the chief of police; it is much more true of the Mayor of Coketown, and of the academic dignitaries.

Now the obvious quality of all these classes is their wealth or the wealth that is spent in putting them into appropriate clothes; whatever form their costume may take it must be expensive, or at least must appear expensive. Even the new bachelor of arts must be adorned with fur; true it is but rabbit or nylon and the B.A. gown is hired for the day, still, symbolically, it is expensive and the embroidery of the Chancellor's gown is, we hope and trust, of veritable bullion.

But the manner in which wealth is displayed upon the person is often very oblique and by no means obvious at first sight. It is here that the analysis of what Veblen calls 'pecuniary canons of taste' is of the utmost value. Veblen has expressed the modes of pecuniary taste under three headings: *Conspicuous Consumption*, *Conspicuous Leisure*, and *Conspicuous Waste*, and to these I add a fourth category which I call *Conspicuous Outrage*. To understand the nature of sumptuous dress we must glance at each of these categories, without which, indeed, the history of clothes is not explicable.

Conspicuous Consumption. Let us start with the basic premise of the couturier – the human body. Can the human body consume in a conspicuous manner? Obviously it can and frequently does and it is interesting to find such consumption, that is to say a tremendous obesity, is much admired in many parts of Africa and Asia. The opposite tendency of feeling, which finds its most striking expression in feminine fashions, abhors bulk and exalts the skinny, twiggy, bony, positively anorectic skeletons of the rag trade. Oddly enough this loss of weight would seem also to involve great expense. It results not from poverty but from expensive treatments aimed at producing poverty's effect. In a world of which much is starving, vast sums which might be spent on making the thin fatter are devoted to making the fat thinner.

The second simplest and most obvious manner of displaying wealth is to take the greatest number of valuable objects and to attach them to the wearer's person.

Westermarck, in his history of human marriage, tells us that:

> A fully-equipped Santal belle ... carries two anklets and perhaps twelve bracelets, and a necklace weighing a pound, the total weight of ornaments on her person amounting to thirty-four pounds of bell metal–a greater weight ... than one of our drawing room belles could well lift. We may without much exaggeration, say with Grosse that the primitive man attaches to his body all the ornaments that he can get, and that he adorns all the parts of his body that can bear an ornament.'*

Plekhanov has pointed out that in a society which knows iron only as a rare and very valuable metal, iron is worn for its beauty just as, in a hunting community, evidence of prowess, as for instance the claws and feathers of the larger predators, will be thought beautiful.† Such valuations seem to be the result of a perfectly genuine aesthetic sentiment. Iron is truly felt to be the most becoming material with which to adorn the person; they are nevertheless subject to the variations of the market. The late Colonel Teed, who knew Africa well at the end of the last century, told me that there were areas in the interior of that continent where any woman who wished to present a respectable appearance wore on her person a prodigious quantity of blue beads; these were sold by Arab traders on the coast who brought their wares inland over a difficult and dangerous route. With the advent of the railway it became possible to import blue beads by the wagon-load. They at once became cheap and being cheap were considered nasty. Henceforward no respectable woman would wear such things.‡

Generally speaking, the naive exhibition of wealth is unusual in Western societies; it is comparable to those large-scale advertisements that are set upon hoardings; the intention is to impress the world at large. It is a method unsuited to a society where persons of the same class meet in privacy and in which a certain income is taken for granted. Thus, at a time when monarchs lived very much in the presence of an unsophisticated public, the wearing of full regalia was much commoner than it is

*Westermarck, *History of Human Marriage*, 1921, I, 498.

† Plekhanov, *Art and Social Life*, 1953, 27.

‡ A. and M. Strathern, *Self Decoration in Mt Hagen*, 1971, describe an almost exactly similar devaluation of traditional values in the interior of Borneo, where sea shells were used for ornament until it became possible to bring them from the coast in bulk; they have now been replaced by Australian currency.

today, when it is reserved for very large crowds and very important occasions. The mediaeval monarch, one imagines, had as it were to act out his role of kingship in full view of the public and for that purpose could hardly wear too many jewels, too much fur or precious metals. Today the more obvious forms of conspicuous consumption persist only in a few places, in the ceremonies of the older Churches, the stage, the cinema, and military operations of an ornamental character, etc. It persists also in a modified form, where individuals have achieved wealth in very humble surroundings, the world of Champagne Charlie and Diamond Jim and, it may be, of the well-oiled sheikhdoms of the Middle East. But if the ornate costume of the *nouveau riche*, intended as it is for the admiration of the vulgar, be transferred to a society more used to affluence, it will itself be accounted vulgar or 'loud'. It is indeed the special glory of the good Savile Row tailor that he achieves an effect of great expense by his very lack of flamboyance; the perfection of his cut is made manifest in its extreme discretion.

But a certain minimal display of wealth is usually considered essential; no excellence of cut, hue, or design will serve to redeem the sin of poverty. A cheap material cannot please, only 'good' materials are permissible, and these must be expensively worked. A 'good' tailor-made, that is to say expensive material worked by hand, is felt to have a virtue which we do not find even in the best products of the machine. In the same way nothing can compensate for the lack of 'real' products, 'real' pearls, 'real' silk, 'real' lace, 'real' mink, etc.; in other words the materials employed must be difficult to obtain or laborious to produce. The same standard of excellence is implicit in the costume of many European peasants; here the merit of the artefact resides, not in the value of the materials employed, but in the enormous amount of socially necessary labour time which has been devoted to the making of the product. Careful and laborious handicraft of this kind commands almost universal admiration; we are astonished and impressed by the prodigious amount of work 'put into' the manufacture of such garments.

Clothes are warmer if they consist of several layers superimposed one upon the other; their value as insulation can be diminished and their conspicuously expensive character enhanced if the protective layers are cut away so as to show how many things are being worn and what expensive things they are. Thus we find the practice of looping up the skirts of a dress in order to show a costly underskirt beneath, of 'slashing' a garment to the same end, or again, more discreetly, of wearing rustling petticoats, the presence of which may be advertised only by a susurrus, or by lining the skirt with some brilliant material which will 'flare' as the wearer passes.

The display of linen has been a feature of masculine dress since the end of the Middle Ages and is frequently found in woman's dress; linen has a particular value as an indication of wealth, in that it betrays dirt at once and must be frequently renewed. The pattern of masculine dress during the past three hundred years has been two or more coverings cut away in layers so that each is displayed, the last covering being a shirt. In the mid-seventeenth century the effect was enhanced by the provision of a hiatus between the waistcoat and the breeches; here the shirt bellied out again as though to guarantee its presence at all levels.

At times conspicuous consumption in dress like conspicuous consumption in old masters has been effected simply by purchasing from the most expensive producer. She who can say 'my dress is an original by Dior' is almost enviable as she who can say 'my still life is by Chardin'. Almost, but not quite, for it is natural to ask for the artist's name and natural to find it on or near his picture; it is only an informed few who will know enough to guess that you are wearing a dress by Dior, nor is it likely that the signature will be so evident, although in fact there have been cases where unscrupulous dealers have used the names of great couturiers in order to sell clothes of inferior quality.

Conspicuous Leisure. The mere demonstration of purchasing power is the simplest device of sumptuosity; much more important is that which Veblen calls Conspicuous Leisure, i.e. visible evidence that one is leading an honourably futile existence, an existence so far removed from all menial necessities that clothes can be worn which make any kind of physical labour difficult if not impossible. Dress of this kind, so long as it is manifestly sumptuous, marks the wearer as a member or a dependant of the leisure class, or at least as somebody who for a time can 'dress the part' of a member of that class. We admire the clothes of indolence almost instinctively, feeling them to be elegant and dignified, belonging, as it were, to a world in which the wolf has been kept far from the door. It is indeed doubtful whether we can conceive of dignity without a certain degree of leisure, and undoubtedly, if we attempt to personify that quality in a graphic image, we shall find that some measure of repose is essential both in the attitude and in the drapery of our subject.

It is perhaps useful to consider the opposite of personified leisure and consider the difficulties which occur when we attempt to find a plastic equivalent for action. The obvious symbolical figure is the warrior, who has of course a long iconological history; but the warrior, in that his activity is essentially destructive and wasteful (hence socially acceptable), does not provide a true antithesis to the man or woman of leisure. The antithetical figure is the workman, the socially useful person, but the dignity of labour is a concept for which we cannot easily find a graphic symbol, because the workman is not socially reputable and therefore has no place in the mythology of art. In fact we usually feel some misgivings when, in an attempt to create an iconography of labour, a Meunier, a Dalou, a Millet or a Brangwyn invests the manual worker with the agonised grandeur of Michelangelo's slaves; such corporeal splendours seem rather to be an attempt to ennoble the subject by means of an artistic disguise, than the actual discovery of some unperceived beauty in the worker. In fact the dignity of labour is a purely moral quality and one not easily expressed in terms of physical excellence. Nothing prevents us from supposing that a feeble and hideous lavatory attendant might be a hero and a saint; but it would be hard to express his moral excellence in visual terms, harder still if it were necessary to do so by showing him with the tools of his trade.

Even a warrior hero whom we may legitimately suppose to be gifted with athletic beauty, may be felt to fall below the requirements of dignity when he is portrayed in action rather than in repose. Reynolds objected to Bernini's David because the sculptor represents the sling thrower in the very act of casting his stone, an effort which has made him so tense that he bites his lower lip. The expression, says Sir Joshua, 'is far from being general, and still farther from being dignified'. Sir Joshua is perfectly right: if you want dignity look at Michelangelo's David; he exists beautifully, he is doing damn all, or, better still, look at Marcus Aurelius, he is doing damn all on a horse, a more expensive and therefore a more admirable waste of time.

These considerations may remind us that no dignitary can be perfectly dignified all the time. We may perhaps imagine a god perpetually seated and perpetually administering the Universe without ever actually exerting himself; but it is hard. Human beings, even royalty, cannot in real life achieve such elegant inertia for very long. Ideally, the socially excellent life is one of perpetual uselessness; to 'sew a fine seam' would be quite as near as the conspicuously leisurely consumer might come to industrial activity. But in fact the exigencies of life are now, and perhaps always have been, such that continuous leisure, even for the privileged few, is impossible and perhaps unendurable. Thus a judge on the bench, a bride at the altar, an archdruid at an Eisteddfod, adopts a new persona and plays a part which, although perhaps it may soon be ended, requires while it lasts a particular costume. So, even the most industrious of men may sometimes discard his greasy overalls and for a season don the white tie of indolence. So too, the well-dressed nymph, queen of an evening's festivity, may cast aside her garland and don the workmanlike denims in which she may best cope with the mess and the confusion of the morning after. Increasingly, Western man plays many different roles and for each he needs a suitable disguise.

Examples of the exhibition of leisure through clothes are abundant, and here I can do no more than indicate a few devices of conspicuous leisure to which the reader will no doubt be able to add many more.

Starting then at the top, the sumptuous hat has nearly always been devised either to give no protection to the head, or to make the wearer helpless in a high wind, or again to blind her with its too flexible brim; the hair, or wig, can be raised to a precarious height, or given an appearance of crushing weight as in the chignon. Women's hats and hair have for long been a jest amongst men; the jest can hardly be made by our younger men today, nor indeed by anyone whose knowledge of history is good enough to remind him of the extraordinary things that men have worn upon their heads, things such as the hat which St George is wearing in Pisanello's picture,* or the vast periwig surmounted by a feathered hat which European gentlemen wore, not only at the court of Louis XIV but at the court of the great Moghul. Even the once ubiquitous top hat is not the most rational head covering in the world.

Descending to the neck, we shall find collars for both sexes which have been devised so as to give the wearer an elegant appearance of being strangled to death. The most notable example is the great ruff of the early seventeenth century, a vast elaborate confection of linen and starch above which the wearer's head seemed as it were to be served up for a new Salome. Less striking, but one may suppose equally uncomfortable, was the 'choker collar' of the late nineteenth century, a shiny cylinder, the sharp edge of which seemed designed to cut into the flesh of the wearer's chin; this was a masculine fashion; but it was thought so charming that it was worn by both sexes. As a mortification of the flesh it seems hardly less effective than those rigid necklaces which, in the Congo, were used actually to stretch and to deform women's necks.

The arm and hand have been incapacitated by means of long trailing sleeves, sleeves of episcopal grandeur, very tight, or fashioned (as in China) to project well beyond the hand. The hand itself must be most carefully tended, the nails being pointed, lacquered, and/or kept scrupulously clean and soft; rings and bracelets help to sustain its genteel appearance, while gloves give further evidence of leisure.†

*Plate 2.

†'It cannot ... be in good taste to squeeze it (the hand) into a glove so much too small for it that it becomes useless for any purpose beyond holding a visiting card ... though the hand is not permanently injured by the tight glove as the foot is by the tight shoe, the effect is ignoble and absurd.' *G. F. Watts*, ed. M. S. Watts, Macmillan, 1912, III, 213.

PLATE 2

Conspicuous Consumption (first half of the 15th century)

In the orient we find the finger-nail allowed to grow to a prodigious length, the object being to show that the hand belongs to one who is not a manual worker or, to apply the common symbolism of America and Western Europe, that the wearer is a white-collar and not a blue-collared worker.

The constriction of the waist, which has at various periods included a deformation of the thorax and the hips, I have already mentioned in connection with the sartorial criticism of the medical profession. Undoubtedly corsets, which in one form or another have been worn by most European women in most historical periods since the Middle Ages, can reduce efficiency but I doubt whether they are to be regarded as instruments of conspicuous leisure except in those periods when very tight lacing has given women a positively fragile appearance (as in the 1830s), or again, when corsets become a kind of solid armour in which women are rigidly encased and clearly hampered in every way, as in the 1880s.

When Veblen wrote *The Theory of the Leisure Class* the world seemed to be divided, almost as by a law of nature, into trousered and the petticoated halves, and for Veblen nothing marked the essentially servile status of women so clearly as the fact that they were condemned to wear that hampering and hobbling device, the skirt. Add to this the fact that the bulk of such a garment could be greatly augmented by hoops and panniers, crinolines, flounces, trains and hobbles, and the picture is complete. It is however historically inaccurate; on the one hand it is necessary to remember that trousers were for centuries worn by both sexes in China whereas in Europe, until the Renaissance at all events, the difference between breeched and petticoated humanity was determined not so much by sex as by occupation. The worker and the warrior hardly could wear skirts, and the warrior's social status was so good that a fashionable biped does emerge in the history of European dress. But for a long time the superior character of leisurely skirts was strongly felt. God himself is a robed and not a trousered being, and this is true of the majority of his angels, although not those who are definitely committed to military service. Look at the Ghent altarpiece and amongst the angels and the apostles, the bishops and confessors, the patriarchs, the prophets, the holy martyrs, the popes, the deacons, the just judges, the holy hermits, and the holy pilgrims, how many legs can you see? Three, I think; one belongs to St Christopher, who has pulled up his robe, the other two belong to warriors of Christ who are in armour. And before leaving that admirable work we may notice that on the outer side of the altarpiece the donor and his wife are equally skirted.* In fact until the sixteenth century it

*The reader will be familiar with this work. My illustration is therefore taken from another master who makes my point with even greater force. (See Plate 3.)

was not only the ecclesiastics who wore skirts; any judge, merchant, prince, official or other civilian was likely to wear skirts and indeed almost certain to do so if a man of mature years. We may still observe a recollection of this old order of things in the dress of our judges, our civic functionaries and our academics. The skirt – or at least the robe – is still a sign of leisure and a symbol of dignity.

Perhaps the most effectual guarantee of social standing is obtained by means of unpractical footwear. Of Chinese feet I shall have more to say, but we may note here that there has never been a more efficient form of conspicuous leisure than the deformed and mutilated foot. In Europe various kinds of more or less uncomfortable shoe, but above all the high-heeled shoe, have been a fairly constant phenomenon. It is odd to note that this kind of shoe, which has frequently been worn by men, seems to have a military origin and indeed to serve a practical need in that the heel is of obvious use in holding a stirrup. It is interesting to note the extent to which poetical tradition seeks to place women upon this particular pedestal. Big solid feet, however beautifully formed, are definitely unromantic, so too are stout workmanlike boots, clogs or brogues. It is felt to be poetically appropriate that Cinderella, whose ugly sisters had condemned her to a socially useful existence, should gain her prince by means of her atrophied toes. The glass slipper is not only a means of identification but a certificate of economic inefficiency. We feel it to be right and proper that she should be translated from the scullery to the throne.

Fashions in footwear do nowadays permit a certain glossy serviceability and this is particularly true where men are concerned, but the pointed shoes of the Middle Ages (see Plate 3) and the heelless slipper of the Turk are quite as unpractical as most feminine modes. In the same way many varieties of men's boots have been so designed that although you may ride in them you can barely walk.

Finally, under this heading, we may notice that kind of dress which may be called 'difficult'. It is of two varieties: that which, like the kilt or toga, requires some art in adjustment and that which has apparently been fastened upon the wearer by an attendant. The latter is the more certainly a dress of conspicuous leisure although both suggest a socially reputable familiarity with the practical problems of wearing fine dress.

Enough has been said to suggest that the sumptuously dressed person is not entirely enviable. It may be held that he is one who goes to great expense and pains to mortify the flesh. It must moreover be borne in mind that the leisurely existence suggested by sumptuous clothes is by no means always a reality. The black-coated, well-starched clerk who runs to catch his train with the temperature at 98° in the shade, and his sister, who endures the agony of high heels and all but naked legs in a blizzard,

PLATE 3

Conspicuous Leisure (15th century)

are very industrious persons; they dress as they do, not because they really have leisure, not even because they have social pretensions, but because their employers demand that their dress should be decently uncomfortable.*

Fortunately there are limiting factors which prevent any extravagance of dress being pushed beyond a certain point. Clothes may be an encumbrance, but always a graceful encumbrance. They must be just wearable, for to exhibit awkwardness argues an inability to deal with the paraphernalia of polite existence, and this would suggest a plebeian lack of address. It is, moreover, important to notice that it is a function of clothes to dignify and add importance to the body of the wearer. This they do very effectively but only when there is a judicious proportion between the wearer and that which is worn. A wide skirt confers dignity and an important air to a woman who, if left naked, might appear dumpy, but an enormously big skirt would have the opposite effect and dwarf the wearer. A train two yards long is impressive, a train forty yards long is grotesque. Again, a really violent exaggeration of the prevailing mode is somewhat like the display of easily convertible wealth upon the person, it is something intended for the multitude and therefore vulgar. (See Plate 4.)

Conspicuous Waste. This of course is a kind of conspicuous consumption, but of a more heroic and dramatic kind; it is important to the historian of fashion, not because it exercises direct influence upon clothes but because it determines the manner of life of sumptuously dressed people.

To drink a lady's health is an act of courtesy, to drink her health and then to dash down the glass, preferably a priceless work of *virtu*, upon a stone floor, thus ensuring that the vessel shall never be devoted to any less noble purpose, may be accounted a romantic gesture and is unquestionably an act of conspicuous waste – unless the glass be made of plastic in which case it is better not to attempt the gesture.

The process may be seen in a very pure form in the Potlach of the Kwakiutl Indians of British Columbia. The Potlach is a confrontation between rival chieftains. The challenger or host demonstrates his superior wealth by giving away or destroying his possessions, paddles, canoes, baskets, copper shields, or in later years, blankets, enamel ware, sewing machines and motor boats; the guest had to outdo the host's prodigality by an even more reckless display of conspicuous consumption, whereupon the host went one better and so on ... until at length one of the two competitors was left ruined and ashamed. The *Moka* of the Mt Hagen tribes is a very similar trial of strength and generosity but with

*I hope that these words are rather less true than when they were first written.

PLATE 4

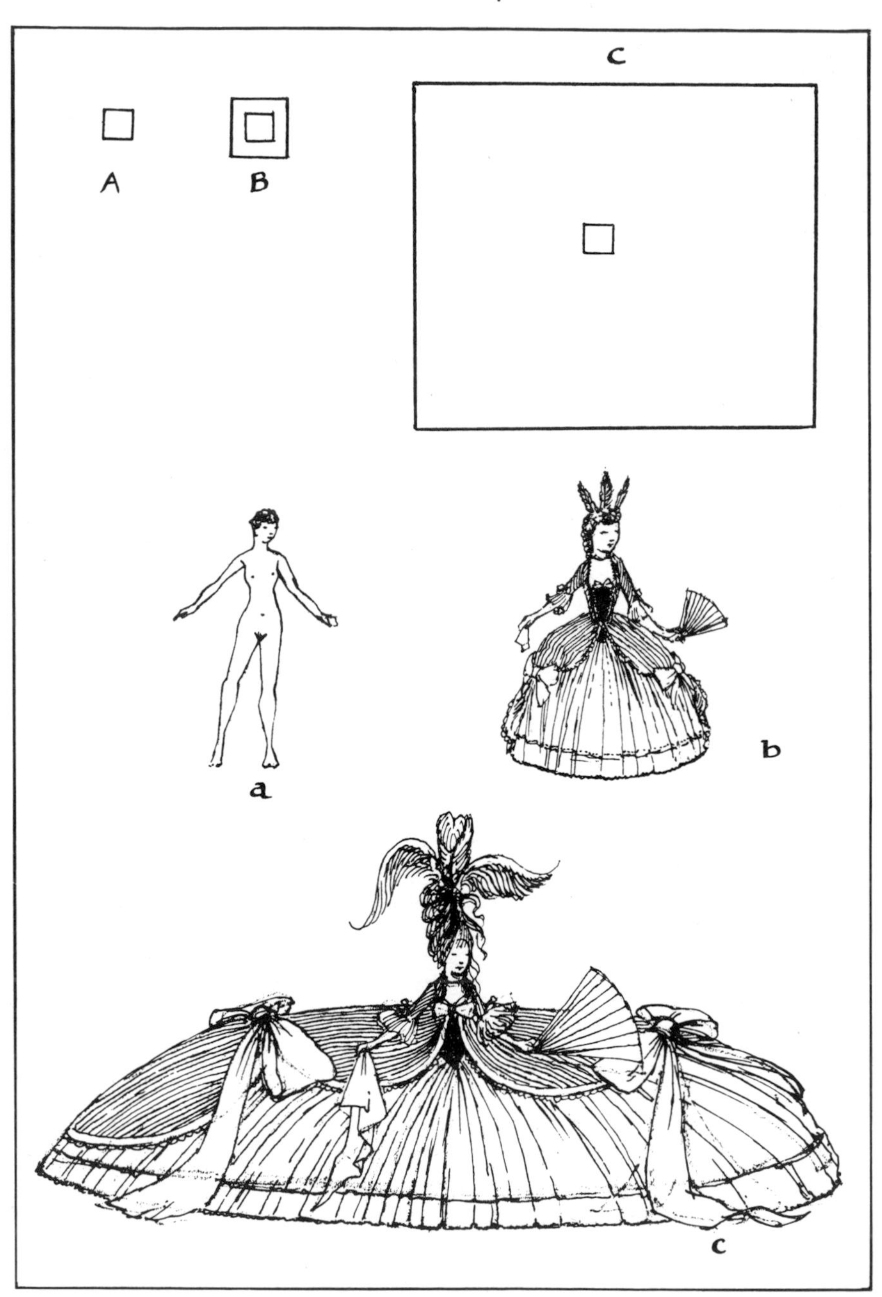

Confluence and Proportion

The apparent size of the rectangle is enlarged in figure B and diminished in figure C. In the same way the nude (a) is magnified by judicious drapery (b) and diminished by an excess of clothes (c) an additional element of dancing and dressing up. A fairly close parallel will be found amongst people living on low wages in our industrial cities who feel that it would be dishonourable, and a matter of lasting shame if, when a relative dies or a son or daughter is married, the family responsible (and in these matters responsibility is pretty clearly defined) did not undertake very large expenses, expenses which in ordinary economic terms would be deemed entirely unjustifiable. The thing must be done in style, parties must be given, flowers bought, photographs taken, presents given and so on, so that a man earning £30.00 a week might easily find himself with a bill of £150.00 before he could see a daughter properly disposed of or an aunt safely underground.

The funeral is perhaps the ideal vehicle for conspicuous waste. This must always have been the case from the earliest times; important people have been followed to the tomb by slaves, animals, furniture, jewellery and much else, and although these objects (they included such luxury goods as the jade casket of a Chinese princess and the golden sarcophagus of Tutankhamen) remained to delight the tomb robbers and the archaeologists, they were in theory and in intention removed from circulation; it was, to put it grossly, money thrown away. Not that our remote ancestors were so purely addicted to conspicuous waste as we are. They after all did suppose that the furniture of the grave would supply the dead and might even constitute a visa to Elysium, whereas we pay the mortician's enormous bills with no such comfortable beliefs but only the sense that money must be paid if honour is to be satisfied.

A man who can spend with no prospect of seeing any return for his money must always command a certain respect. It is, we feel, a fine thing to play ducks and drakes with guinea pieces. In the same way we are mildly shocked by any suggestion that the guineas might somehow be recovered. Thus, when we are told of that Florentine family which in the fifteenth century concluded its banquets by gaily tossing the gold and silver plate off which it had supped into the Arno, we feel that this was magnificent although not a very sensible proceeding. And when we learn that, after the last of the dazzled guests had tottered home, the precious ware was drawn up again in a net, we may agree that this was sensible but somehow it doesn't seem at all glorious. This of course is partly because the family was guilty of deception. But here is a rather subtler offence not involving any serious falsehood:

> The young writers of that era–and I was sure this man was a writer – strove earnestly to be distinct in aspect. This man had striven unsuccessfully. He wore a soft black hat of clerical kind but of Bohemian intention, and a grey waterproof cape

> which, perhaps because it was waterproof, failed to be romantic. I decided that 'dim' was the *mot juste* for him.

Thus, with economy and elegance, Max Beerbohm describes and, in describing, faintly damns Enoch Soames. But why does the waterproofing of the wretched man's cape show us how completely poor Soames failed to achieve the distinction that he so earnestly and in the end so tragically sought? The answer is provided by that fundamental document of the romantic movement – the Preface to *Mlle de Maupin.*

> Nothing is really beautiful except that which is good for nothing; all useful things are ugly, for they meet a need, and the needs of mankind are base and disgusting, as is his poor weak nature. The most useful room in the house is the lavatory.

It is not necessary to accept Theophile Gautier's reasoning in order to measure the force of his opinions. In fact there is nothing ignoble or disgusting about keeping out the rain; but there is something practical and commonsensical (something 'bourgeois') about the umbrella of Louis-Philippe or the waterproof cape of Enoch Soames. They are, in their frank utility, anti-sumptuous and anti-romantic, and there are some articles of use–false teeth, surgical belts, bicycle clips, galoshes–which hardly can be adapted to any sumptuous purpose.

Nevertheless, it is not the fact of being functionally efficient, of serving its purpose well, which makes a garment socially unsatisfactory. If the function that is to be performed is of an honourable (i.e. a wasteful or destructive) kind, then the efficiency of the instrument is no great drawback. Thus there is nothing very romantic about an oven glove, for cooking is a useful art, but a mailed gauntlet is the very stuff of romance for there is nothing more splendidly useless than war. Admittedly, for social purposes an obsolete or old-fashioned kind of war is to be preferred to a more modern conflict (the helmet is an adornment in a way that the gas mask is not). Of the clothes that we most admire on men the greater part are, or were originally, designed to serve destructive or economically futile purposes. These are the noble occupations, of which by far the most important, from our point of view, are war and sport. Hardly less noble are the genteel occupations, some of which approach so nearly to complete futility that they may be accounted noble; for instance those nominally administrative functions which involve hardly anything save the adoption of a distinctive costume and a polite air, also the more ornamental kinds of priestcraft, diplomacy, and even the law. All these have been accounted sufficiently noble to make of their uniforms a token of honour.

Of lesser importance are such occasional vehicles for the expenditure of unprofitable energy as worship, gambling, dancing, etc., which are not whole-time jobs and which, although frequently the occasion for a display of finery, have no very distinctive uniforms; in this category we may place that kind of sporting activity which consists simply in attending sporting events.

The importance of war and sport to the student of dress lies in the fact that these occupations have at various times been the chief and almost the only active employment of entire castes and classes. They have the double advantage of being largely unprofitable and at the same time very expensive. No pains have been spared to make them more so and, although some of the items of expense are utilitarian in the sense of being intended to promote the more efficient prosecution of the campaign or the chase, many are purely futile and exist only that the 'thing may be done in style'.

I shall attempt in a later chapter to look at some of the characteristics of military uniform. Here I wish only to remind the reader that war has an eminent place in the sartorial history of men, and that whereas most writers on costume have much to say regarding the part which women's dress plays in arousing sexual admiration, perhaps equal attention should be paid to the use of military dress for the same purpose. There is a good deal of evidence to show that a handsome uniform exerts a devastating effect upon the opposite sex, or rather that it used to do so. It will be noticed that here as elsewhere pecuniary canons of taste apply. The cavalryman may not be braver than the foot soldier but he is much more expensive and correspondingly important in the social scale; in the same way the foot soldier enjoys much more status than the pioneer. For rather similar reasons an army is usually a good deal more chic than a navy.

Again we shall find that whereas plebeian sports (football, shove-halfpenny, skittles, etc.) set no fashions, golf, yachting and polo have all given their names to garments. Nor is it thought unreasonable, but rather glorious, that the most English of sports and that which has had the most decided effect upon clothes should consist in the pursuit of an 'inedible animal', with an expensive pack of hounds, a great assembly of expensive horses and expensive ladies and gentlemen, many of them wearing a kind of uniform and with a stiff bill for damages at the end. Mr Jorrocks called it 'the image of war without its guilt', and from a social point of view he was perfectly right.

The influence of these two noble occupations has been such that, at different moments in the history of modern Europe, the costume of a gentleman has, with very little modification, been that of an officer or a huntsman.

Conspicuous Outrage. Look at Plate 5. It shows Miss Chudleigh, a Maid of Honour to Augusta, Princess of Wales (who was later to be Countess of Bristol and, through a bigamous marriage, to be called Duchess of Kingston), as she appeared at a subscription masquerade in 1749. 'Miss Chudleigh was Iphigenaia, but so naked that you would have taken her for Andromeda', wrote Horace Walpole; one might indeed, if the print really gives an accurate picture of what she looked like on that occasion, which may be doubted; but if the artist is guilty of exaggeration I do not think that he misrepresents the shock that Miss Chudleigh's costume certainly inspired. It was, by common consent, outrageous.

In every generation there are probably a few individuals who ride out ahead of the fashion, gladly offering themselves as targets for censure and bravely defying the censors. Sometimes this may be the characteristic of an entire society, as I think it was of the generation which reacted strongly against the Puritanism of the Interregnum, that generation which flaunts its charms in the canvasses of Lely (although here again we must not suppose that the liberties of the artist show us what was actually worn in Restoration London). But more usually it is left to a few individuals, the 'forlorn hope' of the *avant-garde*, to challenge the proprieties. Thus we find George Sand in trousers and smoking a cigar, or Oscar Wilde in knee breeches with long hair and a sunflower, Augustus John magnificent in long hair and earrings, or Ottoline Morrell dressing in scraps of priceless brocade, with pearls and plumes and paint that bade defiance to current fashion. It is the note of defiance which distinguishes this kind of social attitude, a kind of aggressive non-conformity which may result in a kind of dress which is simply eccentric or, in the case of an individual like Mme Récamier, simply carries the fashion to a logical conclusion which most people would find unacceptable. The ladies who about the year 1913 appeared on the streets in 'harem skirts' furnish another example.

Perhaps the most typical examples of conspicuous outrage belong to the world of ideas and to fashions in speech rather than in dress. The fashionable adoption of new and unfamiliar ideas in art or religion, or again the acceptance of a scandalously permissive attitude to questions of sexual morality, are fairly common social phenomena. Still more typical is the fashionable preference for coarse terms. The use of the word genteel shows us the kind of evolution that results from conspicuous outrage. To Jane Austen it was a simple term of commendation. Later it becomes a term of abuse applied to those refinements which had become vulgarised by those who felt that to be honest was to be coarse; thus it was an essentially upper-class belief in frank and robust speech which rejected such euphemisms as 'toilet' for lavatory, 'serviette' for napkin, and 'perspira-

PLATE 5

Conspicuous Outrage, 1749

tion' for sweat. Again the general tendency towards obscenity, blasphemy and crudity in language, and in behaviour, represents in large measure the reaction of an upper class against the timidities and prudishness of a slightly less upper class.

In clothes, conspicuous outrage usually takes the form of an affront to modesty, nakedness being, in common apprehension, something shocking. It follows that in courts and capitals, the outsider is most effectively repelled from the *beau monde*, or whatever the local habitation of really well-dressed people may be, by means of clothes which do not cover the person. It is thus that the 'fast set' may most easily show its speed.

Such an outrage is an affront upon modesty; but what, in this context, do we mean by modesty?

Japan may provide an instructive example. The dress of Japanese women in the centuries before Japan opened her doors to the West was both pretty and chaste. Japanese prints frequently show us very obscene acts, but not lascivious clothing. It may be that there are suggestive subtleties to which a Western observer is blind, but certainly there was never, as in Europe, a dress designed to display bare arms or shoulders, bosoms, waists or ankles. The mini skirt is unthinkable in the dress of old Japan, and all those erotic devices of the West, the gown that hugs the waist and thighs, the muted revelations of transparency, the drapery that caresses the bosom, are unknown in the Far East. Here then, on the face of it, is evidence of an extremely modest and discreet civilisation which keeps its sex for private interviews. And yet the same people feel not the slightest shame in seeing each other completely naked; for them the bathroom is a public place in which the chaste purposes so admirably achieved by their clothes are completely forgotten. To them it seems that nakedness, which would be scandalous in the street, is of no account when a lady or a gentleman is being washed. Nor need we find this so very surprising, for we too apply a rather different standard of modesty on a beach to that which we should expect on a bus.

Modesty in fact is not tied to a fixed, an immutable, canon but varies in accordance with the conventions of different cultures and different contexts. To the Chinese an exposure of the feet would seem very gross, whereas Mohammedan ladies will show their feet even when they will show us nothing else, and to them the greatest immodesty is a bare face. It is only in Europe and the 'Western world' that there is no fixed custom, and for this reason Europeans are far more immodest than the people of any other culture. Where customs are fixed and do not change, there is unlikely to be even a small breach of decorum and therefore there is unlikely to be any great immodesty, but in a fashionable, that is to say a mobile situation, one in which there is continual change, the possibilities of conspicuous outrage are far greater, and there is rather less certainty as to what is and what is not sanctioned by custom.

The situation is made more interesting by the fact that, when once an outrageous breach of custom has been effected, it is likely to be followed by a second and even more outrageous breach so that, within certain limits, a fashion tends to get progressively more and more improper. Thus in the late Middle Ages it was felt to be immodest in a woman to show her hair ('if a woman be not covereed, let her also be shorn', said St Paul). As a natural result coverings for the head became more and more exiguous and took more and more the form of jewelled nets and transparent veils. In the same way the fashions of the 1840s imposed a poke bonnet, in shape not unlike a coal scuttle, which had the effect of putting a woman into blinkers and making it very easy for her to avoid the gaze of anyone taller than herself. Thereafter year by year we see the bonnet opening out and set further and further away from the face, until by the 1860s it is set at the back of the head to reveal both the face and the hair. It is not very easy for us nowadays to feel the scandalous quality of such innovations. Even the famous divided skirt of the lady cyclist, which startled the 1880s, seems to us now an object of almost depressing sobriety. But then, this is the natural fate of outrageous modes; when a custom has been broken the breakage itself becomes customary and therefore ceases to be shocking. And yet this is only true in part. It takes a good deal of historical imagination to see anything shocking about bare heads; but it is rather more easy to see the inflammatory potentialities of bare breasts.

The 'low neck' has indeed been with us for a very long time, usually, but not always, as a feature of feminine dress; and the odd thing about it is that, since the fifteenth century at all events, it has been regarded as a feature of high sumptuosity. Something to be reserved for high days and holidays, so that by the end of the eighteenth century it was customary in the upper and middle classes at a certain hour of the afternoon to 'dress', which in effect meant largely to undress. The custom is not extinct, but it was in the period between Napoleon's wars and 1914 that it was observed with almost religious scrupulosity and with results which might astonish an unprejudiced observer.

There is a story, which has been repeated with numerous variations, of a Mohammedan prince visiting London in the 1880s who was taken to an evening party in Kensington which he described more or less in the following terms:

> This assembly, though conducted in an orderly way and without any obscene cries or gestures, was quite clearly the prelude to

> an orgy. I had long been used to the spectacle of Frankish women with uncovered faces and had learnt that in spite of this shameful aspect they are frequently honest, but these females had stripped off the greater part of their clothing leaving their arms, their shoulders and the greater part of their breasts bare, save for powder and cosmetics. Whether these women were sold or allotted in some other fashion to the gentlemen who attended the gathering I do not know for, much to my annoyance, my guide induced me by means of various polite excuses to quit the party before the time of fornication had been announced, nor, such is the hypocrisy of these people, would he by any means depart from the patently absurd story that the guests had gathered to listen to music and to exchange remarks about the weather.

It was surely a pardonable error. The exposure of the body must always carry a suggestion of carnality, but what made it so particularly striking in the London of the 1880s was that clothes worn by women during the daylight hours were most carefully designed to cover every inch of bare skin, save for the face, and even the face would often be hidden by a veil. How was an oriental visitor to account for such a drastic inconsistency? We are here confronted by a fine example of the seeming irrationality of custom, an irrationality which I shall attempt to explain later on. Meanwhile, I would like to say a little more about the exposure of the body.

So much has been written about the 'seduction principle' and 'erogenous zones' and the like that one might almost conclude, from the literature of fashion, that the only people who ever wear clothes are attractive young women. This proposition is indeed confirmed by our leading fashion journals; but it is not true, and it should be pointed out that women who seek to attract men form a minority of the population, that the erotically provocative dress is the product of one particular kind of social environment and something unknown to Islam and the Far East. And, finally, that most of the discussion of the erotic purposes of women has been undertaken by men.

Surprisingly little has been written by anyone about the psychology of clothes, and until some perceptive woman with a thorough knowledge of the history of costume tells us I shall not know whether I am right in supposing that military dress produced, or used to produce, a profound effect upon the female psyche; nor is it easy to know what effect fine clothes have upon a woman when they are worn by a man, or whether women's clothes have an erotic effect upon those who wear them or upon other women. I leave these questions unanswered and proceed.

PLATE 6

Ball dresses, 1885

> A mass of naked figures does not move us to empathy, but to disillusion and dismay.

Thus Lord Clark, and he observes that:

> ... anyone who has frequented art schools and seen the shapeless pitiful model which the students are industriously drawing will know ...*

Indeed we do, even though some of us may think that Lord Clark has been unfortunate and that one has seen models, particularly adolescent models of both sexes, who moved us neither to disillusion nor to dismay. Still, as I say, we *do* know very well the kind of spavined, jaded, long in the tooth, academic warhorse who is the usual occupant of the model's throne. But look at her carefully before the pose ends: why is it that she so surely qualifies as a *remedio amoris*? You will observe that there is a sharp difference of tonality at the point where her clothes usually begin. Above she is brick red, below she is bluish yellow; her breasts sag, her nipples are large and of a purplish colour, her belly hangs in a multitude of wrinkles and runs through several interesting shades of pale yellow made almost white by contrast with her very dark pubic hair; her legs display all the muted blues and violets of raw French asparagus, her knees are a bit knobbly, her toes have been crushed inwards by shoes which are too small for her feet, she is fascinating to look at, but never was there anything less like second-century sculpture or Renaissance painting.

Now watch what happens when the day's work is over. She slips on a blouse and skirt, does something to her hair, adds a cheap necklace, a hat perhaps, stockings or tights, shoes and a scarf. Suddenly she has become a rather attractive woman.

It is as though we could only feel sexual admiration when it is presented in the form of art. As a nude, the model failed because she could not live up to the highly confected nudes of antiquity and the Renaissance; but as a specimen of the current fashion she manages well enough, or well enough at all events to mark a decided improvement. A lot, of course, was concealed: wrinkles, blemishes, hair, spots and so on and then, if our model dresses with art, a great many devices may be used to draw attention to her better features and to conceal her faults. But in addition to this there is, I think, another process at work which we may call generalisation. If we wrap an object in some kind of envelope, so that the eyes infer rather than see the object that is enclosed, the inferred or imagined form is likely to be more perfect than it would appear if it were uncovered.

---

* Kenneth Clark, *The Nude*, 1956, p. 4.

Thus a square box covered with brown paper will be imagined as a perfect square. Unless the mind is given some very strong clue it is unlikely to visualise holes, dents, cracks or other accidental qualities. In the same way, if we cast a drapery over a thigh, a leg, an arm or a breast, the imagination supposes a perfectly formed member; it does not and usually cannot envisage the irregularities and the imperfections which experience should lead us to expect. The art, if one may thus describe it, of the stripper consists in always being about to reveal all; she pursues nudity as Achilles pursued the tortoise, never quite achieving it; the visible charms of her person always being enhanced by those which are yet to be revealed. And this is true also of dress: it heightens the sexual imagination partly by revealing the body but partly by a judicious discretion.

This is so much the case that fashion can offer us a purely artificial and conventional form and persuade us to accept it. Look for instance at Plate 7. The upper part of the dress follows the figure so closely that, although the person is completely covered, this may be accounted a 'revealing' costume, and yet in fact when we consider it against what we know of anatomy we realise that it is not so much revealing as suggestive; no real waist and chest are constructed upon the boldly curving lines described by the lady's stays, the bosom consists of two separable breasts not of one united mass; above all, no real human being possesses such an amazing backside. What we are looking at is an idealisation which in real life would be contrived by means of pulling, pushing and padding. And yet such artifice would, I think, have been accepted by the spectator as reality. We know what the model is probably like from experience, and yet we are willing to suspend our disbelief in favour of the fictions of her wardrobe. Indeed I think that we are ready to go further in the way of self-deception. When we slip on our best jacket and see our deplorably unimpressive shoulders artfully magnified and idealised we do, for a moment, rise in our own esteem.

Aristotle said that Drama was something more philosophical than history, for history tells us only what did happen whereas Drama tells us what ought to have happened. In this sense the dressmaker, like the academic painter, is philosophical. The painter seeks to recreate the body in a state of such perfection that it requires no drapery; the dressmaker seeks to arrange the drapery so beautifully that the actual body becomes a mere starting point and, it may be, a very unpromising starting point.

Poiret, the great French designer of the pre-war epoch, writes thus of one of his models:

> She was as silly as a goose and lovely as a peacock ... in my Salons she appeared as a Messalina, an Indian Queen, preten-

PLATE 7

Day dress, 1885

> tious, majestic, and proud, and her royal port left the real princesses before whom she paraded in a state of wonder ... am I the only one to know that this bird of paradise concealed the vilest of bodies, that her body had gone to pieces, that her breasts, empty and unspeakably awful, had to be rolled up like pancakes in order that they might be packed into her majestic bodice?*

Poiret writes with the pride of an artist. To a very great extent he must have 'created' this model, and one wonders whether such creative efforts are still part of the couturier's business. Clearly though, in such a case, the provocation of apparent nudity must always remain rather in the imagination than in fact.

Essentially the outrageous quality in dress is a reflection of elitist thought. The elite or in-group has its own ethos, an ethos which allows it to challenge the ideas of the vulgar, and as I have indicated this must very often mean ideas concerning sexual decorum. But opinion can be outraged in quite a different way; an aesthetic innovation can be almost as disturbing as a moral innovation. My grandmother boasted that she had never worn a crinoline, G. F. Watts had told her not to, and there was a small, courageous party of ladies who in the second half of the nineteenth century deliberately flouted prevailing fashions and dressed themselves in accordance with the ideas, or what they believed to be the ideas, of the Pre-Raphaelites. It was a kind of anti-fashion which, to a certain extent, actually became the fashion. Its followers hoped to effect a reformation of dress, and their motives were by no means wholly aesthetic. In fact aesthetic dress was too much a fashion to be able to survive, nor did it have any direct descendants. In the early years of the twentieth century we find Isadora Duncan attempting to regenerate society by walking the streets in grecian robes. The artists were offered a more practical opportunity to reform dress by Poiret, who set them to work as designers with enormous success, and by Roger Fry, who produced dresses at the Omega Workshops but was a good deal less gifted as an interpreter of fashionable taste.

The latest attempt to create an aesthetic fashion was inspired by the paintings of Augustus John. In the early 1920s when the fashionable dress for ladies consisted, roughly speaking, of a cylindrical length of material falling straight from shoulders and in no way shaped to the figure, a certain number of art students or artistically minded ladies gathered their skirts to a precisely defined waist above which was a fitted bodice, vaguely quattrocento in character and quite revealingly tense with a great multi-

* Poiret, *En Habillant l'Epoque*. Paris, 1930, pp. 136–7. (My translation.)

tude of buttons. A round neck and elbow-length sleeves added to the effect, and the skirt was gathered with conscious art into innumerable folds. I remember once seeing a young woman who had adopted this fashion (or anti-fashion), it must have been about the year 1925. The effect was very striking.

In this account of sumptuous dress the reader will no doubt discover many omissions – I have for instance said nothing of symbolic clothes, as for instance the 'old school tie' which to the initiated is as eloquent of the wearer's previous career as is the broad arrow of the convict. Nevertheless, I hope I may have accomplished the preliminaries necessary to a study of finery. It must be repeated that in considering the essential virtues of dress I have in truth done no more than analyse the different aspects of one central phenomenon. Always we return to the basic question of expenditure; conspicuous consumption is but the putting of wealth upon the person, conspicuous leisure the display of wealthy ease, and conspicuous waste of wealthy activity. Conspicuous outrage belongs rather to the world of ideas, but the ideas are those of a wealthy class.

Our feelings concerning the right spending of money on dress are however so blended with other emotions, our sense of beauty, of martial glamour, of sexual desirability, etc., that it is not easy to disentangle one factor from another. It is difficult for us to tell to what extent those standards which Veblen calls the 'pecuniary canons of taste' affect our judgment. And yet it is surely that nice perception of financial worth which makes the difference between the civilised man and the barbarian. On the face of it, it may seem that the bejewelled lady of Europe differs but little from the savage with her necklace of beads. But although a diamond cross upon the bosom of a young beauty serves all the purposes of a moroccan charm, leading us, in the one case as in the other, to think well both of her person and her principles, the effect will be totally marred in *our* eyes if the ornament be a tawdry and vulgar thing of glass in 'atrociously vulgar taste'. It will indeed be condemned as 'barbarian' (even though we may surmise that the barbarian commonly has the finer taste). Our sense of value cannot ever be quite divorced from our sense of cost or class.

In conclusion a word should be said regarding the accessories of sumptuous dress. Here the difficulty is to know where to draw the line, for the term 'finery' may legitimately be extended to embrace such things as hair styles and wigs, cosmetics, eye-glasses, fans, scents, walking sticks, umbrellas and parasols. Perhaps we may also use it to describe the vehicles, the furniture, the interior decoration, the architecture, the habits of speech, the ideas and all the other belongings of a people in so far as they assist in producing an effect of sumptuosity. I will however confine myself to those portable belongings which are definitely intended to subserve the costume. They will on the whole be found to exhibit conspicuous leisure. The handkerchief which is too small for use, the fan which does not refresh, the hypertrophied muff, the unnecessary walking stick, the labour-creating lorgnette, etc.

Perhaps the most interesting accessory of fashion is the domestic, or rather the ornamental, animal. The laws regulating the use of animals for sumptuous purposes are the same as those which govern the use of clothes: expense and futility are the criteria. Although the number of species which has been pressed into service is very great, it will hardly ever be found that these are of an outstandingly useful kind. Sheep, pigs, ducks, hens or goats seldom become household pets or the ornaments of a gentleman's garden, while deer will be more esteemed in his park than cows or any save the most expensive horses. Preference is given to exotics such as parrots and canaries, monkeys, goldfish and other more or less futile creatures. The cat is an exception, although even here those varieties which are more expensive than useful will be preferred.

A comparison between the cat and the dog is highly instructive. The cat is the most polite of domestic animals. Its life in the home is almost a kind of symbiosis. It is very clean in its habits; on the whole it pays its way and is frequently of more service than disservice to its owner.

The dog on the other hand has not shown the cat's power of adaptation to life in houses and cities; it belongs in the kennel, but is seldom found there when used for purposes of decoration. As Veblen has said: 'He is the filthiest of the domestic animals in his person and the nastiest in his habits. For this he makes up in a servile attitude towards his master, and a readiness to inflict damage and discomfort on all else.'

That there is some truth in this can hardly be denied; nevertheless for all social purposes the dog is vastly superior to the cat. What Veblen calls the dog's 'servile attitude' is of primary importance, for a dog is, far more than a cat, manifestly the property of its owner, while the carefree incontinence of the species makes work (the honourable because wholly futile work of taking the dog out) for its owner. But what makes dogs sumptuous above all other animals is their connection with socially reputable forms of sport, their sequacity, which makes them in effect a part of the costume and, above all, the extreme malleability of the species when subjected to selective breeding. Dogs are the fashion because we can fashion them to our will. Dogs, much more than cats, can be made objects of conspicuous waste; they can be rendered completely incapable of fending for themselves and become, manifestly, objects of continual expense and care (whoever saw a cat wearing a little coat in the cold weather?) The highly bred dog can have its whole frame twisted and distorted into shapes of the most astonishing kind and can in fact become an ornamental monster. An uninstructed observer would suppose that the owners of such crippled and unhealthy animals must of necessity be very cruel. On being further informed that the monstrosity fanciers are amongst the most resolute critics of vivisection, he would set them down as hypocrites. Such an accusation would however be unjust; the owners are genuinely devoted to their victims. Fashion, as we have said, has a morality of its own; and the cruelty involved in breeding deformed animals, like that involved in blood sports, is redeemed by the economic futility of the motive; that involved in scientific experiments is felt to be odious because of its unpardonable utility.

3

The Nature of Fashion

'As good be out of the world as out of fashion'
COLLEY CIBBER

In discussing the character of any particular costume, no contextual factor is more important, or at times more misleading, than that of the changing fashion. Dress which is sumptuous but not fashionable is easy enough to explain in Veblenian terms, but that which is in a continual state of flux and so unstable that, in the course of a few decades every manifestation of sumptuosity is transformed, constitutes a problem mysterious in itself and vital to our entire argument.

In most circumstances fashion is the essential virtue in a garment without which its intrinsic values can hardly be perceived. We may allow the merits of dresses which make no attempt at fashion, but that which is positively démodé or which attempts and fails to be in vogue is damned without further discussion. We are indeed such creatures of fashion that we tend to accept its influence almost as a law of nature, a tendency which has been the undoing of many theorists. To avoid making that mistake it may be as well to begin this chapter by looking at a part of the history of dress in which the influence of fashion has been so slight as to be barely perceptible; the exercise should enable us to place the phenomenon of fashion historically and geographically, to measure the value of many of the generalisations that are commonly made concerning fashion, and finally to approach the problem of its causation.

Now the most obvious and convenient antithesis to the costume of the Western world (by which I mean Europe and all those countries which have accepted European costume) is China. Not that we cannot find many other examples of cultures which in their dress are equally opposed to ourselves, but in that ancient civilisation we have the oldest continuous society, one which has developed apart from our own and one which has pushed the art of living and the polite arts to a degree of perfection which we in the West have but recently approached.

China* has produced sumptuous dress which in many respects is

* i.e. China up to and including the Manchu Dynasty. Costume in the People's Republic of China would certainly be an interesting subject of study. It is not one that I am qualified to undertake.

similar to that of Europe. The long silk robe of the Mandarin, with its projecting sleeves designed to frustrate manual labour and its high stiff collar, is entirely Western in its demonstration of conspicuous leisure. The more extravagant forms of sumptuosity are perhaps less common than with us; gaudiness is a Manchu rather than a Chinese characteristic. The refinement of the Chinese, like that of Western man during the past 150 years, tends towards a sober 'goodness' of quality. In most respects the clothes of women resemble those of men, the same robe and trousers (in the North at least) and the same sobriety of taste, with this important distinction: where Europeans have demonstrated conspicuous leisure in a variety of ways, constantly shifting their attention from one part of the body to another, the Chinese have concentrated nearly all their attention upon the foot (I am talking now of women's dress). For many hundreds of years – the origins of the custom are lost in the mists of antiquity – the celestial lady had tottered painfully upon feet which had been horribly mutilated in early youth. Thus, in theory at all events, she was debarred from almost any task of social utility. The deformed member which, to the European eye, is almost too disgusting to contemplate is, or was, an object of intense erotic delight. As in Europe, so in China, protests were made. Several scholars of the eighteenth and early nineteenth centuries assailed the practice, which indeed was forbidden by a law of the Emperor Kang-Hsi. The Manchu ladies did not at first bind their feet, nor did the practice become general amongst them (it must be remembered that theirs was a ruling caste), nevertheless the Emperor Chien Lung found it necessary to forbid them to follow the Chinese custom. In the nineteenth century the Empress Dowager also attempted, and failed, to abolish the practice.*

It will be seen that the sumptuous dress of China, like that of Japan, bears a great similarity to that of Europe in that it is manifestly a dress of conspicuous leisure, but it differs in two important respects: it is modest and it is static.

Chinese erotic imagination has played upon the atrophied foot, but this was unseen both in public and in decent art. So too was every other part of the body save for the face, hands, and, sometimes, the neck. By this I mean not simply that the person was clothed but that no part of it was revealed or suggested, as it would have been in Europe. In fact there was the same invariable chastity that we have already noted in Japanese dress. The nearest approach to the Chinese practice to be found in the West is in the dress of Spanish ladies of the late sixteenth century – the invisible foot and legs, the shape of the body masked and deformed by a patently

* See Robert K. Douglas, *Society in China*, 1894, 361. Lin Yu Tang, *My Country My People*, 1936, 158–61. Howard S. Levy, *Chinese Footbinding*, 1970, *passim*.

unnatural corset, the breasts weighted down to flatness by leaden plates, just as they were flattened by the chest-binding jacket of China, only the face and hands visible; here, however, the resemblance ends. If Europe had worshipped the foot as China has, more and more of it would have been revealed to us, increasingly daring modes would have come into vogue until at last, our pedestrian lusts satiated, the 'erogenous zone' shifted elsewhere. In China, when once the bound foot had become 'fashionable', if one may use such a word of Chinese dress, it was there to stay.

No doubt there were variations in Chinese dress from dynasty to dynasty of a kind that Western eyes would hardly notice. Certainly there have been importations, and the Manchus in particular effected some important changes. Nevertheless, when all allowances have been made, the extraordinary fact remains that the Chinese family of the last century looked very much like a Chinese family of the classical age. It is as though we in Europe had made no substantial alteration in our dress since the time of the Punic Wars.* Nor is this the full extent of the difference. Western costume is like a river: throw in a novelty and it will flow downstream. Chinese costume on the other hand is like a pond: that which it floats it keeps. Thus when at the beginning of the nineteenth century the Europeans discovered the charm of Egyptian ornaments, they floated the idea with enthusiasm, adapted it and, presently finding other things to amuse them, let it sink. When, on the other hand, the Manchus imposed the pigtail upon their Chinese subjects it remained unaltered for the best part of three centuries, in fact until the revolution of 1912 when that which had been a mark of servitude had become honourable through long use and was most unwillingly abandoned by older men

To say that Chinese dress is entirely static may not be quite accurate. Change may well occur but it occurs at the speed of a rather hesitant glacier and, when compared with the West, it can fairly be described as something rigid and unchanging. I have already said that this is largely true of Japanese dress; it is true also of the cultures of India and the near East, of Ancient Egypt, of the Pre-Columbian civilisation and of all pre-literate societies; it is true to a large extent of the Classical Antiquity; in fact the static situation of which China forms the most notable example is the normal situation. It is we in the West who are peculiar; fashion is probably our invention. At all events we and we alone have given it that dizzy speed which we now take for granted.

When we speak of fashion in dress we speak not only of an unusual, perhaps a unique, situation in the history of dress, but also of something

* *See* Williams, *A Short History of China*, 1928, 79.

comparatively recent in the history of culture. The beginnings of fashion were so gradual that it is very hard to say at what point the machine really started into motion, but the process can hardly be said to have been at work in the time of Charlemagne and was definitely active by the beginning of the thirteenth century. From then onwards the rate of change accelerates until in our own times it has become prodigious. Simultaneously, with the increase in pace goes an increase in scope; more and more people are affected by the fashion, and that which in its beginnings was a matter for a few wealthy people in the courts of monarchs has gradually become the concern of millions so that in industrialised societies it governs the dress of the entire population. With the increase in social depth goes an increase in diffusion; European fashions have accompanied European enterprise and spread throughout the habitable world, not, it should be said, with equal success, for some cultures have resisted European dress more resolutely than others. There has also been a development towards increased centralisation. At times the different capitals of Europe have each had their own fashions and dictated to their own separate areas. A local fashion might be found in Florence and another in Venice, in Madrid, Brussels, Amsterdam or Nuremberg. By the nineteenth century, styles were to a very large extent set by two centres: Paris and London.

In a general way it is probably correct to think of the rate of fashionable change as something which has been gradually accelerating since fashions first began; there have, however, been periods of sudden catastrophic change, and also deceleration amounting almost to complete paralysis; but fashion always evolves, it never makes a completely new departure. Usually it will be found that any particular garment or feature of a garment develops in the direction of greater and greater distortion, and then disappears or changes direction. In masculine dress we can frequently discover atrophied members, the relics of previous stages of evolution. In the contemporary work of a London tailor there are buttons, flaps and incisions as useless and as historically interesting as the male nipple or the appendix. To take one example from many: the hat band, both that which we find outside nearly all hats and that which we sometimes find inside hats, was formerly useful in keeping the stuff of the headdress upon the head, as we see in Arab headdresses to this day. On a modern felt hat it has entirely lost its original use. The band is sewn on to the side of the crown; no one would dream of untying the bow, but the maddest of hatters would not dream of omitting it. In women's dress, which in recent times has been far less conservative than that of men, the retention of archaic features is less noticeable. Nevertheless here too we do find the same kind of process at work, but in the opposite direction.

Thus the hat band, instead of being atrophied, suffers hypertrophy; it becomes a brilliant decorative motive, an excuse for streamers or for a large and quite unfunctional bow.

Broadly speaking we may say that conservatism in dress consists in this: utilitarian features are retained, but only on condition that they cease to be useful; they are transformed into discreet ornaments (like the two buttons in the small of a gentleman's frock coat, which used, when it was a riding habit, to secure his tails so that they would not flap in the wind) or they are retained as highly sumptuous features, like the long fringe of a silk shawl, which originally was the loose end of the warp.* Another example, the safety-pin, may serve to show how a given article can evolve in both directions. Crude but recognisable safety-pins can be found at a very early period of history; at this stage the thing is both useful and ornamental, frequently it is made of bronze or gold. It becomes the conspicuous brooch, a device for displaying a jewel, usually made without a safety guard. It also becomes the modern steel safety-pin, which is hidden away from public gaze; to wear it as a fastening for a dress is thought very ignominious.

As has already been said, the distinction between the sexes has become very much more marked with the development of fashion, particularly during the past two hundred years. Today that distinction seems to be becoming less important, so that it may be that the radical differences between the clothes of the sexes which were so very evident in the nineteenth century mark a temporary phase in the history of clothes. Certainly in Ancient Egyptian, Sumerian, Assyrian, Chinese, Hellenic and Byzantine dress there is no very sharp distinction. In the history of fashion since the fifteenth century an increasing division into clearly defined sexual areas is noticeable, although we still find many epicene modes, such as the ruff and the high heeled shoe which are worn by both sexes in the sixteenth and seventeenth centuries.

It may also be said that with the growth of fashion there is a growth in specialised dress or, as one may call it, 'occasional dress'. We have already said that one of the characteristics of fashion is its tendency to govern the dress of more and more people. This tendency shows itself, in the case of a workman who has an occupational dress, in the adoption of 'Sunday best', a special dressing up for a socially important occasion; in rather the same way that people of a higher social class would make occasions for dressing more ambitiously, so that we get such phenomena as evening dress, garden party dresses, dressing for the performance of, or for watching sports, dressing for seaside holidays, or for yachting and

* See W. M. Webb, *The Heritage of Dress*, 1907.

so on. At the same time we get the invention of specific naval and military uniforms.

It will be seen that the development of fashion is a process considerably wider in scope than the mutation of various styles of garment. But even if we look at it only from this restricted point of view, it is clear that it is not just a factor in the recent history of dress but an overall determinant. Under the influence of fashion we have, in the course of the past 140 years, seen women completely change the shape and texture of their garments and as it would seem of their bodies. They have, at one time or another, looked like milk churns, like spinning tops, like inverted flowers and like boys, they have been through a most extraordinary series of incarnations.

Of the many factors which determine the design and use of clothes – protection, convenience, sexual advertisement, beauty, and those which we have described as being characteristically sumptuous – all are influenced and dominated by the prevailing mode; the demands of convenience and protection are restrained, the form taken by sexual display directed hither and thither about the person, and the specifically sumptuous characteristics enlarged, altered or abolished by this immanent force. As climate is to flora and fauna, so is fashion to dress.

And yet the word 'fashion', because it implies change and mutability, suggests something frivolous and inconsiderable. A judgment based upon fashion is felt to be less serious and less reputable than one based upon those eternal values, those enduring truths which, as we like to suppose, we can all recognise and in the light of which we can relegate fashionable opinions to their proper and inferior place. 'It is fashionable to maintain . . .' – such a beginning allows us to anticipate that the speaker will soon refer to something more permanent than fashion. A fashionable artist is certainly one who will abide our judgment. Such assumptions may be, in fact certainly are, true; nothing is so mortal as fashion, no flower carries within it more plainly the seeds of its own destruction; the only trouble is that when we seek for the eternal verities against which we can measure the shortcomings of fashion they may be rather hard to find. But if in condemning fashion we imply that it is the produce of a light-weight emotion and one that can easily be disregarded then we may fall into a very grave error.

Fashion for those who live within its empire is a force of tremendous and incalculable power. Fierce and at times ruthless in its operation, it governs our behaviour, informs our sexual appetites, colours our erotic imagination, makes possible but also distorts our conception of history and determines our aesthetic valuations.

Because it is a transitory thing, it is not weaker in its operation than are the immutable customs which govern static societies. Because it is continually changing its laws, we are able to perceive something of their monstrous absurdity, but we are not for that reason better able to defy them. The absurdity of fashion serves only to make its enactments more patently cruel and more obviously irrational.

Here a concrete instance may help. There was a time when I used, almost every day, to see a girl whose face was pretty enough to be called charming and whose figure was, in almost all respects, admirable. But she suffered from some kind of malformation of the leg so that, below the knee, she wore an ugly contraption of steel and leather. Although she dressed and carried herself bravely it was difficult to look at her without a shudder; one sensed that she was aware of this and one was sadly conscious of her distress. And yet the problem (I am sure that it was a deeply pondered and infinitely melancholy problem) of confronting and distressing the passer-by on the pavement could have been solved by means of half a yard of material and forty minutes' work with a needle and thread. With skirts that fell to within two inches of the ground she would have been remarkable only for her prettiness and for an inability to move gracefully. If she had lived in the nineteenth, or indeed in any previous century, her deformity would have been barely visible. Today fashion would offer her a refuge in the 'maxi'. But she had the misfortune to be young at a time when fashion would allow no alternative to the short skirt.

This anecdote, which is alas true, should be borne in mind when people speak (not without a certain reason) of fashion as a device for making people look beautiful or for attracting the opposite sex. The statement may tell us something about the purpose of fashion but not about its operation. Fashion is at best a tyrannically democratic force. Fashions may be adopted because they are acceptable to the majority (although even this may well be doubted) but the wishes of the minority are not consulted. However much a fashion may hurt the individual, the individual has nothing for it but to obey.

And yet, can one truthfully say this? In the melancholy case that I have cited it would seem unreasonable to believe that the poor girl *chose* to follow the fashion that did her so much injury; but equally, to say that she was compelled to do so – if we are thinking of any kind of legal compulsion – is untrue. And yet there was some kind of compulsion. The effort of wearing unfashionably long skirts would I presume have involved her in distresses and embarrassments greater than those involved in that painful submission to custom for which in the end this victim felt obliged to opt. Some kind of compulsion there must be and it is severe.

This happily is an unusual example of the punitive power of the mode, but it would be quite wrong to regard it as something utterly uncharacteristic of fashion. No doubt there are some people who, as they say: 'can wear anything and look good in it'. But they are the happy few; the great majority need some assistance from their clothes, and that assistance must be of different kinds for there are many different ways of being imperfect. Obviously if fashion favours one type it will penalise another; it is bound to hurt someone because it is in its very nature a kind of uniformity. The reign of the mini skirt is but recently over, and I think I may safely appeal to those who lived through it and ask them whether their memories of that epoch are not of two kinds – on the one hand a nostalgic recollection of angelic thighs and on the other the unwelcome display of some quite frighteningly ugly hams; we lost on the roundabouts that which we gained on the swings. Looking further afield, say to the fashions of the year 1927 or those of 1810, these imposed a style which was very hard on age and obesity; stout elderly matrons were forced into clothes which could not but appear ridiculous except when worn by sylphs. On the other hand, in most periods, it is youth that has been cheated of its due. How many beautiful necks have been cruelly hidden beneath the compulsory collar or ruff? What beautiful thighs have been hidden by skirts which gave never a hint of their splendid proportions, what lovely legs have gone unseen to the grave?

Where there is a legitimate grievance we expect to find some kind of protest; but the laws of fashion seem to be accepted without a murmur, and the leaders of fashion seem to be incapable of raising a finger in their own defence. The Empress of all the Russians might cut off heads and annexe provinces, but could she raise skirts by a matter of twelve inches? She could not. To this you may reply that there is not the faintest evidence of her ever having wished to do so, and if it could be shown that a Czarina or even a mere Czar had ever seriously wished to do such a thing, she or he would surely have the social authority to change the fashion.

To this I reply with an historical anecdote. The Empress Elizaveta Petrovna, autocrat of all the Russias (regnat 1741–62), lived in a period when a lady's skirt was both long and voluminous and in which her legs were inferred but not seen. The Empress possessed an uncommonly fine pair of legs and an exceedingly strong desire to show them to the world, this much we know. We do not know whether she ever contemplated leading a new fashion which would enable her to display her charms; if she did she must have abandoned the notion or failed to carry it into effect for in fact she hit upon another device, the '*metamorphose*'. The *metamorphose* was an occasion when the sexes exchanged clothes, as in the Saturnalia of the Romans; this meant that a lady might sport knee breeches and silk stockings, and it was exactly what the

Empress needed. Elizaveta Petrovna held an almost continuous succession of *metamorphoses* at St Petersburg and no doubt her legs were much admired. But it was a servile and an imperial solution. Servile in that the Empress continued to be obedient to a fashion (which no doubt came from France) and satisfied her vanity only by the expedient of pretending to be a man. Imperial, in that the solution was devised to please the Empress and her alone. Evening after evening the dowagers of the Imperial Court (most of whom of course had legs which had better have remained hid) had to expose their deficiencies to the public. Evening after evening elderly ambassadors and sedate administrators had to struggle with hoops and panniers, stays and petticoats. It may have started as a joke but it became a prodigious bore. If only her Imperial Majesty could have restricted the metamorphosis to her own person. That she could not was presumably due to the fact that it was a kind of excuse. It affected everyone and just happened, most conveniently, to affect her. It allowed her in effect to continue to obey the fashion while managing to make the fashion play into her hands (if that be the metaphor). So that in a sense the answer to my original question is not that the Empress *couldn't* alter the fashion but rather that she didn't want to. This is a point to which I must return when we come to a consideration of the causation of fashion. But the hardship of fashion is indeed caused by this, that we all want to be beautiful and that fashion so distorts our sense of beauty, decorum, etc. that by disobeying the fashion we seem to make ourselves ugly.

The particular cruelty of fashion results from this: that fashion, being mobile, does give us a glimpse of possibilities other than the present fashionable solution. Thus, for instance, a lady gifted with an exceptionally pretty bust and exceptionally large feet might in the year 1926 have regretted the fashions of the year 1904, even though the year 1904 would by that time have seemed terribly dowdy. For in 1904 bosoms were displayed while feet were hidden, whereas twenty-two years later bosoms were 'invisible' while feet were much in evidence. The situation of a Chinese lady of the Ming Dynasty endowed with the same physique would have been even more unfortunate. The aesthetics of China would have left her to suppose that she was hopelessly ill-favoured but, unlike the victims of the 1920s, she could not have conceived that things could have been otherwise; she was just plain ugly. Without fashionable change she had no former mode to remember with regret and no possibility of some future development that might work to her advantage.

The hardships imposed by fashion are even more radical than I have suggested, for fashion is, or at least fashion can be, more than clothes deep. At several times during the past thirty years I have made the experiment of showing students between the ages of seventeen and twenty-three pictures of the fashions of previous generations and of listening to their reactions. A group which in 1947 was asked to comment on fashions of the period 1925–30 was both amused and distressed by the exhibition of so much ugliness and wondered what anybody could ever have found charming in such dismal, shapeless, sacklike garments. Their own taste was formed by the pinched-in waists, the low-set shoulders and the long skirts of the 'New Look'. Nineteen years later a similar group, a little older, was equally loud in its denunciation of the New Look and, while admiring the boyish fashions of the later 1920s, felt that they were being revived in the fashions of their own time.

There is nothing particularly surprising in this. What did astonish me, though, was the feeling expressed by both groups that the models employed to exhibit the clothes of the epochs which they condemned were exceedingly ill-favoured. 'Was everyone so plain in the 1920s?' or 'why did Dior choose such awful girls to model his clothes?' are typical of the reactions of both groups.

To some extent this is a criticism of the fashion itself: models are no doubt chosen because they are of a build which will best exhibit current fashions. But I think that the tendency, already noticed, by which we infer an ideal form beneath the clothes which we see, is affected by fashions. Thus when Goya painted his *Maja desnuda* he painted her breasts in a position which is anatomically impossible, for they are thrust apart as indeed they would have been by the underclothes of that period; so that it is conceivable that the painter intended a pleasantry on the subject of nudity.

Again, if we return to the 1920s and look at the treatment of the female nude in academic painting and sculpture or in illustrations to such journals as *La Vie Parisienne*, we shall find that the ideal woman is a very streamlined, thick-waisted, flat-chested, long-legged creature, and if we compare her to the opulent charmers of twenty years earlier she looks as thin as a tram ticket. It would be extremely interesting if someone with a knowledge of psychology, art and literature could trace the influence, if there is an influence, of these very different ideals; on the one hand the essentially heterosexual, maternal and (so far as Western art is concerned) traditional, image of womanhood which must have informed the imagination of the Edwardians, and on the other the epicene, virginal, immature nymphet of the twenties. Such a work is beyond my powers but I believe that it might prove rewarding. That the literary imagination may to a very large extent be governed by the working of fashion I am sure. I offer the following examples as evidence.

Vanity Fair appeared in 1847, a year in which trousers, side whiskers, poke bonnets, buns and ringlets, sleeves low on the shoulder and volu-

PLATE 8

Fashions for 1815 translated, 1847

minous skirts were very much in evidence. All these things appear in Thackeray's own illustrations to his novel so that, without reading it, one takes it for granted that this is a novel of 'modern life', that is to say of the year 1847. But of course this is not the case. *Vanity Fair* is an historical novel and is indeed specifically dated as such; for the battle of Waterloo falls bang in the middle of it. Thackeray knew perfectly well that any kind of historical accuracy demanded far fewer trousers, quite different hair styles, higher waists and exiguous skirts. But to be faithful in 1847 to the fashions of 1815 demanded too much heroism; the fashions of twenty years back were impossibly dowdy (see plate 8).

When Thackeray came to write *Esmond*, a novel which is set in the early eighteenth century, he experienced no such difficulty. The styles of the reign of Queen Anne had been for so long abandoned that they had ceased to be dowdy, they had become romantic; and Thackeray made studies in which the clothes of that epoch are very sympathetically described. On this occasion it was not he, but Du Maurier, who made the completed illustrations, and Thackeray was content that his illustrator should try for historical accuracy.

Nevertheless when, in 1891, Du Maurier himself came to write and illustrate a novel he found himself in just the same predicament as that in which Thackeray had found himself half a century earlier. *Trilby* is a deliberate essay in nostalgia. It deals with Du Maurier's youth as an art student in Paris about the year 1856, and one would have thought it necessary, if the atmosphere of the past was to be effectively rendered, that Du Maurier should have evoked the fashions of the mid-century. But when it came to the point Du Maurier could no more put his Trilby into crinolines than Thackeray could give Amelia a high waist. The illustrations to *Trilby* follow the fashions of the 1890s (see plate 9).

The cases of Thackeray and Du Maurier are interesting because, where other artists have taken historical liberties without being really conscious of what they did, these must surely have known what they were about, for they belonged to an epoch which, like ours, has a clear image of history.

And now, if the reader will bear with me I will describe, by means of a personal anecdote, what I mean by the image of history.

It happened in broad daylight. I was walking through the cloisters adjacent to one of our great cathedrals and I was alone in my environment, a wholly mediaeval environment which was by no means disturbed when, presently, I saw a nun talking to someone who remained hidden behind the pillars of a gothic recess. Then, with startling clarity, the nun's companion became visible. He also was entirely appropriate; but in a dreadful way, for in his hose, his doublet, his liripipe, his long pointed shoes he belonged wholly and inexplicably to the past and not at all to the age

PLATE 9

Fashions for 1856 translated, 1894

PLATE 10

The Homeric Age, translated by the 15th century

from which, like those ladies at Versailles who were said to have strayed into the eighteenth century, I seemed to have wandered.

'Either', said I, 'I am seeing things (at such moments one's remarks are not always very brilliant) or else . . . .' but at this point the young gallant offered the nun a cigarette and it became obvious that there would be – as of course there were – cameramen in attendance.

It was the kind of thing that could have happened to anyone. To anyone that is who shares our position in history, a position in which, more or less consciously, we dress each age in its appropriate attire, seeing the story of Western man as a kind of long continuous fashion parade. It is not of course an assembly that we all perceive with the same degree of clarity, but almost anyone would be sufficiently well informed to know that there must be something unusual about a fourteenth-century gentleman appearing in our midst. This need not always be the case. The ghost of a nun wishing to appear with éclat in a nunnery would have to rely upon something beyond the resources of her wardrobe; the same would be true of a Chinese or Japanese spectre. Even in a society which has experienced fashionable change, but has only experienced it as a comparatively slow process, the sense of anachronism in costume may be lacking. There is a work in the National Gallery which used to be ascribed to Benozzo Gozzoli and is now given to a follower of Fra Angelico (Plate 10). It is a pretty picture of courtly fun and games in the fifteenth century, and it comes as something of a shock to discover that a scene which belongs so evidently to the painter's own epoch is intended to represent the homeric age. This is in fact the Rape of Helen. I do not think that the artist has used the fashion of his own age for the reasons that led Thackeray and Du Maurier to do likewise. There seems to be a genuinely naive feeling here, such as that which enables northern artists* to set their holy families and biblical scenes in that costume and amidst those Flemish houses and landscape that would have been most familiar to the painter himself. In those days sacred art had a quality of nearness and intimacy, which seems to have been lost, and at the same time history, as we know history, lacked the imaginary furniture with which we now endow it.

Mantegna, I suppose, was one of the first to look for 'correct' historical detail, and in the High Renaissance something of the old naivety of the quattrocento has vanished. But in his search for ideal forms a painter like Raphael, while avoiding the contemporary look of his predecessors, manages also to avoid any very precise epoch of any kind. Drapery is

* And Italians also – see Elizabeth Birbari, *Dress in Italian Painting*, London, 1975, pp. 1–14.

in a vague way classical. Something approaching Roman armour serves to adorn a military figure, but we are far from historical exactitude, and in Raphael's cartoon *Feed My Sheep* we find vaguely classical robes set against frankly modern architecture or, as in much Venetian painting, the intrusion of highly fashionable contemporary dress. The first painter to come anywhere near conscientious historicism is Poussin, while his baroque contemporaries offer us the strangest mixtures of Roman body armour, Caravaggesque rags, Raphaelesque robes and full-bottomed wigs. In the eighteenth century it was still possible for Tiepolo to dress Pharoah's daughter as a Venetian lady of the late sixteenth century, but by this time the opportunities and problems of costume were beginning to make themselves felt. We now find painters like Copley, who celebrate the heroic events of modern life in the dress of modern life and without using the props of the High Renaissance. The same artist also painted Charles I in the House of Commons demanding the arrest of the five members, and in France the painter Vincent took a not dissimilar theme from the history of the Fronde (*The Arrest of le President Molé*). Both of them attempt, by putting their figures into correct seventeenth-century costume and into correct architectural settings, to show us, not that which a baroque artist would have provided – a noble version of history as it ought to have been – but rather a glimpse of the past as a witness might have seen it who was present at the time of the event. It was an idea which was to be thoroughly exploited by the painters of the nineteenth century and by the film makers of our own time.

But this new appreciation of the historical possibilities of dress raised problems. Reynolds, the last apostle of the grand style of the High Renaissance, could not contemplate a form of art that lent itself to the vagaries of fashion. Fashion had begun to move so fast that its self-destructive qualities were becoming obvious. In fact Reynolds was conscious of the dilemma which Thackeray was to confront. While urging the painter to avoid all local and particular details he felt that this advice was even more important for the sculptor.

> Working in stone is a very serious business; and it seems to be scarce worth while to employ such durable materials in conveying to posterity a fashion, of which the longest existence scarce exceeds a year.
>
> However agreeable it may be to the antiquaries principles of equity and gratitude, that, as he has received great pleasure from the contemplation of the fashion in dress of former ages, he wishes to give the same satisfaction to future antiquaries; yet, methinks, pictures of an inferior style, or prints, may be con-

PLATE II

Raphael

Timeless Dress

PLATE 12

François-André Vincent

Historical Reconstruction

> sidered as quite sufficient, without prostituting this great art to such mean purposes.

He then, rather unkindly, cites Cheere's statue of the Duke of Cumberland as a horrid warning.

But Reynolds, while urging the sculptor to avoid modern dress, failed to consider the alternatives, or perhaps one should say the alternative which, sixty years later, left his commentator in a condition of some perplexity.

> The statue of the Duke of Cumberland in Cavendish Square has, however, found a worthy compeer in that of George III in Pall Mall East, which proves sculptors are not so easily deterred as Reynolds supposed. Nor is the pig-tailed monarch of Wyatt more ridiculous than the bishops' wigs by Chantrey. What can appear more absurd than a lump of stone behind the human head like a half cheese or a porters knot? In painting, many things can be tolerated, and even rendered useful, from their colour or the treatment of the back-ground, but sculpture has less assistance than even the dryest style of painting, and therefore requires to be more chaste and pure: it is 'not for an age but for all time': otherwise the fashions of one century will remain a laughing-stock to the succeeding. In Greece, the climate, and the games, and customs of the people, brought them more in contact with the exhibition of the naked figure; and therefore, even a priest of Apollo officiating at the altar could be represented undressed, as in the sculpture of the Laocoon; but it is a very different affair with us in England; an English admiral cannot be represented naked boarding a seventy-four without creating a smile; nor chiseled out at full length with a Queen Anne's wig on his head and Roman cuirasse on his stomach, without our present laughter, and yet these are the absurdities but of yesterday. The Romans have represented many of their figures in the costume of the time, but it must be remembered that the dresses of their senators and their generals were unchanged and of ancient origin; while ours are subject to a sliding scale, more changeable than the moon. This will always make it an affair of the greatest difficulty in sculpture; something must be conceded to the taste of the time and for the sake of resemblance, and something to give the dress the air of drapery and antique simplicity. Reynolds has recommended this course in portrait painting, and Chantrey has made admirable use of it in dressing his figures: the soldier in his mili-

> tary cloak and the professor and divine in their gowns, are an extension of this principle; and where his subject has neither, he has adopted a robe de chambre, which is a nearer approach to drapery than a coat and waistcoat. This, however, like every shift, wears out, and it would be ridiculous to dress every man in a morning gown: it is necessary, however, to allude to it here that the student may take advantage of the hint, and that the general reader may make every allowance for the difficulty.
>
> REYNOLDS, *Discourses*,
> Ed. Burnet, 1842, 182–3

Remembering the Balzac monument one cannot but wonder whether Rodin ever read Burnet. But as Burnet remarks, it would be ridiculous to dress every man in a dressing gown and the problem remains. As we have seen, a certain dissatisfaction with modern dress makes of the nineteenth-century painter a natural dress reformer, and although the twentieth-century painter may rise superior to such considerations, still I suspect that a certain realist heroism is required of the painter, and still more of the sculptor, who undertakes to immortalise a natty piece of gents' suiting from a West End tailor.

These perplexities arise, as I have already suggested, because the pace of fashion has become noticeable, so noticeable that the fashions of a man's youth could look dowdy by the time that he was middle-aged. Under such conditions it is natural to declare that modern clothes are 'ugly and inartistic' – the statement is made in all sincerity and yet it has to be qualified by the equally true statement that we love the current fashion, and indeed we love it so much that it is the glass through which we look at the past – a glass which distorts that which we see and makes it tolerable to modern eyes.

I can best exemplify this truth by pointing to the history of costume in the performing arts. Look now at Plate 13; what is it?

'An eighteenth-century actress playing the part of Lady Macbeth,' you reply. But you say this only because you are exceptionally intelligent and well informed and because you noticed that the lady was armed with a couple of daggers. Most people I can assure you would have puzzled their heads in vain, for in whatever dim regions of the darkest ages we may choose to situate Lady Macbeth, we do not usually think of her as a highly fashionable person of the year 1770.

But it was thus that the eighteenth century treated Shakespeare. Some characters, as for instance Falstaff, had traditional costumes; sometimes actors would appear *à la romaine*, that is to say in Roman body armour, buskins, helmets and full-bottomed wigs; but on the whole actors, and

PLATE 13

Dramatic Licence

even more, actresses, paid little heed to historical propriety and naturally enough wore that which suited them best; for actresses this meant the grandest and smartest clothes from Paris.

It was Kemble who, in his production of King John in 1824, employed the learned Planché to bring pageantry and historical probability to the theatre. It was still possible in the early years of this century for Mme Tetrazzini to sail on to the stage of Covent Garden dressed as though she had come straight from a dinner party, although the opera in which she was to sing was *Lucia di Lammermoor*. This however was exceptional, a last operatic assertion of old liberties. Throughout the nineteenth century the work which Planché had begun was continued with great thoroughness; historically accurate costume was a matter of great concern to producers. And yet, historical accuracy as seen through the distorting glass of fashion, is a relative term.

Now look at Plate 14. After your brilliant identification of Lady Macbeth you will not find much difficulty in seeing that this must be a scene from *Antony and Cleopatra*. There are in fact certain architectural details which are quite convincingly Egyptian. But, and this is the really interesting thing, the picture provides information of a different kind. We can date it. Observe Cleopatra, her hair style, her waist, her full, tiered skirts and you will arrive at the correct answer. Yes, this was staged in the 1840s, to be exact in 1849.

At the time when this production was drawing crowds to Sadler's Wells it was acclaimed as a triumph of scholarly and archaeological exactitude. We cannot quite agree, but at least, in 1849 historically correct decor was a new thing and not so very much was known about Egypt in the time of the Ptolemies; it is not hard to find excuses if excuses be needed. Two much more recent examples of the distorting power of fashion are more difficult to explain. In Plates 15, 16 and 17 we have stills from *The Birth of a Nation* made by D. W. Griffiths in 1915; *Gone with the Wind* made by Metro Goldwyn Mayer in 1939, and a photograph of a lady and gentleman taken in the United States in 1861, the year in which the American Civil War began. Both the films purport to show us what Americans looked like at the time of the Civil War. The film makers, unlike the producers at Sadler's Wells, had abundant evidence, photographs, pictures, actual specimens of costume, and the recollections of old people who had lived through that period. But do they in fact make a much better job of it than the gentleman who designed the costumes for *Antony and Cleopatra*? The two versions, which are utterly unlike each other, are both very different from the originals on which they are supposed to be based, nor I think should we have any difficulty in distinguishing the version of 1915 from that of 1939. Miriam Cooper wears deflated versions of the

PLATE 14

Dramatic Interpretation

PLATE 15

Miriam Cooper in *Birth of a Nation*

PLATE 16

Vivien Leigh in *Gone With the Wind*

PLATE 17

Fashions for 1861

crinoline, broad-waisted, flat-chested and very close in their floppy, unironed, unfitted way to the Paris fashions for 1916 (Plate 39). Vivien Leigh, with her incredibly broad shoulders, her 'page-boy' hair style, is very much in the fashion of 1939. Neither, it would seem, results from a serious attempt at historical reconstruction although it is probable that the makers of *Gone with the Wind* did hope that they had achieved something of the kind.

In this connection the case of Britannia is worth our consideration. Britannia is, or was – for we do not see very much of her these days – a national symbol used in our coinage and in the more serious designs of the cartoonists. Taken from an hellenic prototype she was, as it were, a sister of Athene Parthenos. She wore a simple chiton and over it a peplos falling to her knees; she wore the helmet and sometimes the breastplate of Athene, and in place of a spear carried a trident. With so clear a classical origin and embodying as she did a permanent national idea one would not expect her to be much influenced by fashion.

Nevertheless, if you look at Plates 18, 19 and 20, all of them taken from *Punch*, it is clear that she can be dated in each example by the dress that she is wearing. Leech, in 1854, gives her a high enough waist and sufficient petticoats to suggest a crinoline; Tenniel, in 1872, gives her a bustle; we do not at first realise that she must be wearing an 'improver' beneath her dress but if one considers the position of the drapery in its relation to her foot it is I think necessary to admit that her backside has been artificially enlarged. At the same time her bosom matches the flamboyance of her rear and her hair, again in sympathy with prevailing fashions, hangs half-way down her back. In 1914 Bernard Partridge produces a Britannia who is noticeably more Roman, hence more imperial, than her predecessors (her helmet, breastplate and cothurnus are all roman) but in her general line and use of drapery she manages to follow the current fashion, exhibiting a continuous line from breast to ankle, with little emphasis on the waist and a rather daring display of leg. La France, as is proper, is even more fashionable and might almost have come from chez Poiret.

Finally I would like to show that fashion exerts its influence not only on our perception of history and our ideal images but upon the supernatural. Plate 21 is a photograph of a fairy; it is one of a number of photographs which were shown to the late Sir Conan Doyle who pronounced them to be perfectly genuine photographs of perfectly genuine fairies. Some years ago I showed this photograph to Miss Anne Buck of the Museum of Costume in Manchester, who modestly suggested that these fairies had been photographed somewhere between 1918 and 1922. She

PLATE 18

Britannia in 1854

PLATE 19

Britannia in 1872

PLATE 20

Britannia in 1914

arrived at this date by an examination of the hair style. In fact the photograph was published in 1920.

At the risk of being accused of materialism I would venture to suggest that someone was pulling someone's leg and, if so, if, that is, there were an element of fraud in the pictures, then it seems probable that the last thing that the manufacturer of fairies would want to do would be to suggest that these immortal creatures were in any way influenced by fashion. The fashionable hair style must therefore have resulted from an unconscious impulse. An even clearer case is provided by the celebrated Vermeer forgeries of Van Meegeren; the forger, as Mr Benedict Nicolson has very acutely pointed out, modelled the heads of his figures upon fashionable beauties of his own time, that is to say, on celebrated film stars. Here, manifestly, the artist had every motive for wishing not to give a clue to the actual date of his work; the fashionable element crept into the work without the artist wishing it.

If we now come back to the *Antony and Cleopatra* and consider Cleopatra's dress, which is I think the most emphatically fashionable thing in that picture, we may say, as we observe the way in which Cleopatra's neckline sweeps low across her bosom and falls to reveal a graceful shoulder: 'how very 1849'. Meaning, of course, that the Egyptian robe echoes perfectly the cut of a fashionable evening dress of the period. But would anyone in 1849 have said: 'how very 1849'? I doubt it. What they would have said then would have been 'how becoming' and, if the dress had been a little more accurate in its historical detail, this would probably be felt simply as a rather disappointing lack of charm. Fashion is easily equated with beauty, and the fashionable way of representing something appears simply as the most attractive way of representing something.

Thus it happens that when we dress an actress in historic costume, or find the clothes for a national emblem, or a fairy, or invent a face for a spurious picture, we quite naturally make the thing represented as beautiful as we can while at the same time making it as historically correct as possible. What we find it so hard to realise is that the two aims are in a subtle way incompatible; the more we beautify the more we bring our reconstruction into line with current taste and the more we take it away from the taste of the time that we are trying to recreate. At the time when the reconstruction is made both the artist and the spectator are unaware of the kind of concessions that have occurred. When taking the Egyptian Queen or Vivien Leigh, or whoever it may be, and putting them into an appropriate disguise, we at the same time make sure that they shall look as charming as possible. But when the fashion ceases to charm, when the mode becomes dowdy, then the spurious element becomes painfully obvious. Anyone can tell a fraud when the attractive

PLATE 21

Fashions for Fairies, *c*. 1920

element has become repellent; it sticks out like a sore thumb. But to distinguish the essentially modern beauty in that which is supposed to be beautiful in an antique style is not so easy.

The history of art in the West is the history of an ever-changing conception of beauty, an aesthetic which is continually dying and for ever being renewed. All our achievements and all our theories are governed by that changing impulse; so too our whole conception of art history itself. Fashion in fact is the grand motor force of taste.

4
Theories of Fashion

'No one should formulate any theory of fashion which fails to take into account its partial or total absence in other civilisations, and also its previous importance among the males of our own. To do so must lead to conclusions as unreliable as those of a critic who refuses to see more than one act of a play. His verdict might be right, but it would have a very good chance of being wrong.'

DORIS LANGLEY MOORE

What then sets this incredibly powerful evolutionary process into motion, what maintains and increases its velocity, gives it its vast strength and accounts for its connected phenomena? The historians of dress tend to be vague upon this point; they produce secondary factors of undeniable importance, but insufficient to supply a complete answer. Resolute attempts to produce a theory of fashion are rare. Of Veblen's account (which is not mine) I will speak later; here it may be useful to discuss other systems which, though they appear to me to be radically unsound, are by no means unilluminating or without value. These theories may be said, roughly speaking, to fall into four groups: (1) those which explain change of fashion as the work of a few individuals; (2) those which see in fashion a product of human nature; (3) those which find in it a reflection of great political or spiritual events; (4) those which suppose the intervention of a Higher Power.

Very few writers on fashion see in the action of individuals the principal cause of fashionable change. Nevertheless, the view is fairly widespread that certain people, and notably the 'leaders' who set the fashion or the businessmen who 'create' it, are of primary importance.

Obviously no history of dress would be complete without a mention of Beau Brummel or Mlle de Fontanges. That these, and others, were leaders is indisputable, but to conceive of them as despots, able to do whatever they wanted, is I am sure to put the cart before the horse. No one creates a fashion, for we are born into a society in which fashion already exists; it exists because it pleases and, because it pleases, our aesthetic affections are predetermined for us. As we have already seen, the Empress of Russia was powerless to change the fashion, not because she couldn't do so, but because, being herself a creature of fashion, she didn't want to do so. Thus, during the 'seventies and eighties' of the last century the Princess of Wales was able to exert a considerable influence upon feminine dress. But it would have been quite impossible for her to have reintroduced the crinoline or, even, in 1885 to have reverted to the fashions of 1875 for the sufficient reason that these outmoded fashions had become odious to the fashionable world, and of course to her, as to everyone else. The leader must therefore be a follower; he may alter details, but he cannot either arrest or reverse the process.

One of the most fashionable of our monarchs, Charles II, did indeed make a conscious effort to bring fashion to a full stop. In 1666 he introduced a form of masculine dress, 'a fashion of clothes which he will never alter'. It would appear that this garment was inspired by oriental sources: it was 'a comely dress after the persian mode', says Evelyn. With the king himself setting the fashion and the court following, the success of this venture seemed assured. And yet it was short lived; the vest was soon forgotten and Englishmen like Englishwomen again took their fashions from France. It is indeed possible that the 'vest' was killed by Louis XIV; for in November 1666 Pepys records that:

> ... the King of France hath, in defiance to the King of England, [with whom he was at war] caused all his footmen to be put into Vests, and that the noblemen will do the like; which, if true, is the greatest indignity ever done by one prince to another, and would incite a stone to be revenged ... This makes me mighty merry, it being an ingenious kind of affront.*

If an Englishman, and one who had actually purchased the 'vest', could laugh, the laughter was no doubt general and that was the end of this royal fashion. But whatever the circumstances of its demise, it certainly did die, and it is hard to imagine that Charles II or any other monarch howsoever influential could have actually brought the fashion to a halt.

It has been said that it is the dressmakers who impose a new fashion upon the public in order to stimulate the market and thus fill their pockets. The suggestion has a reasonable air, for it is after all the great firms and not their customers which design and create the fashions. But there are insuperable difficulties in the way of such an explanation. If the makers of women's clothes profit by continual changes in fashion, why is it that the makers of men's clothes do not do likewise, or rather, to put the diffi-

* Pepys, November 22, 1666. See also Laver, *A Concise History of Costume*, 1969, p. 116.

culty more accurately and more strongly, why was it that men's fashions for centuries followed the same changeable and expensive course as women's fashions and then, presumably to the great disadvantage of tailors, became very conservative? If fashion was a profitable sauce for the goose why not for the gander?

Again one may doubt whether the fashion industries serve their own interests very well. A vogue for simplicity which makes it possible for the woman with a sewing machine to compete with larger concerns must surely be to the disadvantage of the trade, and even more to the disadvantage of those who manufacture ornaments for dress, and yet it was at a time when the trade was very highly organised that the very simple style of the 20s was at its apogee and skirts at their height. The designers did in fact attempt to bring back the long skirt as an article of daily wear; but they failed. Many other attempts of the same nature, fashions launched with adroit and costly propaganda, have been tried without success.* Finally it must be realised that the process of change began at a time when most clothes were made in the home and that it has continued through many phases of organisation and mechanisation which, though they have increased the scope and velocity of change, have not altered its essential character.

In a free market the relationship between the consumer and the producer is in its essence one of unity. The great houses dictate; the orders of fashion are issued through them. But the great houses are great only because their clientele makes them so. It is only because they please that they prosper and if not prosperous they cannot command.

Here is the testimony of M. Paul Poiret, and if ever there was a dictator of fashion he was one. Speaking to an audience of ladies in the United States, he said:

> I know that you think me a king of fashion. It is what your newspapers call me, and it is thus that I am received, honoured and feted everywhere by great multitudes of people. It is a reception which cannot but flatter and of which I cannot complain. All the same I must undeceive you with regard to the powers of a king of fashion. We are not capricious despots such as wake up one fine day, decide upon a change in habits, abolish a neckline, or puff out a sleeve. We are neither arbiters nor dictators. Rather we are to be thought of as the blindly obedient servants of woman, who, for her part, is always enamoured of change

---

* See Nystrom, *The Economics of Fashion*, New York, 1928, 13–17; 82; 299–301 *et passim*. See also Stuart Chase, *The Tragedy of Waste*, New York, 1925, p. 92.

> and athirst for novelty. It is our role, and our duty, to be on the watch for the moment at which she becomes bored with what she is wearing, that we may suggest at the right instant (*à point nommé*) something else which will meet her tastes and needs. It is therefore with a pair of antennae and not with a rod of iron that I come before you, and it is not as a master that I speak, but as a slave, a slave, though, who must divine your innermost thoughts.

In another lecture we find the following profoundly significant anecdote:

> There are signs which allow one to proclaim the end of a fashion. Very few people can recognise them. Thus when I announced that hats would henceforth be plain, it was because I saw them to be smothered with leaves, fruit, flowers, feathers, and ribbons. All fashions end in excess. Nevertheless, on the morrow of that announcement I received a delegation of manufacturers, makers of flowers, fruits, ribbons, and leaves, who, like the burghers of Calais, came to implore me to restore trimmings. But what can one do against the wishes or the desires of women? Hats continued plain, and are so still, and I am heartily sorry for it.*

The essential difficulty in the way of any explanation which sees an individual, whether he be a monarch or a tailor, as the prime mover in the history of fashion is, not that these autocrats have frequently been unable to stand against the current of taste, but that we are still left with no explanation as to why the leaders should desire to make a change or the followers be willing to obey them.

This brings us naturally to the theory of human nature, of which Paul Nystrom is the ablest exponent. Nystrom concludes his examination of human motives with the following summary:

> ... The specific motive or factors for fashion interest and fashion changes, in addition to the physical reasons for change such as occur at the end of each season, are the boredom or fatigue with the current fashion, curiosity, desire to be different or self-assertion, rebellion against convention, companionship and imita-

* Poiret, *En Habillant l'Epoque*, Paris, 1930, 265/266, 271. The whole of this chapter is of the greatest interest and importance. It should perhaps be said that M. Poiret makes some prophecies which have not been wholly fulfilled.

> tion. There may be other factors in human nature promoting fashion interest, but these are sufficiently effective and inclusive upon which to build a practical theory of fashion.*

This is no doubt true enough as far as it goes: it is a sufficient catalogue of human motives; but obviously it also leaves a great deal unexplained. If fashion were a universal and constant phenomenon in the history of dress, so that all men and all women in every land and in every age had always shown a restless desire for change, a desire to be different, a desire to rebel, a tendency to be bored by the end of a season, then indeed we might say that fashion results from the mutability of human nature. But, as we have already seen, this is not the case. The conditions in which fashion occurs are, taking the history of mankind as a whole, exceptional conditions. As a rule men and women have been content to wear that which their fathers and mothers wore before them. In fact it seems that those traits in human nature which result in a change of style can only become effective given special circumstances; it is not fashion which results from human nature but human nature which is itself subject to fashion.

In this connection it seems proper to consider those theories of dress which relate the outer man to the inner mind. The very important bearing which sexual display and the related feelings of modesty have upon clothes is discussed in a learned work by Professor J. C. Flugel, who shows very clearly how the erotic imagination plays upon clothes, their putting on, their taking off, the phallic shapes which they assume, both in the conscious and the unconscious apprehension of man. It would seem, in the light of his researches, that the sexual differentiation which is so marked a feature of modern dress may well be of central importance in our imaginative equipment. But however valuable these investigations into the use to which our conscious and unconscious minds put our clothes and those of our neighbours may be, they do not help us to understand the forces at work which change the form of these symbols. (In fairness to Professor Flugel it must be said that he makes no such claim.) What the psychologists do show is the enormous importance which attaches to the history of dress. The sexual impulse may after all, broadly speaking, be regarded as a constant affect upon the course of history, but we are here dealing with something which is by definition a variable. If we are to look for causes of fashionable change we shall surely find them among those historical forces which are themselves in a perpetual flux,

---

* Nystrom, *op. cit.*, p. 81.

such as can, for instance, explain why men's fashions became stable while those of women continued to evolve.

In considering the role of the unconscious, a concrete instance may not be amiss. Let us take a favourite of the psychologists, the high-heeled shoe. Flugel explains the persistence of this fashion on the ground that it gives an upright carriage, that it effaces the abdomen, that it gives additional height without breadth (i.e. a youthful figure), that the size of the foot is thereby diminished and that the heel provides a phallic symbol.

But it is necessary, in considering an explanation of this kind, to remember that it has got to be efficient in more than one context. As an explanation of why women in the twentieth century have worn high heels this may work; but we have to remember that high heels have been worn by both sexes, and we have to consider whether the analysis of motives here offered will account for the high heels of Louis XIV.

The main difficulty however is this: supposing that Flugel's explanation is perfectly correct and that certain conscious and unconscious demands can be supplied by a certain kind of shoe – or whatever it may be – this may tell us why the high-heeled shoe came into fashion, it cannot tell us why it went out of fashion. And yet this does happen.

To say that mankind is fickle and shifts its attention from one fetish to another is again no answer, for mankind is not always fickle and, as we have seen in the case of China, under certain conditions mankind, far from being fickle, will remain constant to its fetish for hundreds of years. Once again we find that any explanation which depends upon a theory of human nature leaves us, as Plekhanov pointed out a long time ago, just where we started. In studying fashion we have to look for the determinants of human nature itself.

This brings us naturally to a consideration of events which lie outside human nature such as climate, commerce and international trade, accidents, wars, revolutions and the emergence of new moral and political ideas.

Of climate little need be said; it is only under protest that men will change their clothes in a new country. It took many years to persuade Europeans that a special fashion is needed for life in India. The form of clothes may sometimes originate from climatic needs, but it develops almost in defiance of climate. To my mind the most extraordinary and the most lamentable victory of Western fashions is that described by Charles Campbell Hughes in his account of Eskimo life. The Eskimos have evolved a type of clothing which is severely practical and highly efficient. One would have supposed that no people on earth could have better reasons for not wanting to make a change; and yet the clothes brought in by traders, although it is realised that they are much less well adapted to the needs of the Arctic than is the traditional dress, have gradually been adopted. Shivering and disconsolate, but happy to think that they are chilly with the best people, the Eskimos are losing their old dress-making skills and accepting the inadequate weeds of the foreigner.*

Trade and foreign influences, especially foreign conquests, certainly play their part in the development of dress. The effect of conquest can be measured fairly well in the history of China. Here, for instance, the Tartar conquest brought the Tartar cap. In the same way the barbarians who overran the Roman Empire influenced, and were influenced by, the Roman dress. But once such a conquest has been completed the process of change stops. Foreign influences are sometimes hard to distinguish from fashion itself. Wherever a more sumptuous style is encountered it tends to be imitated: the history of German fashions is very largely a history of foreign influences. But if the flow of importation stops, it does not necessarily lead to any further development. This has in fact been demonstrated in the more backward of the Latin American states, where European importations have created static local costumes.

Trade, in the sense of the importation of new materials, does not seem to create new fashions, although it may sometimes affect those already in existence, as in the case of Indian stuffs at the beginning of the eighteenth century; it may be fairly classed as a secondary influence, subordinate to the general trend of fashion and itself deeply affected thereby – witness the ruined ostrich farms of South Africa.

Accidents would seem sometimes to determine details. The victors of Steinkirk were so hurried in their toilette that they inadvertently set the style for a new cravat. Lord Spencer burnt his coat-tails and set a new fashion in jackets. But the continuous and regular development of fashion does not suggest that it owes its direction to a series of accidents, but rather that a fashionable accident has to be of a kind that will meet the needs of the moment.

The theories of fashion which we have so far considered lead us naturally to look for a more probable explanation in those larger historical movements which, since they exert an influence upon us all, may perhaps be the efficient cause, if not of fashion itself at least of the direction that it takes.

Such theories have been extremely popular during the past fifty years, and it may be that they received a certain stimulus from the very dramatic evolution of fashion in the first thirty years of this century, an evolution

*See Charles Campbell Hughes, *An Eskimo Village in the Modern World*, Cornell, 1960. See also Roach and Eicher, *Dress, Adornment and the Social Order*, New York, 1965, pp. 308–11.

which might be paralleled in the no less remarkable developments in feminine fashion which took place during and after the Napoleonic Wars. On this basis certain generalisations seemed possible. It was asserted that a Great War will invariably exert a profound influence upon the clothes that women wear. In particular it favours the simpler and more youthful styles of dress. Likewise it was believed that currency inflation might affect clothes in much the same manner.

The phenomena which in the first place led theorists to associate certain developments of fashion with war, that is to say Directoire and Empire styles and the style of the late 1920s, to which more recently have been added the fashions of the past twenty years, will be discussed in a later chapter. I will only anticipate that discussion by saying that it is not in my opinion easy to establish a direct and unequivocal connection between the fashions which followed either the Napoleonic Wars or either of the recent world wars. But even if it were, these are but three conflicts out of many that have afflicted humanity. Even if a clear correspondence could be established in these cases it would hardly prove a general rule concerning the relationship of war and fashion. Conversely, if we find that any armed conflict produces an effect upon the development of dress, then the imperfect connection between some recent wars and some recent mutations of fashion will hardly affect the generalisation as a whole.

Look then at the history of fashion and trace the influence of the major European conflicts. The difficulty of course is to find any epoch which may be called peaceful and which may serve as a contrast. If we find, and I think that we do find, no recognisable influence exerted by the Hundred Years War or the Thirty Years War, it may be because there was so little peace to let us know what, under happier circumstances, the fashions would have been like. But in later periods the opportunities for obtaining clear evidence are more favourable. Between the War of Independence and 1917 the United States experienced one vast war and two minor conflicts. What effect did they have upon the clothes worn by American women? None at all. Between the Napoleonic Wars and 1914 England had only one war with a European power. Did the Crimean War have any effect upon the clothes worn by Englishwomen? None at all. Neither the War of the Spanish Succession, the Seven Years War, nor the War of 1870 seem to have had the slightest effect upon the history of costume in any of the belligerent or non-belligerent countries. I cannot help feeling that this particular generalisation is rather too narrowly based.

The relationship between clothes and inflation has been stated thus:

> It is a curious fact in human history, and one well worthy of

> more attention than it has received from the social psychologists, that the disappearance of corsets is *always* accompanied by two related phenomena – promiscuity and an inflated currency. No corsets, bad money, and general moral laxity; corsets, sound money, and the prestige of the grande cocotte – such seems to be the rule.*

There is a poetical charm about this generalisation, a touch of agreeable fantasy which makes it seem obtuse and heavy handed to measure it against anything so coarse as a fact. And yet, students treat such theorising with such portentous solemnity that it does seem necessary to try the effect of a little economic history.

It is no new thing to debase a currency. Henry VIII of England debased our money to a scandalous extent, and it was left to his daughter Elizabeth to restore the value of the pound. There is no reason to suppose that she tightened her stay laces in the process; but perhaps this was not inflation in the modern sense of the word. Modern inflation hit the United States during and after the Civil War, say from 1862 to 1868. I am willing to believe that this was a period of great moral laxity (after all, one can believe this of almost any period) but was it also a period in which there were no corsets, was it even a period in which corsets became perceptibly less restrictive? It was not; indeed the tendency of fashion during this period was rather in the opposite direction. At this time American women, like European women, followed a policy of controlled deflation.

On the other hand, if we compare Paris fashions for the year 1904 with those for 1914, we shall discover that during the first decade of our century corsets were, so to speak, losing their grip. I would not say that they were abolished; some women continued to wear some kind of more or less rigid infrastructure, and this I think will be found to hold good for pretty well any period of European dress. Nevertheless, a recent biographer is hardly exaggerating when he says that Poiret dispensed with the corset and 'gave women a new figure'.† There was undoubtedly a great loosening up of dress, and if we are to accept the theory 'no corsets bad money' the franc should, by 1914, have been severely shaken and falling steadily on the world's market, whereas in fact it was perfectly healthy.

These examples may serve to remind us of one of the main difficulties that confront any attempt to build generalisations concerning fashions which are based upon the supposed influence of political events, or even upon the prevailing ethos of any given age. If the proposition 'no corsets

---

* Laver, *Taste and Fashion*, London, 1948, p. 101. My italics.

† Palmer White, *Paul Poiret*, 1973, p. 11.

bad money' be accepted it would not have been possible in the 1860s for French fashions to have been imported into the United States; or if the proposition 'corsets sound money' held good at the time when Poiret was making a fortune in England and Russia, it would have been necessary for him to export inflation together with his models. In the same way there would, if the generalisations concerning fashion and war held good, surely be some marked difference between the fashions of the belligerent and the non-belligerent countries. In fact it is extremely hard to discover any substantial differences between the fashions of different countries in recent times. Some differences do exist, and to a specialist they may seem so important that it is possible to consider English nineteenth-century fashions for women as something quite different from French fashions of the same period; but this is the kind of distinction that is much more obvious to the expert than to anyone else. Provincial centres may imitate the metropolitan areas of dress slowly and clumsily; in earlier centuries local customs may be sufficiently apparent. But the ordinary reasonably well-informed spectator confronted by a dozen or so photographs or fashion plates of the last century would find it hard to say which came from London, from Paris, from Vienna or from Milan. On the other hand it is clear that Italy, Austria, France and England had at this time very different political histories. Nor is this all; each country may be said to have had a rather different 'ethical atmosphere'. The point needs to be borne in mind when one evaluates a statement such as this:

> In any investigation of the precepts which have governed feminine fashion, it will be found that, in every country and at all periods of time, the mind of woman has been strongly affected by the ethical atmosphere of her time, and, consciously or unconsciously, has formulated a record of history in her dress.*

The mind of woman – without pausing to subject that rather puzzling concept to rigorous scrutiny, what, one may ask becomes of the mind of man? Why should he be neglected; surely the ethical atmosphere of the age of Elizabeth is as well represented by Leicester as by the Queen? Louis XIV is as much to the point as Mme de Montespan, Sir Brooke Boothby as Mrs Andrews. Why then, about the beginning of the nineteenth century, was the continually changing course of history echoed (I do not think that one can truly say that it was recorded) in terms of petticoats, while the mind of man became so dull, indeed so absent that, so far as waistcoats and top hats are concerned, it barely changes at all? If we had the answer to this question it might be rather easier to say

* J. M. Price, *Dame Fashion*, 1913.

just what we mean when we describe the mind of women as being strongly affected by the ethical atmosphere of her time.

It is in fact the kind of statement which, unlike those which relate fashion to a specific historical phenomenon, such as warfare or inflation, is rather difficult either to accept or to reject. This is even more true of another and much more recent formulation which I will quote:

> ... modes are but the reflections of the manners of the time. Any serious student of costume history must admit that this is true; otherwise he is driven back on the long exploded idea that fashion's changes are purely arbitrary, or the equally untenable notion that such changes are the conspiracy of half a dozen leading designers in Paris. ... In the perspective of costume history it is plain that the dress of any given period is exactly suited to the social climate of the time, and indeed bears a close relation to such things as interior decoration and even architecture. It is impossible to imagine Louis XIV in the top hat and frock coat of Napoleon III; it is impossible to imagine the Empress Eugénie in the short skirts of the 1920s. Examples could be multiplied indefinitely.*

Certainly there is much here that is undeniable. In Western cultures fashion is itself an important part of history. To those of us who see history in terms of images this must seem self-evident. In the history of man few things can be more important and few things will be found more characteristic of an age than the outward aspect of man himself. It is this which furnishes that which I have called the 'historical imagination'. At the same time it is as well to remember that the historical imagination can play us false. Certainly when we think of the Empress of the French we imagine her as Winterhalter painted her, emerging bare-shouldered from a sea of crinolines, and we forget that this was but one aspect of the fashions of her youth and that in fact, living on until 1920, she was to appear in a great many other disguises. But the real danger of such image making is that it suggests a causal connection which may not in fact exist. Supposing you had twisted your ankle and had a bad cold, it might well appear that these maladies, in that both made you miserable at the same time, were connected. But one would not begin to believe that this was the case unless you always had a cold when you sprained your ankle, or unless you never had a cold unless your ankle was sprained. And even if this melancholy coincidence were frequently repeated you might still be wrong in believing that you had some kind of foot and mouth

* Laver, *A Concise History of Costume*, 1969, p. 272.

disease. The fact that we are bound to associate Louis XIV with periwigs and high-heeled shoes does not necessarily mean that there is a causal connection between the two. Are they both manifestations of the 'social climate of the time'? And what do we mean by a social climate?

We have already seen, in the specific cases of war and currency inflation, that social conditions are not always precisely mirrored in the history of dress. Does the same difficulty occur when we look at those larger commotions of the social climate which themselves seem to govern the character of wars and other social disturbances? I am thinking here of two major historical affects: religion and nationalism. It is appropriate to take them as subjects for examination because both are clearly influential in the history of costume. The Sikh, the Muslim and the Quaker all exhibit, or used to exhibit, their religious opinions by means of their dress. There are few, if any, of the older nations which do not have some kind of national dress, nor is this an unknown phenomenon in the new world. Where religion and nationalism have exerted a direct effect upon dress they have established, not fashions, but uniforms; and in fact because they represent ideas which are held to transcend history, to belong either to eternity or to the semi-eternal character of race or country, they must be inimical to fashion. We have already seen that fashion is in a large degree international. It would seem therefore to be totally opposed to nationalism and, in so far as religious faith varies from one state to another, it is opposed also to religion.

Now when we consider sixteenth-century dress, the dress of Christendom at the moment when it was being torn apart by rival sects, it becomes very hard to find any clear trace of that fearful conflict in the clothes which were then being worn in Europe. Very probably there was a certain sobriety in the fashions of Edinburgh and Geneva which would not have been found in Florence or in Venice; but in the massacre of St Bartholomew the Catholics had to invent a badge that would distinguish them from their victims, and throughout the latter half of the sixteenth century Protestant England and Calvinist Holland, while carrying on a desperate struggle against Spain, carefully imitated her fashions. Despite the distinction in dress (a distinction which has been exaggerated) between Cavaliers and Roundheads, the fierce wars and persecutions which in the seventeenth century divided Christian from Christian found but little reflection in the fashions of the time.

The nineteenth century provides an even more striking example of the way in which dress fails to mirror the social climate of an age; indeed the case is such that one is tempted to look for some kind of negative correspondence between nationalism and fashion. In the past 200 years nationalism has been one of the most important political, social and aesthetic forces in the world, it has inspired wars and persecutions, it has made and destroyed nations. At the beginning of this period every European nation (including many nations that did not yet exist) had a national costume; by the end of the period such costumes had become all but extinct, national dress was something kept for patriotic holidays, tourist junketings and travel posters.

To take one example; the Irish (and no one will accuse the Irish of being indifferent to the claims of nationalism) wore tall pudding-shaped hats, cutaway jackets, and knee breeches during the first half of the nineteenth century. These were so completely extinguished by the end of the century that I used to imagine that they were the invention of political cartoonists and the music-hall stage. Nevertheless, George Moore refers to them as the ordinary dress of the Irish peasantry in County Mayo during his youth, i.e. in the 1860s. It was with Parnellism, the Land League and the Celtic Revival that Ireland lost her knee breeches.

Much the same sort of thing happens today in those African and Asian countries where Europe, America and all their works are violently denounced by young enthusiasts who have exchanged native dress for the civil and military uniform of the West.

The oddities and anomalies which present themselves when we begin to consider the relationship of fashion to the social climate of an age need not force us altogether to abandon the notion that there is such a relationship, but I think that it must oblige us to admit that the connection is not one of mechanical causality. Indeed so far is it from being so that the determining force, the spirit of the age, who may be dignified with the appellation of Zeitgeist, may by some theorists be endowed with a volition and a personality. To all our objections it may be replied: 'That is the way the Zeitgeist works; we are not dealing here with a simple weathercock which turns mechanically to all the spiritual winds of humanity but with a hidden and mysterious force which chooses the vessel into which it will pour itself, which need not respond immediately to some stimuli but acts when and where it pleases.'

If we accept these premises and allow the Zeitgeist a free hand there can be no objection. But the argument then resolves itself into a tautology; fashion is what it is because the Zeitgeist makes it so. The theory of ideological causation then becomes, not an explanation based upon facts, but one based upon a supernatural hypothesis. If on the other hand we attempt to find a rationale of ideological causation; if we attempt to correlate the ethical, religious, political or aesthetic ideas of men and women with the clothes that they wear and have worn, we shall come to a standstill because, inevitably, we shall find that fashion cuts clean across ideological frontiers.

The supernatural hypothesis has been carried a stage further by the late Gerald Heard, a daring speculator who explains fashion as the product of the Life Force or Evolutionary Appetite, as the work, not of man, but of God. 'The thesis of this book is that evolution is going on no longer in but around man, and the faster because working in a less resistant medium.'

> ... the statement that in clothes we are still witnessing creation at work, that in the people's 'Sunday Best' alone it is still not resting from its labours, that in a matter held so insignificant the supreme force of the universe is alone visible, that the same dynamo-design which once made our bodies for good or ill and now seems to have left them to be maintained at our costs or cut down, is still moving mysteriously though faintly in, of all unlikely things, our garments, the *ignis abyssi* smouldering but alone alight on, of all unlikely altars, a tailor's bench – such a contention may seem to the ordinary well or ill dressed man simply ridiculous.*

It is an attractive argument, neither does it lack force. There is, as we have seen, an astonishing similarity between the development of clothes and that of bodies; the same slow development of forms, the same increase in specialisation, the conservation of vestigial members, the same mysterious force.

Mr Heard was one of the few writers to consider the problems posed by Chinese dress. He attempts to solve them by invoking a racial theory. 'At once we see we are faced with a people who for some reason are rational, consciously utilitarian in a way that we have hardly ever attained.' Hence their indifference to fashion, or, as on this theory we may put it: their failure to evolve.

> The bound foot of the Chinese woman is shaped and shod so as to resemble a hoof, and is a late importation; it may be as late as and associated with the horse hoof sleeve and cuff which conceal the Chinese hand and are said to be a Manchu totemistic fashion, as they, through their irresistible cavalry, mounted the celestial throne from horseback. What more natural then, that the heightening of sexual charm should be obtained by a distortion with the same tendency? A race memory of immeasureable age was roused by the recollection of late national glory.†

* Gerald Heard, *Narcissus: an Anatomy of Clothes*, 1924, p. 16.
† Heard, *op. cit.*, p. 74.

There are grave historical objections to such an account. But the real trouble about China, from the 'Heardian' point of view, is that which attaches to any racial view of dress; for how, on such a hypothesis, are we to account for the abandonment of traditional dress which accompanied the Meiji restoration in Japan and was already evident in China between the time of Sun Yat Sen's revolution and the Communist seizure of power?

The evolutionary view of dress as presented by Heard is, however, open to more sweeping objections. The process of evolution in living things is one in which the fittest survive and in which the claims of utility are inexorable. As we have seen, the contrary is true of dress; if we were able to find some animal which had evolved in the direction of greater and greater unfitness for existence, until finally it was reduced to a condition in which it had to depend upon the goodwill of other species for its support, then we should have an exact parallel to the evolutionary process (as regards any given phase of fashion). Certain Japanese poultry do indeed fulfil these conditions, but they are the product of artificial, not of natural, selection.

It may, however, be argued that some animal finery is only in a special sense utilitarian. The tail of the peacock, the gorgeous rump of the mandril, would appear to be sexual stimulants useful only in courtship. May we not, then, suppose that the brilliant mating colours of animals have been evolved in the same way as the fine dress of humans and for a similar purpose? I think not. When any peacock meets any peahen it would seem to require a certain manifestation of splendour before it can cooperate in the reproductive process. Are we to suppose that a similar necessity exists as between ladies and gentlemen? And if that be the case, must we not believe that a singular frigidity pertains among the higher income groups of the Western world? It is indeed an awe-inspiring thought that the frantic distortions and encumbrances in the dress of the wealthy and their liveried servants result from a genteel difficulty in procreation. Happily this does not seem to be the case; although there are certainly economically determined standards of sexual charm, such as small hands and feet, daintiness, and delicacy of complexion, there is abundant evidence that the classes can interbreed freely, and do so without any apparent loss of fertility.

The evolutionary hypothesis breaks down because evolution deals in species, whereas dress is divided neither by races nor by nations, but by classes and groups of classes.

This chapter has been very hard to write and will probably be equally hard to read because I have found it necessary to make use of a rather wearisome method of argument. I have put up a series of arguments and have then shot them down again; in so doing I have used the same weapons again and again. These weapons are taken from the history of fashion and clearly any theory must fit those facts. But there are in addition some other difficulties which are not immediately relevant to the theories that I have discussed, but which must be borne in mind when in my next chapter I attempt to outline what seems to me a workable theory.

The facts which have somehow to be accommodated are briefly as follows:

Fashion, as we know it in the West, is not and never was a universal condition of dress. It is a European product and is not nearly as old as European Civilisation. It is an expanding force, it affects an ever greater number of people in an ever greater part of the world. And yet the expansion of fashion has not been a regular phenomenon. One of the most remarkable things about the development of fashion is that from the end of the eighteenth century the history of men's clothes has been quite different from the history of women's clothes. Fashion is an international thing and has tended to become more and more international; at all events until very recently the tendency was for styles to be set by fewer and fewer centres. Although there have been many convulsions in human history which seem to have no effect upon fashion at all, there have been some which certainly do appear to have had a profound effect. Of these the French Revolution seems to be the most obvious example. We may also find a sartorial influence at work in the Puritan Revolution of 1644 and perhaps in the war and post-war periods: 1914 to 1930 and 1945 to 1960. Fashion is an extremely powerful force and yet it can be checked, and in certain circumstances we shall find that archaic forms survive in spite of fashion.

I hope I have shown that a consideration of the history of fashion makes it impossible to start with generalisations about human nature if that entity is to be considered as something universal and unchanging. I hope also that I have shown that the role of the individual in the history of fashion can never be of paramount importance. Also it is impossible to arrive at a complete correspondence between the political history, the race, sentiments, ideals or institutions of a nation and its fashions. We can accept a theological explanation only if we agree in advance that no explanation is required. Nor can we allow the development of fashion to be the result of some or all of the factors here discussed acting in combination. Many of them do no doubt play their part in shaping fashion; but since these factors will be found in almost any culture, and since fashion in its origins at all events is purely European, it seems impossible to suppose that there is not some other force required to put all these factors into operation, to start the engine of change and, having started it, to accelerate it in an ever-increasing degree. This other force is not far to seek, and when once we have seen what it is and how it operates, I think it will be quite easy to construct a theory which accounts for all the historical phenomena that I have listed. The nature of this force is to be found by returning to Veblen. It is by the application of his theories that we can meet all the difficulties here proposed and thus come to an account of fashion which will at least tally with the salient facts in the history of clothes.

5

The Mechanism of Fashion

'Does not the world love *Court Guides*, and millinery, and plate, and carriages? Mercy on us! Read the fashionable intelligence; read the *Court Circular*; read the genteel novels; survey mankind, from Pimlico to Red Lion Square, and see how the Poor Snob is aping the Rich Snob; how the Mean Snob is grovelling at the feet of the Proud Snob; and the Great Snob is lording it over his humble brother. Does the idea of equality ever enter Dives's head? Will it ever? Will the Duchess of Fitzbattleaxe (I like a good name) ever believe that Lady Crœsus, her next-door neighbour in Belgrave Square, is as good a lady as her Grace? Will Lady Crœsus ever leave off pining for the Duchess's parties, and cease patronising Mrs. Broadcloth, whose husband has not got his Baronetcy yet? Will Mrs. Broadcloth ever heartily shake hands with Mrs. Seedy, and give up those odious calculations about poor dear Mrs. Seedy's income? Will Mrs. Seedy, who is starving in her great house, go and live comfortably in a little one, or in lodgings? Will her landlady, Miss Letsam, ever stop wondering at the familiarity of trades people, or rebuking the insolence of Suky, the maid, who wears flowers under her bonnet, like a lady?'

W. M. THACKERAY

The easiest manner of approaching our problem will, I think, be to look at the manner in which one particular garment has undergone mutation. Thus we shall be able to see, in an admittedly diagrammatic way, how and why the mechanism works.

Somewhere about the middle of the nineteenth century the Duchess of Fitzbattleaxe was pleased to extend the already large area covered by her skirts by means of a light metal contrivance called a crinoline. The crinoline enabled her to increase her volume without adding to her weight; it made possible an extension which, under normal circumstances, would have been virtually impossible. For the crinoline came

Vulgarisation of the Crinoline

opportunely at the end of a long process of aggrandisement, which may be said to have started (we can draw no line) in the twenties and thirties of the century. For many years skirts were expanded by the addition of more and more petticoats, then in the forties pneumatic hoops made their appearance, but even these could not sustain the dimensions of the true crinoline which, at its greatest width, filled rooms, blocked doorways, and overflowed from carriages. To have walked in one of these must, in a high wind, have been a considerable feat of navigation. It will be seen that the thing was undoubtedly an instrument of conspicuous leisure.

The example of the duchess was, of course, sufficient for Lady Croesus; clearly the crinoline was 'being worn', so she wore one; then, of course, Mrs Broadcloth must have one too, and if Mrs Broadcloth why not Mrs Seedy and Miss Letsam, until finally Suky the maid also has one, just as she has flowers under her bonnet (see Plate 22).*

By the time that the crinoline has made its way into the servants' hall, with results depicted by Leech, it has in the strictest sense of the word become vulgar. What then is the duchess to do? It is unthinkable that she should be seen wearing the same costume as that of Lady Crœsus, not to speak of Mrs Seedy and Miss Letsam. The obvious reply is to forbid her pushing neighbour to wear any such thing. This in effect is what her ancestors did; if we look at the sumptuary laws of the Middle Ages we shall find again and again that their overt purpose is to ensure a proper degree of class distinction in dress.† But, as we have seen, these laws were disregarded; the Crœsus family seems to have been too resolute, and in time the legal struggle was abandoned. What then could be attempted? The obvious thing was to increase the size of the crinoline. This had two advantages; in the first place it altered the fashion so that the duchess again became its leader; in the second place it made the crinoline still more unpractical and therefore more difficult to imitate. But of course this move led to a repetition of the emulative process. The circumference of the duchess expands until we get the situation pictured in Plate 23.

The process did not of course proceed in jumps; there was always a restraining influence to prevent the vulgarity of eccentricity, and there were also other ways in which the fashion could be altered, changes of colour and material, in hats, in sleeves, and in the dressing of hair. It will moreover be found that as an aristocrat the duchess did not hesitate to outbid her rival in a generous display of shoulders and bosom. Here

---

* Crinolines were actually worn by girls working in the fields in East Prussia in 1865; see von Boehn, *Modes and Manners of the Nineteenth Century*, III, 52.

† See von Boehn, *Modes and Manners*, I, 251 *et passim*.

indeed Mrs Broadcloth, whose husband perhaps was a dissenter, may have been frightened out of the game, but Lady Crœsus would not have hesitated to try a show-down with the duchess. This device of conspicuous outrage worked with more effect in the seventeenth century than in the nineteenth and is, because of its narrower scope, pushed to less extreme limits in any one direction; but, as we have already noticed, in the history of feminine dress the focus of attention shifts continually from one part of the person to another and there is, in consequence, always some new manner in which a dress can be shockingly immodest and therefore fashionable.

As we have seen, throughout the entire process of development disapproving voices are raised, jokes are cracked, sermons preached, the medical profession invoked, etc. It is by no means certain that these criticisms are a deterrent to the fashionable, and that they are not rather in the nature of encouragements. For the leaders of fashion are attempting to escape, as much as to compel, imitation. To those who feel strong enough to leap them the barriers erected by the Church and the press are welcome. Moreover it is the imitators rather than the innovators who incur the chief censure; it is as though the hurdles were set higher after the leaders in the race have cleared them.

Nevertheless, on this occasion, the protests came from a quarter which, supposing the pre-eminence of the individual, might well be thought authoritative. Not only did Queen Victoria abjure the crinoline, but, what was much more important, the Empress of the French, with whom it is always associated, did likewise.* Both attempts failed; the thing persisted, despite the efforts of both sovereigns, until about 1866 when, after a continual development of about twenty years, the duchess was, so to speak, pushed to her extremities. Mere enlargement being rendered impossible, as a result of those limiting factors to which we referred in Chapter Two, the crinoline declined. But its end like its beginning was slow. First the skirt was looped up in front to show an elaborate underskirt; it then tailed away into a long train which was eventually gathered up into a bustle, which in various forms constitutes the basis of feminine fashions for the next twenty years, and which provided a sufficiently conspicuous encumbrance and effectively impeded the wearer's movements. Whereas in the 1860s a lady's skirts were too wide for her to pass up a narrow stairway, in the 1880s they were so tight that she could not mount a steep flight of steps. At every stage of its development the dress maintained its sumptuous character. At each point the duchess was more

---

* Nystrom, p. 279. von Boehn, *Modes and Manners of the Nineteenth Century*, III, 70.

PLATE 23

Hypertrophy of the Crinoline

fashionable, more ladylike than her competitors, at each stage the emulative process was at work.

In its broad essentials such a view of the mechanism of change is very far from being new or revolutionary. Hazlitt described it in terms which cannot be bettered.

> Fashion is an odd jumble of contradictions, of sympathies and antipathies. It exists only by its being participated among a number of persons, and the essence is destroyed by being communicated to a greater number. It is a continual struggle between 'the great vulgar and the small' to get the start of, or keep up with each other in the race of appearances, by an adoption on the part of the one of such external and fantastic symbols as strike the attention and excite the envy or admiration of the beholder, and which are no sooner made known and exposed to public view for this purpose, than they are successfully copied by the multitude, the slavish herd of imitators, who do not wish to be behindhand with their betters in outward show and pretensions, and then sink, without any farther notice into disrepute and contempt. Thus fashion lives only in a perpetual round of giddy imitation and restless vanity. To be old fashioned is the greatest crime a coat or a hat can be guilty of. To look like nobody else is a sufficiently mortifying reflection; to be in danger of being mistaken for one of the rabble is worse. Fashion constantly begins and ends in the two things it abhors most, singularity and vulgarity.

This is admirable, but perhaps the essayist may be thought a little too severe when he goes on to say that:

> [fashion] ... is not anything in itself, nor a sign of anything but the folly and vanity of those who rely upon it as their greatest price and ornament ... fashion is the abortive issue of vain ostentation and exclusive egotism: it is haughty, affected, trifling, servile, despotic, mean and ambitious, precise and fantastical all in a breath – tied to no rule and bound to conform to every whim of the minute.*

Hazlitt over-simplifies the motives of those who follow the fashion, and that today is all of us, as I also have over-simplified in the account of mutation given above. I have of course stated the process of competitive emulation in too plain a way. It is an account of actions rather than of

* Hazlitt, *On Fashion. Complete Works* (1933), Vol. XVII, p. 51.

motives, of classes rather than of individuals. Such a degree of ratiocination and so conscious a pursuit of competitive advantage are not present in the mind of the duchess when she chooses a dress, or in that of the housemaid when she buys a reach-me-down. No snob ever describes his own particular form of emulation as snobbery. Indeed the word 'snob' is too harsh, and I need, but cannot find, some other term with which to describe that great majority which follows fashions. Nor am I supposing that those manifold emotions of the 'snob', the desire to be decent, to be 'in the swim', as good as the next man, smart, up-to-date, respectable, etc., are paramount considerations in the mind of the consumer. Beauty, in its purest sense, sexual advertisement, modesty, utility even, may be of the first consideration when the purchase is made. Nevertheless there is a constant determinant, to some extent imposed by the producer, to some extent immanent in the sartorial morality of the consumer, which guides his or her choice inexorably in the fashionable direction. I believe that this truth is capable of experimental verification. If two retailers were to compete at the same prices I think that he who neglected the fashion would not only lose custom, but would find his wares adjudged less pretty, less becoming, and even, when he had lagged too far behind, less modest and less practical than those of his rival, for at a certain point in their development we are unable to find any quality in the creations of the past but a grotesque dowdiness and a dreary indecency (that particular mode of fashionable outrage having ceased to be customary).

If we allow the mainspring of fashion to be the emulative process whereby the members of one class imitate those of another, who in their turn are driven to ever new expedients of fashionable change, then, I think, we shall find that the first three of the objections raised in our last chapter can be resolved without difficulty.

Clearly if our account be true, fashionable change can occur only when wealth is so distributed in a society as to allow more than one class to afford the luxury of sumptuous dress. There must, in addition to the ruling class, be a middle class, and this middle class must have the power, financial and political, to vie with that above it, to imitate its dress and defy its sumptuary laws. Such a class must be constantly increasing in power and in wealth in relation to the highest class; otherwise a point must soon be reached at which it is distanced in the race, obliged to fall into a secondary rank and forgo emulation. In other words the society which produces changing fashions must itself be a society which is changing. Surely we have here the obvious difference between the civilisation of Europe and that of China.

It may be that fashion owes its origins in Europe to the importation of sumptuous foreign clothes from Byzantium, and later, with the Crusades, from the Levant. This would appear to be the view of Herr von Boehn, but in discussing the changes which supervened at the beginning of the fourteenth century he says:

> The chief change was the apparent loss of a standard of what had so far passed for propriety. In the arrogance of its newly acquired wealth the rising middle class recognised no bounds, it must and would enjoy life. It did not desire to emulate the knights, but to outshine them. This aim naturally manifested itself most obviously in dress, for dress is the agency through which any new consciousness of the world and one's particular *milieu* is most speedily proclaimed. Not only did new modes arise, but they changed with far greater frequency than before; fashion, in the sense of incessant fluctuation, perpetual striving after improvement, now came on the scene.*

I quote from the impressive and scholarly text of Herr von Boehn, a writer who has no ideological axe to grind, because at this stage of my argument I want all the heavy artillery that I can bring to bear. In fact von Boehn is simply describing the earlier stages of a process which Thackeray picks up again four hundred years later. The 'arrogance of newly acquired wealth' is but another name for the ambitions of Lady Crœsus. Thackeray's model is rather more complex and rather more extensive than one would be likely to make if one were trying to give an account of social pressures in the fourteenth century (or so I suppose); certainly the distinction between Lady Crœsus and Mrs Broadcloth would be less evident, and the emergence of Suky, the maid, as an important social phenomenon, is something new. But the essence of the situation is the same. In both cases we have a stratified society, and in any stratified society you are almost certain to have a classification of dress, the upper ranks being, of course, more sumptuous than the *hoi polloi*. In both cases you have a situation in which it is possible for the lower strata to compete with the higher strata, to challenge the situation of its social superiors by adopting that form of dress which in principle was reserved for its 'betters', and in this situation you find 'fashion', in the sense of incessant fluctuations, perpetually striving after improvement. All right, you say, but why go on labouring a point which is not in dispute?

The answer is that, although we do all seem to be in agreement when we try to describe the mechanism of fashion, there are a great many of us who are not ready to accept the implications of that position.

---

* Von Boehn, I, 215.

Come back now to the historical characteristics of fashion which I outlined on an earlier page. Fashion, I said, is not and never was a universal condition of dress. It is a European product and is not nearly as old as European civilisation. If we accept the foregoing account of the emulative process then this makes perfectly good sense. Emulation occurs where status can be challenged, where social groups become strong enough to challenge the traditional pattern of society, in fact in those places where a strong middle class emerges to compete with the aristocracy and, at a later stage, a strong proletariat emerges to compete with the middle class. This surely is the grand characteristic which distinguishes Western civilisation from the static authoritarian societies of the East, those societies in which there is a place for everyone and everyone knows his place. It also distinguishes the evolving competitive society from preliterate or savage cultures. And from this it follows that all theories of fashion based upon human nature, the ethical climate, or any kind of ideology, go straight out of the window. It is true that they may be allowed back again; but only when they have been re-examined in the light of the really important overall determinant in the history of dress, the condition of the class struggle.

Take for example this kind of remark: 'The desire for novelty in dress is but a manifestation of human nature, all men desire novelty.' Or the even sillier variant: 'All women love novelty in dress.' Statements of this kind are demonstrably and obviously untrue. A man or a woman in a stratified society, whether at the top or the bottom of the social scale, is so far from desiring novelty in dress that he hardly conceives it to be possible, and when he does encounter it his reaction is one of shock, astonishment, ridicule or disgust. But now take the much more interesting situation of the individual who is able to perceive the possibility of change and is half inclined to break with tradition –

> Now is now, and then was then:
> Seek now all the world throughout,
> Thou kens not clowns from gentlemen:
> They are clad in black, green, yellow and blue
> So far above their own degree.
> Once in my life I'll take a view;
> For I'll have a new cloak about me.

It is worth remembering that in the sixteenth century, a little later than the probable date of this poem, the rebellious peasants of Germany demanded the right to wear red cloaks like their masters. This personal rebellion was put down, as must often have happened, by the rebel's wife; she had a strong sense of social propriety and declared that

It's pride that puts this country down:
Man, take thy old cloak about thee.

The role of the individual is of course an important, in fact a vital part of the mechanism of fashion. The arguments between the cowman and Bell his wife, multiplied many thousands of times over many years, decide the fate not only of other individuals, such for instance as the man who is trying to sell them new cloaks, but also of the fashion, and indeed of fashion in general. And yet if one measures the strength of any one individual against those probably impersonal forces which have brought him to the frontiers of fashion's empire, that is to say the historical movements which make it conceivable that he should have any choice in the matter of clothes whatsoever, he appears a helpless creature of history.

In much the same way an understanding of the mechanism of fashion helps us to understand the anomalies which appear when we try to explain the history of dress in terms of ideology and ethical climate. That there will be some correspondence is obvious. The relationship of social groups within a society must itself affect not only dress but the ethical climate in general and, in specific terms, such phenomena as nationalism and religion. Thus, for instance, the comparatively low temperature of war in the eighteenth century (and by low temperature I do not mean that these wars were free from atrocities but that, at a certain level, they were conducted with mutual civility) arose from the fact that they were no longer wars of religion and they were conducted by opponents of the same social class. Thus, it is entirely typical of the eighteenth century that *Pandora*, a doll, who was sent from Paris to London and other capitals wearing the latest Paris fashions, should have been accorded a safe conduct by the opposing generals. It was in the new spirit of nationalism engendered by the French Revolution that this courtesy was brought to an end.

The nineteenth century, the century in which nationalism emerges as the great overriding force in Europe, produces the oddest possible contradiction of motives where dress was concerned. Look for instance at the situation of the Italian patriot. On the whole the backbone of the Risorgimento was the Italian middle class, more particularly the active and industrious bourgeoisie of Northern Italy. The peasantry was, by contrast, relatively indifferent to a struggle which, whatever its ultimate results, could in the immediate future mean only that a Bourbon or a Hapsburg would be replaced by the royalty or the politicians of Piedmont. And yet, in terms of dress, it was the various regional peasant costumes which represented something truly Italian and something which, in the eyes of the painter, seemed intrinsically valuable. Theoretically therefore the Italian middle-class patriot could choose between playing the traditional emulative role of imitating the aristocracy, which in effect meant imitating whatever the Rue de la Paix might provide, or of dressing in a truly Italian style. In fact there was no choice. The peasant style could not be imitated because it was the style of social inferiors; the patriots opted for a French style (or in the case of men for an English style) even at a time when French troops supported the temporal power of the Popes in Rome. Faced by the same kind of choice the pan-slavs of Russia, and the makers of the Second Reich made the same choice. Even the Third Reich, more virulently committed to racialism and nationalism than any nineteenth-century movement, sent its conquering hordes not simply to occupy France but to provide a clientele for the *Maisons de la Haute Couture*.

Where nationalism in dress has succeeded in retaining its own forms it will, I think, be found that those forms have, not simply a cultural but also a social importance. Thus in the dress of Eastern peoples we find that the older forms resist Western influence when they are connected with caste or status, and in much the same way we find the kilt surviving, alone amongst the regional clothes of the British Isles, because it is associated with certain expensive and socially excellent forms of sport.

It is because dress is above all concerned with status that it becomes hard to find any exact correspondence between its development and the demands of ideology. It is for this reason that the Elizabethan gentleman imitated the dress of Madrid even while opposing the religious and national claims of the Spanish Monarchy, and for this reason that the French Protestants, drawn from very much the same class as their Catholic opponents, were not distinguished by a peculiarly protestant form of dress. So much becomes clear when once we realise that the mechanics of fashion are dependent upon the class structure of the society in which they operate. What is less clear, and cannot be explained simply by a study of the mechanism of change, is certain catastrophic developments in the history of dress, the curiously uneven development of the dress of the two sexes, the persistence of certain archaic forms, and some recent developments in the history of fashion. These then will form the subject of my next three chapters.

6

Revolution

> 'There is to be a ball on Friday at Windsor for the Prince's birth-day, which has not lately been noticed there. Lord Lorn and seven other young men of fashion were invited to it. It seems they now crop their hair short and wear no powder, which not being the etiquette yet, the youths, instead of representing that they are not fit to appear so docked, sent excuses that they were going out of town, or were unavoidably engaged – a message one would think dictated by old Prynne or Tom Paine, and certainly unparalleled in all the books in the Lord Chamberlain's office.'
>
> HORACE WALPOLE to Miss Mary Berry
> August 8, 1791

It will be generally allowed that the revolutions of 1642 and 1789 were not without their effect upon the dress of the men and women of the time, and that this fact accords well enough with the view that whatever the actual cause of mutation, the forms to which it gives birth do have a direct relevance to the ideas within men's minds.

It was thus that I began this chapter when I first wrote this book. Today I hesitate; I am less certain than I was concerning what actually took place about the time of the English Civil War. The picture which I too easily accepted thirty years ago of drab-coated, crop-headed, white-collared Puritans in steeple hats opposed by Cavaliers in silk velvet and a baroque orgy of plumes, lace, curls and ribbons is attractive but, I suspect, pretty inaccurate. I was then fascinated by the idea that here we had, for the first and only time, a war in which non-combatants of the same nation adopted opposing styles of dress. Also I was ready to concede that here there really was a case for thinking that an ideological as opposed to a class distinction was of paramount importance. I now think that I was ready to concede too much.

> The Puritan costume, before the Restoration, was by no means as fantastic as later satirists often depicted. 'When puritanism grew into a faction the zealots distinguished themselves, both men and women, by several affectations of habit', but those who eventually arrived at prosperity then forsook their peculiar

> modes. Thus, the Parliamentarian Colonel Hutchinson wore his hair long over his shoulders and in the House of Commons in 1650 appeared in 'a habit which was pretty rich but grave', of dark cloth trimmed with gold and silver points and buttons, while the Puritan General Harrison on that occasion wore 'a scarlet coat and cloak both laden with gold and silver lace, and the coat so covered with cliquant [metal foil] that one scarcely could discern the ground'.*

That Puritan dress was less a distinction of religion than of social class is a statement fully in accord with everything that I have said about the nature and history of dress; but perhaps in dealing with this period the distinction is in some degree unreal. Religion was then so much identified with social attitudes that Stubbs's *Anatomie of Abuses* may surely be seen as an attack either upon the idle rich or upon immoral pleasures as such.

The important thing, from our point of view, is not that the Puritan rejected the vanities and luxuries of the world as that (in sartorial matters) he offered a mundane alternative. It is here that he differs from the mediaeval zealot who retired from the world altogether and sheltered beneath the habit of a monk. The Puritan, in effect, declared that it was not mundane existence in general but the noble in particular who was unworthy of admiration. In place of aristocratic admiration there was something better.

> Costly thy habit as thy purse can buy
> But not expressed in fancy; rich, not gaudy:
> For the apparel oft proclaims the man.

Polonius is, in his infinitely discreet way, revolutionary: for he attacks the very principle of emulation; he does not withdraw from the fashionable world; he offers a respectable alternative and comes very near to describing the sober middle-class dress of the solid, solvent, self-respecting candidate for salvation. The kind of person whom we imagine as a pillar of parliamentary strength in the city of London. I say 'imagine' for in fact the Puritan portrait is not easy to find in England and one relies, perhaps unwisely, upon the pictures of Hals or Lievens or De Bray. I think that it is probably not illegitimate to think of the English middle

---

* C. Willett and Phillis Cunnington, *Handbook of English Costume in the 17th Century*, 1955, p. 11.

class of the mid-seventeenth century as reflecting contemporary Dutch models while the Cavalier style, popular though it no doubt was with many gentlemen on the other side, was mainly French.*

The Dutch do in fact have a wonderfully middle-class white-collar aspect, although if one seeks the origin of their style one must go back to the fifteenth century. In the Middle Ages both sexes had worn the most brilliant colours and had carried a great deal of jewellery. The tinctures of dress were like those of the escutcheon, with dazzling effects of *mi parti* to enliven the effect. The use of black began in the Burgundian court and is recorded as early as 1468, so that in its origin it can hardly be connected either with the Reformation or counter-Reformation. But such a connection may perhaps be traced in the adoption of this fashion by the Spanish successors of the Burgundians, and certainly the popularity of black among the Dutch Calvinists, who took their style from their Catholic adversaries, may be connected with a religious motive. And although, in the second half of the century, France became more and more important as a centre of fashion while the Spanish influence steadily declined, both in England and in Holland the more sober style, the style of the 'white-collar worker', remained to some extent as an alternative to the higher sumptuosity of France.

Here, in passing, we may notice what seems to be a marked tendency of the bourgeoisie in modern Europe and a characteristic of its own form of sumptuosity, namely personal cleanliness. Not that a certain nicety of person has not always been well thought of, especially among the Islamic peoples. But in Holland, in England, in the Scandinavian countries, and in the United States soap and water have marched hand in hand with protestantism, commerce, expansion, industry, and a sober but spotless attire. Whether it be that the result of tireless scrubbing is pleasing to those who set industry high among the virtues, while dirt is considered shiftless, feckless, unprincipled, and insolvent, I do not pretend to say. But there would certainly seem to be some affinity between the bourgeoisie and the bath. In the great Catholic monarchies on the other hand and wherever a more or less feudal society persists, stinks are not only in evidence but of small account, and dirt a frequent concomitant of sumptuosity.

The subject of smells brings us naturally to that of Versailles. Even before Louis XIV attained his majority France had displaced Spain as the lawgiver of fashion, and the seal was set upon this victory by the crea-

---

* *See* Laver, *17th and 18th Century Costume*, Victoria and Albert Museum Catalogue, 1951, p. 4.

tion of the palace of Versailles. Never before had Europe seen so magnificent a setting for conspicuous leisure. The palace itself carried no vulgar taint of administrative convenience, nor was the site of any particular beauty; better still, the ground itself was unsuitable for building, and many workmen lost their lives in its construction. The water for the fountains could only be conveyed at great expense, the building was well away from any vulgar habitation, and the mere act of getting to Versailles supposed a certain expenditure. Saint Simon, who was there for so many years, speaks feelingly of the discomforts, the damp and the glaring heat.* But then Versailles was built not for ease, but for Glory.

The same may be said of the courtiers who dwelt therein. In the beginning, when the king and his mistresses were younger and the palace was only beginning to arise from its foundations of bog and sand, there was, no doubt, much to please in the life of the court; but that was far from being the case during the long, tedious, and disastrous reign of Mme de Maintenon. The life of the king and of his courtiers was then devoted to a succession of solemn fatuities. Reading the accounts one is astonished at the amount of time wasted by so many talented people, to whom no professions were open save those of arms, the Church, and occasionally diplomacy or administration (but these latter were commonly entrusted to members of the middle class). Take the career of Saint Simon himself. He left the army at the age of twenty-seven, because men of lesser birth were promoted before him; explaining his action to Louis, he said that he wished to be nearer His Majesty the better to court him.† This courtship consisted in hanging about Versailles, quarrelling, intriguing for ceremonial advantage, and running into debt. Never, until the king's death, did he obtain any kind of real power, and even during the regency his greatest achievements were in matters of precedence. He was a man of outstanding gifts, but unless his memoirs had been published we should never have heard of him.

This honourably futile existence was of course accompanied by enormous expenditure both personal and national. It would almost seem that the canons of pecuniary taste influenced Louis in his conduct of war; the king was never fond of pitched battles, which, however glorious, were bound to involve much toil and confusion. The campaigns in which he appeared in person, with the ladies, centred upon the capture of some strong place; M. le Prince or Turenne could be trusted to amuse the opposing army while the engineers ran parallels to the enemy walls, and battered a breach. Then the king, very much the centre of the picture, watched the defenders march out in brave array and received the compli-

* *Memoirs*, ed. Cheruel, XII, 80–2. † *Ibid.*, III, 227.

ment of the hostile commander. The entire ceremony was expensive, decorous and glorious.

This kind of thing went on for many years until France was exhausted. When peace was made and there was a breathing space, Louis found it necessary to hold manœuvres so lavish and so grandiose that the expense was greater than that of an actual campaign in the field.

Saint Simon says of Louis that he loved splendour, magnificence, and profusion in everything. Intentionally he made this a matter of principle. He liked to see indulgence in entertainments, in equipage, in building, and in gambling; he put a premium on luxury, for at bottom he liked to see everyone being ruined.* Saint Simon saw in this a calculated policy aimed at the reduction of the nobility, and most historians agree with him. But it must be said that the nobles needed but little encouragement in the matter. The easier and more self-indulgent life of Paris or their estates was open to them, but they clung desperately to Versailles; nothing could console them for banishment from a place which they well knew to be both tedious and ruinous, and they spent further thousands upon questions of precedence without any encouragement from the monarch.

In the end the king wearied of his own grandeurs; he decided to make himself a little place in the country where he could be quiet with his widow lady. He left Versailles for a discreet valley shut off from the world; there, from Wednesday to Saturday at rare intervals, he might find solace from the intolerable tedium of the court which he had created. So he went to Marly.

But the machine was too strong for its master; bit by bit Marly too had to be enlarged, forested, and furnished. Marly became the inner paradise of courtiers, grander, because more select, than Versailles and as big a bore.

I have dwelt at some length upon the court of Louis XIV because it is not only the home of a multitude of fashions, but provides also one of the finest illustrations to the Theory of the Leisure Class, especially during those years when its creator was alive. Here we have the life of unproductive labour in its purest form, carried on with a disregard for the comfort of those who led it and of those who were exploited in order that it might exist, which leaves one wondering how anyone could have tolerated it for so long. For despite a moment of relaxation under a regent too pleasure-loving for the higher futility, the life of Versailles continued until 1789. Versailles was the cynosure and admiration of Europe throughout the eighteenth century. Attempts were made to reproduce it in Caserta, Potsdam, Schönbrunn, and Tsarskoye Selo. Only in England was its influence resisted with success.

* *Memoirs*, ed. Chervel, XII, 78.

The effects of Versailles are still with us, for in certain respects that amazing essay in conspicuous consumption (backed of course by the real military and economic potency of France in the seventeenth century) succeeded. France then gained and to a very large extent held that authority in the sumptuary arts which for a time had belonged to Italy and to Spain, so that even today, despite the challenge of other centres and the frequently announced downfall of Paris, France still draws the buyers and the journalists to her 'collections'.

In the business of designing women's clothes this pre-eminence has been maintained, despite a revolution in the very capital of fashion. Before attempting to describe that revolution, the most violent in the history of dress, I must return once more to the question of causation even though it has already been rather fully discussed. The neo-classical style, that is to say the slim, high-waisted, rather plain style which appears in about 1795 and lasts through the Directoire, the Consulate, the Empire and the first years of the restored Bourbon regime, has been described as one of those feminine styles which shows the influence of war on dress. In so far as the Napoleonic Wars were a social convulsion this is true; in any other sense it is false. The wars themselves were anticipated by no one; the French Revolution on the other hand was, in a sense, the product of social and political ideas which we can trace far back into the eighteenth century. In the same way the shape of women's clothes, which are my main concern in this chapter, and of men's clothes, which I shall also discuss but of which more must be said in another chapter, already becomes visible before the actual revolution.

The masculine fashion of Versailles at the height of its glory was a fine example of conspicuous leisure tempered by martial futility. The enormous peruke, heavily cuffed and embroidered coat, ruffled breeches, and high-heeled shoes were just not too unsuitable for the more genteel kind of military operation.

But the tendency of the eighteenth century is one of slow but steady simplification; the bulky breeches dwindle into small clothes, the sleeves are diminished and both coats reduced, the inner one becomes a waistcoat, the shoes flattened, plainer and darker colours replace brocade. In nothing is the change more visible than in the wig. (The head is always a most sensitive index of fashionable change.) Wigs which were so vast in the late seventeenth century, decline with only one short revival, until they are reduced to the vestigial tie wig of the late eighteenth century and finally disappear altogether. This decline and fall is portentous; ever since the days of Elisha men have been deeply sensitive to the crowning injustice of nature; the wig gave them a century and a half of immunity. Dignified, not too unpractical in its later stages, above all discreet, it was

PLATE 24

Sir Brooke Boothby

one of the most flattering contrivances ever invented, and yet it went. By the middle of the nineteenth century even the Established Church had given it up; such is the steady tidal influence of fashion.

In addition to this growth of simplicity we may notice two other eighteenth-century innovations in masculine dress. First an increasing tendency to make a sharp distinction between the dress of business and that of ceremony; a change which was in part compensated by the increasing use of ceremonial dress, which became 'evening dress'. Secondly, the divorce between army uniform and civilian dress.

It will be noticed that these innovations were very much to the advantage of the middle classes; the fashion permitted an occasional sumptuosity on the part of those who led a more or less industrious life. More important still, it placed the civilian upon a footing of equality with the army officer.

The resultant costume was, however, based upon a notion of Conspicuous Waste; for it was in its essentials the dress of a country gentleman. It demonstrated a life largely, though not wholly, futile, devoted to the honourable pastimes of the countryside. The sword goes out of fashion, but it is replaced by the riding-crop of the foxhunter, from whose attire modern evening dress is still recognisably descended. The sportsman has become the ideal type in place of the soldier.

Look at the portrait of Brooke Boothby by Joseph Wright of Derby (no painter was ever more of an aeolian harp or more exquisitely attuned to every light intellectual breeze of his century). The young man has thrown himself upon the ground and this for the excellent reason that he wants to return to Nature. Above him the freely growing trees of the forest; by his side the running brook; beneath his hand a MS copy of *La Nouvelle Héloïse*. He wears the mildly amiable look of a virtuous philosopher; he also wears a suit cut by a first-rate tailor. It is a suit carefully designed for a Natural Man who is also the eldest son of a baronet; it is no way gaudy or ostentatious, it has an air of high luxury (a quality so evident that we cannot but wonder anxiously whether, when the young man gets up, he will not discover that he has been lying on a cow pat) and this derives entirely from its beautifully discreet cut. These are the clothes of the future; it is thus that the bourgeoisie will attain high sumptuosity.

Now, at first sight, this triumph of a middle-class fashion would seem to contradict all that has been said concerning the mutation of forms. Here we have the bourgeois refusing to imitate his betters and imposing a style of his own. But emulation depends obviously upon a complete acceptance of the social hierarchy, and this was precisely what was vanishing throughout the eighteenth century. Or rather, to put the matter more exactly, the sartorial standards of England, a country in which the class structure of the *ancien régime* had never existed in its entirety, were slowly adopted by France, where that regime was gradually drifting to disaster. Here indeed we can find a pretty close correspondence between the ideological and sartorial influences of the age. The Anglomania which culminated, in the years immediately preceding the Revolution, in the most grotesque parody of English habits, was echoed at every point in the dress of Frenchmen.

There is, however, a further difficulty; in feminine fashions the emulative process remained almost normal. Women's dresses remain aristocratic, in the sense of demonstrating conspicuous leisure, all through the century and right up to the year 1914 or thereabouts, with only one violent though short-lived fluctuation at the time of the French Revolution. The coiffure again marks its development. At the beginning of the century the high headdress named after Mlle de Fontanges (against which Louis XIV fought in vain for twenty years) gave way to a mode of relative simplicity which was compensated by an increased volume of skirts; throughout the century the hair (or wig) grew again until by the 'eighties it had reached a wild degree of size and fantasy, as had the entire structure of a lady's dress (see Plate 1). It is as though the men were sacrificing their hair, and indeed all their finery, for the benefit of women.

We must postpone an explanation of this remarkable phenomenon to our next chapter; here it will be more convenient to examine that momentary deviation from the general line of development which, for a time, caused the dress of women to follow the same course as that of men.

There was a pre-revolutionary moment when the ladies of Paris succumbed to Anglomania. Fashions of greater simplicity, with a certain outdoor influence, the precursors of the modern tailor-made, came into fashion and with them natural hair reappeared. With the Revolution itself, that is to say in its terrific moment, fashion came almost to a full stop. For a time the exhibition of sumptuosity was checked, and with it emulation. It is with the Directoire that the revolution in clothes begins again. At that moment the situation was one in which the possibility of emulation had returned, but the old social hierarchy had vanished. The fashion was for a time headless. Eventually a fashion was born which met the demands of sumptuosity (largely through conspicuous outrage) while maintaining a revolutionary form.

The concessions to revolutionary sentiment were indeed of a pretty far-reaching nature. One has only to compare the dress of 1785 (Plate 1) with that of 1805 (Plate 25) to see to what an extent conspicuous leisure, and even conspicuous consumption, had been abandoned. By its rejection of artifice the dress of those times seems to assert the equality of women;

it is, in consequence, very unkind to age and to corpulence. But in spite of this, and in spite of the fact that a fashion from Paris must have been felt to have a Jacobin air, the 'Directoire' style swept across Europe even more rapidly than did the armies of the Republic. We have already seen that in some degree the influence of fashion can transcend ideology and this is surely a remarkable instance of that truth, but perhaps it can in part be explained by the fact that this style had a particular charm. It was felt to be, in a quite special sense, beautiful. It appealed not only to the smart world but to the artists and art critics. In most periods we can discover some affinity between the paintings, the applied arts and the architecture of the time. But neo-classical dress is in a very high degree congruous with neo-classical painting and a neo-classical decoration.

There is a danger here that, with certain ultra-fashionable examples before us, we may overstate the case. We may doubt whether there were many ladies who managed to be quite as archaeologically correct as Mme Récamier in her simple chiton, her bare feet and her Roman hair style; it was not very long before all sorts of unclassical trimmings and stitchings, sleeves and ruffles, plumes and gloves began to mar the classical purity of the effect. Nevertheless, the general line of the period, the plain high-waisted robe, short hair, sandals, did come very near to an idea of antiquity which was acceptable not only to the fashionable world but to the artists from whom it was, in a sense, derived.

Looking at Blake's ideal figures, at Flaxman's angels (if such very feminine creatures can be angels) and at the figure of Truth from Goya's *Desastres de la Guerra*, we might almost suppose that they all went to the same dressmaker. Perhaps that is saying too much but certainly they all bear a strong likeness to Mme Récamier. The fashion may be traced back to the paintings of J. L. David, in whose pre-revolutionary work we may already find a forecast of the fashions of 1796. Look for instance at those high-waisted figures on the right-hand side of the *Oath of the Horatii* (1784). But in fact we may go further back, to David's master Vien, whose singularly inept composition *Le Marchand d'Amours* already prefigures the Directoire style in 1763. It is not simply that Vien and David take their ideas from classical antiquity. The slim youthful line obtained by drawing a chiton smoothly over the breasts beneath which it is fastened, and then allowing it to fall ungathered at any point to the ankles, with no chlamys or peplum to break the continuous line, was certainly not unknown in antiquity, and Vien might have found models in work such as the Euterpe or the Danaids in the Vatican.* But it was

* He does not use the costumes provided by the pompeian original from which the subject is derived.

Madame Récamier in 1805

PLATE 26

Fashions for 1804

The Neo-Classical Style in Dress, 1

PLATE 28

The Neo-Classical Style in Dress, 2

PLATE 29

The Neo-Classical Style in Dress, 3

far from being the commonest form of dress either in Greece or Rome. On the whole the ancients preferred a much more complex system of folds and superimpositions; it is thus that Poussin dresses his nymphs and goddesses. The slim youthful line was chosen not only by the neo-classical 'history' painters but it is at all events suggested by Reynolds, when he is mixing history with portraiture as in *Three Ladies adorning a Term of Hymen* (1774), or Wright of Derby, *Mrs Sacheverell Pole and her son* (*c.* 1771). Here the artist takes the unusual step, for a fashionable portrait painter, of going somewhat against the current fashion, for fashion, right up to the time of the Revolution, keeps a rococo complexity of style, favours big and elaborate headdresses, a natural waist, wide skirts and a great deal of ornament.

The neo-classical style marks a reaction against rococo artificiality; it is emphatically natural, the kind of dress that the ancients would have worn if they had had the advantage of being able to read the works of Rousseau. It was not something which was invented by the Revolution, and there is no reason to think that it had anything to do with the wars which resulted from the Revolution; rather it was something which lay ready to hand in the pictures and sculptures of what was then the *avant garde*.

Nor was the style tied to a political ideology. We have already seen that it travelled ahead of the revolutionary armies; indeed it reached capitals which those armies never visited – St Petersburg, London and the cities of the United States. Also it survived the fall of the Empire and continues an unbroken development under the restored monarchy.

In the French Revolution and, to a lesser extent, the Puritan Revolution, the political passions of the age did receive sartorial expression, and the development of fashion was, up to a point, connected with current ideologies. But this, given the mechanism of fashion and the class-bound nature of dress that we have described, is surely what one would expect. In each case the political event was also a social event and one which affected the very principle of emulation. On each occasion the change has been towards a kind of simplicity, very different kinds to be sure, but similar in their rejection of the claims of sumptuosity. On each occasion there was a sudden sharpening of the class conflict, with its inevitable repercussion upon the emulative process. If the process is dependent upon the aspirations and development of a resurgent middle class, then it is only natural that a conflict such as that which occurred in 1642 or 1789 should exercise a much more potent influence upon dress than the numerous wars, *coups d'états*, religious convulsions, aesthetic movements, and dynastic changes in which the resurgent middle class has played a subordinate or negligible part. In our next chapter we shall attempt to show that the converse is true, and that a silent industrial revolution unmarked by any supreme political convulsion has effected a transformation in dress far greater than that of the French or Puritan Revolutions.

Origins of the Neo-Classical Style in Dress: David

Origins of the Neo-Classical Style in Dress: Vien

PLATE 32

Origins of the Neo-Classical Style in Dress: Reynolds

7
Vicarious Consumption – Archaism

'"Rot ye, ye great lumberin' beggar!" exclaimed Mr. Jorrocks, furiously indignant; "Rot ye, do ye think I'm like Miss Biffin, the unfortunate lady without harms or legs, that I can't 'elp myself?" continued he, dashing the wet out of his spoon cuff. "Now that's the wust o' your flunkey fellers," continued he in a milder tone to Mrs. Muleygrubs, as the laughter the exclamation had caused had subsided. "That's the wust o' your flunkey fellers," repeated he, mopping his arm, "they know they'd never be fools enough to keep fellers to do nothin', and so they must be constantly meddlin'. Now, your women waiters are quite different," continued he, "they only try for the useful, and not for the helegant. There's no flash 'bout them. If they see a thing's under your nose, they let you reach it, and don't bring a dish that's steady on the table round at your back to tremble on their 'ands under your nose. Besides," added our Master, "you never see a bosky Batsay waiter, which is more than can be said of all dog un's."

'"But you surely couldn't expect ladies to be waited upon by women, Mr. Jorrocks," exclaimed his astonished hostess.'

R. S. SURTEES

Forty years ago I was refused admission to the stalls of the Paris Opera because I was not wearing evening dress. I do not know how matters may stand in Paris, but today, in the Royal Opera House, Covent Garden, you may look in vain for a black tie in the stalls – the few that remain are in the boxes. And yet, if you come to think of it, this is not quite accurate: there still are black ties, and indeed white waistcoats, in the orchestra and amongst the servants of the Opera House. In fact you will find evening dress still being worn in quite humble bars and restaurants, but never by the clients, always by the waiters and barmen, so that here it has become a thoroughly practical device; you can tell who is supposed to be serving.

All this we know well enough, but it is not quite so easy to say why it is that the sumptuous disguise of the consumer, the 'toff', has become the uniform of the servant.

The process is one that interests Veblen and led him to invent the term 'vicarious consumption'. Like so many of his ideas it seems obvious when stated, but its far-reaching implications are often overlooked.

It is a commonplace that we are hardly less sensitive to a lapse of sartorial morality in someone 'belonging' to us than in our own persons. The father of a family might complain bitterly of the sums which he was expected to spend upon clothing his household, but he would have been the first to complain of any shabbiness or impropriety of dress on the part of his wife, his children, or (if he should have such things) his men-servants or his maid-servants. Generally speaking, his concern will be much greater where the person affected is bound to him by a tie of economic dependence. The clothes of parents, business associates, brothers, sisters or colleagues are, comparatively speaking, a matter of indifference; but those of wives or children unable to earn their own living, or of domestic servants, affect him more nearly perhaps than those which he wears himself.

Nevertheless, the social tensions that can arise from a vicarious concern for other people's appearance are capable of enormous extension. It is easy enough to see how, in the days of domestic servants, it would have been horrible and unforgivable if the parlourmaid had come to the door in a filthy apron or the butler's trousers had come down. Here the fault lies clearly with the employer who should have managed things better. But consider the following case: Mr and Mrs A invite Sir Charles and Lady B to dinner; Miss C, a niece of Mrs A, is a guest of the As staying in the house. When Miss C (or Ms C as she calls herself) comes down to dinner with her hair in a dirty tangle and her jeans in rags, Mr and Mrs A, although they are in no way responsible for Miss C's noisome condition, feel it nevertheless as a slight upon themselves and their guests, a gesture of social hostility none the less forceful for being silent; and of course Sir Charles and Lady B are not unaware of the distress of their hosts and thus are themselves distressed as they might not have been by the mere fact that Miss C looks as though she had spent the night in a rubbish bin; and the realisation that the Bs are sorry for them makes the misery of the As still more intense, while Miss C, glowering and silent, is perhaps the most unhappy of them all, for she feels that her gesture has in some unaccountable way misfired. I will dwell no further upon the miseries of this most unlucky entertainment except to point out that it demonstrates the extent to which a social gesture can go beyond the immediate concerns of her/him who makes it, so that the wearing of the 'right' clothes can become a matter of the greatest importance, not only to the wearer but to all who are socially involved with the wearer. It is this extension of feeling which makes Vicarious Consumption so important a social device.

The display of sumptuosity through the agency of a third person is, of course, nothing new. At a very early moment in history people of wealth found that their own backs were not broad enough to bear the weight of all the sumptuous dress that they would have liked to display. The priest or chieftain, not content with dressing finely himself, employed servants, or persons in a servile position, to dress for him; these vicarious consumers (wives, eunuchs, retainers, etc.) were at first employed in productive or military tasks. But here too the law of conspicuous waste came into effect. It is patently more futile to put a servant into a fine dress and bid him do nothing than it is to have him usefully employed, and the same, of course, applies to a wife. Thus we find that notable magnates supported a number of wives out of all proportion to the demands of concupiscence; these ladies served to glorify their owner simply by their quantity. In the same way it became usual to employ servants whose duties were purely nominal and whose only role was vicarious consumption. In some cases the futility of these occupations had an ennobling effect. Thus we find such survivals as the bridesmaids and best man at weddings, or the grooms, equerries, almoners, ladies of the bedchamber etc. at a court, theoretical servants whose duties, when they have not been changed out of all recognition by later developments in the art of government, consist almost entirely in the wearing of sumptuous dress, and who would be ill thought of were they to perform the manual labour originally entrusted to them.

An extremely illuminating story is told (I hope it may be true) concerning those two celebrated courtesans, Liane de Pougy and La Belle Otero. La Belle Otero is said to have made a triumphant appearance at the Opéra heavily laden with the precious stones given her by her admirers, thus entirely outshining her unfortunate rival. But on the following evening Liane de Pougy appeared with an equally impressive treasure, not on her own person, but on that of her servant; she herself being dressed with the utmost simplicity.* There was of course a particular and personal motive for this tactic, but, in a more general way, it shows how by means of vicarious consumption the employer can, so to speak, have it both ways, and can be at once extravagantly gorgeous and discreetly tasteful. This in fact is what gentlemen (gentlemen as opposed to ladies, servants

---

* The story may be connected remotely with that of Louis XIV and Charles II (q.v.s.) which it would seem was used by Steele (*Spectator*, No. 8) in his account of Brunetta and Philis.

and children) achieved during the last century. The great innovation of that century was in fact the new role of the gentleman; he now consumes vicariously and he does this because he is no longer a nobleman.

The nobleman, like the lady, was a creature incapable of useful work; war and sport were the only outlets for his energy, and a high degree of conspicuous leisure was expected of him. Equally, it was important that he should in his own person be a consumer; if he had relied simply upon the vicarious consumption of his household, it would have appeared that he was working to support them. He had to establish the fact that he was a rentier (which until the eighteenth century almost implied the ownership of land). But now in the society which emerged with the Industrial Revolution idleness was no longer the usual sign of wealth. The man who worked was not infrequently in receipt of a larger income than the men who drew rents off him; an industrious life no longer implied a poor or laborious existence and ceased therefore to be dishonourable. It was sufficient, therefore, that a man should demonstrate by means of his black coat, cylindrical hat, spotless linen, carefully rolled umbrella, and general air of refined discomfort that he was not actually engaged in the production of goods, but only in some more genteel employment concerned with management or distribution. Masculine dress betokened a complete abstention from industrial labour, but that was all; it was not 'highly sumptuous'.

This masculine escape from the task of displaying the higher sumptuosity naturally mitigated to a great extent the necessity for emulation, or rather it made the process vicarious instead of being direct. The masculine attire which established itself with the industrial system changed very little; we may almost say that it is with us today in the more conservative forms of masculine dress. Despite some vestiges of its rural origin, it has for many years become increasingly an urban dress, a black uniform to be worn with white linen.

This then was the long-delayed triumph of the drab Puritan over the gaudy Cavalier. The aristocratic style was abolished, a completely civilian mode took its place. Nor is it only the brocade of the nobleman which has gone, but also the peasant's smock, the carpenter's hat, and all the other regional and traditional clothes of mankind; for the discreet armies of black-coated businessmen have gone to the ends of the earth. The fashion was born in England along with the Industrial Revolution; wherever the capitalist system has been established, the London fashion has gone with it.

But the demands of conspicuous consumption remain. Men might escape them, but women could not. Attached to each industrial breadwinner was his vicarious consumer; on all public and social occasions it was her task to demonstrate his ability to pay and thus to carry on the battle, both for herself and for her husband. For her the task was even harder than it had been before. Since although the actual styles of the new age were not in themselves more impractical than those of the eighteenth century, the occasions upon which it was essential to appear in ceremonial dress were more numerous and the effort was required of a larger class.

The difference between ceremonial and daily dress in the period which followed the revolutionary and imperial styles becomes very marked. Daily dress, especially in the mid-nineteenth century, seems designed to shield, to protect the wearer, and to obscure her figure beneath a pyramid as shapeless as, though more obtuse than, that of Mohammedan women. The face is hidden by extensive blinkers and the entire get-up is suggestive of a retiring modesty. By night the very opposite effect is obtained by a décolletage suggestive of either extreme leisure or of an imminent collapse of the entire dress.

Despite its occasional variations this fashion is consistent in its very high degree of conspicuous leisure, and it harmonises, both in its modesty and its particular form of outrage, with a romantic and idealistic view of women. To the romantic idealist, woman, that is to say financially reputable woman, is a dead-weight upon society. She is above all things a consumer; she is incapable of any bodily exertion, and requires assistance in the performance of any physical task. She must be handed in and out of carriages, not because she is a person of rank, but because she is debilitated. She is of necessity dependent upon a person of means, and her place is 'in the home'; here she produces an expensive family and is frequently in a condition of interesting and costly ill-health. She is trained from girlhood to consume in a decorous manner, to perform difficult tasks of a wholly futile nature called 'ladylike accomplishments'. It is something in her favour if her stupidity when confronted by the practical problems of life verges upon complete imbecility. You will find her in the novels of Thackeray, Dickens, and Disraeli, and from a less flattering angle in those of Surtees. It is to be remembered that she existed contemporaneously with women who worked twelve or more hours a day in factories and mines.

The ideal of womanhood, of women that is as instruments of vicarious consumption, dominates the dress of the century. Conspicuous outrage is, however, never completely absent and we find, especially in France, another ideal, that of the expensive harlot, which embodies in a different manner the same economic principle. In consequence conspicuous leisure is always a leading characteristic.

If we consider the evidence provided by nineteenth-century dress, or to be more accurate, dress of the period 1830–1906, it is hard not to conclude that there was at this time a more complete opposition between the sexes than has ever been before or since. I am not saying that this was in fact the case, indeed I think that pretty obviously it was not; but it is what one might fairly conclude from a study of the costume of the period.

Look at those sober hard-working men in their sober hard-wearing clothes, with never a hint of prettiness or provocation, colour, carnality or caprice; the body sufficiently liberated for the purposes of business and yet in no way displayed, the hair, as the century progressed, shortened almost to penal brevity above, trimmed to luxuriant but masculine ferocity below. Perhaps, in their way, they had a sober dignity which we lack; nevertheless, seen in conjunction with their partners they resemble those moths of the genus *Nyssia* – the Brindled Beauties which, when they emerge from the pupa, are, if feminine, as lovely as their name, elegantly mottled with feathery antennae, discreet in repose, exquisite in flight, but which, when male, remain dingy, wingless earthbound grubs.* In the case of the moths this is clearly a disposition of nature, but the odd thing is that although we know that in nineteenth-century costume this division is something temporary and artificial, to the nineteenth century itself it seemed an arrangement almost as natural as that of the *Nissidae*. It was felt to be right and proper that men should form a sober black and white background to the various, lustrous and many-coloured ladies, that woman should submit to the bondage of her stay maker, display her neck, her arms and an appetising portion of her bosoms to the public, spend in one year on dress that which her husband would spend in twenty, and embark on twenty changes of fashion while he had barely completed one. All this I say was felt to be normal and natural. And while the first brave effort at emancipation, the 'divided skirt', was greeted with unkind derision, the merest hint of femininity in a man's wardrobe was regarded with deep visceral aversion. Even today, after twenty years of permissive innovation, older people, at all events, are still shocked by long curls, cosmetics,† bracelets or necklaces on a man, so thoroughly have we been indoctrinated with the belief that it is only women who should, in a direct manner, be consumers.

This attitude is one that would have puzzled our more remote ancestors and which we ourselves discard when we can escape from the conventions of industrial society. Unconsciously we adjust ourselves to a different standard of values when we consider the fashions of the past or modern

* Wrong again. It is in fact the female who grows no wings, but the mistake was a 'natural' mistake and suits my argument; let it stand.

† A well-informed American writes: 'male cosmetics . . . has become a rather major large-scale industry, in the U.S.'

dress which has survived from a past epoch. At no time in the nineteenth century would the frilly petticoats of prelates, or the plumes and polish of guardsmen, have excited the least disgust.

To recapitulate: I would suggest that the differentiation between the dress of men and that of women, which begins as a variation of development throughout the eighteenth century and culminates in the schism of the early nineteenth century, arises from the fact that the exhibition of wealth on men no longer depended upon a demonstration of futility; this change was made possible by the emergence of a wealthy manufacturing class. On the other hand, the women of this class, having no employment and being entrusted with the business of vicarious consumption, continued to follow the sartorial laws already in existence.

The concept of Vicarious Consumption will also help us to understand other seemingly anomalous practices, for it is not only his wife and his mistress whom the modern producer wishes to see well dressed, there are also his children.

The dressing of very small children gives us an example of vicarious consumption in a very pure form. The 'long clothes' of silk, satin and lace, adorned with ribbons and bibbons on every side, which the children of the very rich may be seen wearing at christenings, etc., are presumably a matter of indifference, or perhaps even of vexation, to those who wear them. Indeed, the pretty clothes of small children generally would seem to be a matter of more pleasure and concern to the parents than to the instruments of display. In pre-industrial society a boy, as soon as he was breeched, wore what was in effect a miniature of adult clothing, even down to the rapier. Girls have usually worn clothes not very different from those of their mothers; boys on the other hand, being neither producers nor yet girls, had to be dressed for vicarious consumption in a new style, masculine, yet more sumptuous than that of their fathers. A great variety of styles was introduced, varying from kilts and sailor suits to lace-collared imitations of early seventeenth-century dress; there were also various school uniforms of a more or less futile character (see Plate 33 and Colour Plate III).

Servants no less than children are instruments of vicarious consumption, especially where their duties consist mainly in an exhibition of decorative idleness. As was only to be expected, the nineteenth century, which chastened the dress of the employer, left the flunkey in all his glory. It was an age of gorgeous footmen. What is staggering is to find the bourgeois dressing his servants as aristocrats, to discover the fashion of Versailles preserved in the Servants' Hall. Charles II has certainly been avenged in a most decisive manner. It would be tempting to perceive in this curious transformation some obscure apprehension of the class

PLATE 33

Instruments of Vicarious Consumption

PLATE 34

THE HEIGHT OF MAGNIFICENCE

Sir Gorgius Midas. "Hullo! where's all the rest of yer gone to?"

Head Footman. "If you please, Sir Gorgius, as it was past Two o'Clock, and we didn't know for certain whether you was coming back here, or going to Sleep in the City, the hother Footmen thought they might go to Bed——"

Sir Gorgius. "'Thought they might go to Bed,' did they? A pretty State of Things, indeed! So that if I'd a' 'appened to brought 'ome a Friend, there'd a' only been you Four to let us hin, hay!"

conflict. Tempting, but not, I think, justifiable. The powdered flunkey was felt to give an aristocratic air to the household of his employer. He was, as it were, a piece of period furniture; his livery had, or was supposed to have, an armigerous significance.

The recent tendency which we have already noticed, whereby the more obvious forms of sumptuosity are increasingly reserved for a large audience, and in time come to be regarded as vulgar in private houses, has affected this form of vicarious consumption. The liveried man-servant is almost extinct, even in the most ostentatious houses; where he survives he adopts an increasingly severe style of dress. We still expect a butler to look like a gentleman whatever may be the aspect of his employer, while maid-servants in cap and apron survive here and there, but high sumptuosity persists only in places of public entertainment in the dress of doormen, waiters, commissionaires, and those vicarious consumers who adorn our cinemas and our aeroplanes.

The dress of footmen brings us naturally to the subject of archaism in general; their eighteenth-century aspect is not an isolated phenomenon. It is characteristic of a number of survivals which mark the catastrophe of the French and Industrial Revolutions. The change in dress which then occurred was so violent, and its revolutionary implications such, that many older people clung to the fashion of the past, letting the young go forward with the new style. It is not surprising, therefore, that many of the survivals which remain, or remained, with us dated from the period immediately preceding those events. They persist as though fossilised by the cataclysm of which they are, in a sense, the memorial. This was the fate of official Court Dress, the dress of jockeys and of lawyers, of the uniform of Chelsea Pensioners, of certain military and naval uniforms. It will be observed that all these, save the last, are the uniforms of servants, in the broadest sense of the word. Few archaic dresses have altogether resisted the influence of fashion; in the majority of cases archaic clothes are worn only upon ceremonial occasions or for a particular purpose.

It will be found that, although nearly all forms of archaic dress are considered beautiful, 'historic' or 'old world', none can survive against the emulative process unless some degree of compulsion be applied by an employer (it may be an institution) who can enforce conformity throughout the period when, far from being romantic, they are simply dowdy; and perhaps even this compulsion must at times be assisted by a break in the fashion caused by radical change.

The hardiest survivals are found where the badge of servitude is also a badge of honour. In this connection it is interesting to note that, while several old-established grammar schools in this country have an ancient and sumptuous school uniform, the fashion in pedagogic wear has been set by Eton; so great indeed has been the social prestige of that institution that for a long time it set the juvenile fashion altogether.

Of the socially reputable professions, two, the Army and the Church, deserve special attention. As has already been pointed out, the sumptuosity of military men is very similar to that of ladies. A certain degree of wasteful expenditure is necessary; so too is a sufficient degree of discomfort and unpracticality (see Plate 35). It is interesting to notice that in both cases the display of pecuniary merit is felt to be particularly glamorous; there is held to be an erotic allure about a full-dress uniform just as there is about a fashionable evening gown. The expenditure, the discomfort, the futility, in a word, the high sumptuosity of the former is felt to be particularly manly; in the latter it conveys a notion of feminine fragility. The main difference between them is the much greater conservatism of the military dress.*

The idea of giving the soldier some form of badge or distinguishing mark so as to enable him to tell friend from foe is no doubt very ancient. But the provision of uniform clothing (as distinct from the livery of the feudal men at arms) is comparatively modern. It was obviously desirable from the first, for the man in uniform – quite apart from the moral qualities which uniform seems to confer – could not easily change sides at a critical moment, or desert and become a non-combatant when he felt that it would be prudent to do so. The invention of military uniform gave commanders a much greater control over their men and created a most important distinction between the army and the populace. But, economically, it was hardly possible to reclothe a great host of men who, at the end of the campaigning season, would be demobilised, and it was not until standing armies were created in the seventeenth century that the military tailor comes into his own. When uniformed armies were created it would seem that the uniforms provided were, apart from their distinctive colours, to which individual colonels soon added regimental facings, not unlike the dress of civilians. But already, by the beginning of the eighteenth century, the idea of using military clothes as a form of conspicuous consumption had become established, and with it the idea that it was the particular duty of the officer and the non-commissioned officer to impose regular and exact conformity with sartorial regulations.

As we have already noticed, conservatism – and a regimental sergeant-major must by reason of his functions be highly conservative – takes the form of the retention of certain features of a dress which in their origin

---

* In the following passages I have relied heavily upon Charles Francis Atkinson's article in the 12th Edition of the *Encyclopaedia Britannica*, s.v. Uniforms.

PLATE 35

THE NEW HUSSAR HESSIANS AND PANTS.

"See, I've dropped my Handkerchief, Captain de Vere!"

"I know you have, Miss Constance. I'm very sorry. I can't Stoop, either!"

Conspicuous Leisure, feminine and military

were purely utilitarian, but which become reputable either by being made obsolete or by being transformed into something so futile as to be no longer recognisable as an object of utility. Thus we find the soldier's hat, originally much like any other hat, fastened up on one side and becoming a cocked hat, plumed, fringed, braided and decorated. The regimental facings and cuffs, originally useful flaps which could be buttoned across to protect the wearer from the weather, become brilliantly decorative motifs, sewn flat upon the uniforms and therefore no longer serviceable but highly ornamental.

One might have thought that the principle of conspicuous leisure could hardly operate in the dress of a man whose essential business it was to march, to ride and to fight; but it does. A really smart uniform had to be made really tight; Frederick the Great, who had won his battles by developing the rapid fire power of his infantry, introduced in his old age such tight-sleeved uniforms as to cramp the arms of the wearer, a policy which may perhaps have borne fruit at Jena. In the same way and for the same reason the Life-Guardsmen of the British Army were at one time so constricted by their jackets that they were unable to practise their sword exercises.

Probably the brilliant colours of most eighteenth-century uniforms were useful and did not become a positive disadvantage until the rifle had replaced the musket. Until that time there can have been little chance for concealment, usually an opponent was in sight long before he was within range of small-arms, and in the confusion of a smoke-filled battlefield where hand-to-hand engagements were common, it would have helped a soldier to be able to tell friend from foe. But the elaboration of uniforms, the weight of heavy bearskins or towering 'sausage ornaments', the hussar's pelisse, the tassels and the embroideries, went far beyond any tactical convenience in recognition.

It was in the first half of the nineteenth century that military dandyism became most outrageous, and a first reaction came after the experiences of the Crimean War; but it was not until the Boer War that it became painfully obvious that eighteenth-century uniforms made a perfect target for the twentieth-century marksman armed with a breech-loading rifle and smokeless powder.

Reformation of uniforms, like reformation of drill, is hard to achieve, even when it results from the dreadful lessons of war. The uniform has a spiritual value which is cherished for its own sake. A dingy, mottled, baggy, inconspicuous garment may make for efficiency on the battlefield but it does not accord with our notions of what constitutes a smart soldier-like appearance. Changes were made in the early twentieth century but they were made reluctantly. The British compromised by keeping a sumptuous 'full-dress' uniform for ceremonial occasions while sending their armies to fight in khaki. But even in khaki there is scope for a kind of modified sumptuosity, and opportunities could still be found for polishing, whitening and generally smartening up the soldier's appearance, embellishments which had to be justified on grounds of discipline and morale rather than of actual efficiency in combat. At the same time our lingering affection for a decorative rather than a utilitarian army results in the continued employment of ornamental soldiers, equipped as though for Salamanca or Inkermann, who still beautify our streets and lend dignity to our public ceremonies.

The wearing of appropriate clothes has been so important a part of devout observances for so long a time that it is very difficult to speak of religious clothes without trespassing upon the dangerous ground of theology. The priest is known by his cloth, and this has usually been an instrument of conspicuous leisure. Veblen sees therein simply the livery of God's service, and there can be no doubt that there is much truth in this view. In their various ways the Churches have provided the greatest vehicle for futile expenditure in the history of the world. Along with the desire to propitiate and honour the Deity there has frequently been a particular delight in the exhibition of wealth, whether by an individual or by a community, in the building and servicing of houses for God. To this end not only have great treasures been amassed and great institutions endowed, but an army of ministers has been supported by the sacrifices of the faithful. These persons are thus, in a sense, in the ornamental position of flunkeys or women.

There is, however, another tendency in established religious institutions which makes of the priest a rentier, a man of property and of fashion. This tendency, which is natural enough where a strong vested interest is concerned, is repugnant to those who have found the money, not for an individual, but for God.* Again and again throughout the Middle Ages we find contemporary moralists complaining that the clergy dress in secular fashion; despite many attempts at reform this practice continues up to and beyond the time of the Reformation. From a sumptuary point of view that movement is important, in that it led the Roman Church to make strenuous efforts to impose sartorial discipline upon her priests, and among the Protestants to an abolition of purple and fine linen, i.e. to the abolition of conspicuous consumption, which in the case of the extreme Protestant sects was effected by the abolition of priesthood as a whole-time job. In neither case did the reformers wholly fail or succeed. Among the older Churches we find wigged and powdered ecclesiastics

* See Samuel, I, ii, 12–17.

until the time of the French Revolution, at which point the Roman Church appears to have undergone that process of fossilisation to which we have already alluded. Amongst the Protestants, especially where a vested interest was established and the clergyman became genteel, we usually find some kind of modified uniform.

The effect of this double process of enrichment and reform is to make ecclesiastical dress a fascinating museum of past modes. In the Roman Church we find vestigial forms such as the pallium and the dalmatica; in the dress of some orders the costume of the dark ages; in that of others the extravagant headdresses of the late fifteenth century, while the fashions of the Renaissance are commemorated in Geneva bands and dog collars.

In recent years the Churches, wishing no doubt to decrease the distance between clergy and laity which must always be felt when the former assumes the aspect of a historic monument, have made attempts to modernise their uniforms. Indeed the wind of change has blown so hard that some orders of nuns have raised skirts 18 inches or more above floor level. Personally, and from a religiously ignorant point of view, I doubt the wisdom of such measures or rather half measures, for the designers of ecclesiastical dress are never going to go to all lengths in their imitation of current fashion. By lifting the skirts of nuns they abandoned the safe ground of tradition and abandoned what is, after all, a very beautiful type of dress, but at the same time they could hardly introduce a conventual mini skirt, so that the final effect looked rather like a dowdy version of the then fashion. But the mere idea of falling into step with fashion is dangerous and may have unexpected results. No sooner were the short-skirted nuns able to show their legs to the world than the maxi skirt began to chase the mini skirt out of favour, thus defeating the original purpose of the innovation. I myself have seen a company of young women, one of whom, a nun, was distinguished from the rest by her unfashionably short skirts.

A uniform which is aligned to fashion is almost a contradiction in terms and probably, if people in holy orders wish to abolish or diminish the divisive effects of religious uniform, they would do better to abandon sartorial regulations altogether and dress as everybody else does, more or less in the current fashion. This does seem to be the tendency of a great many clergymen of the Church of England, many of whom try as far as possible to minimise the distinctions of dress which separate them from the laity.

The dress of the Church of England is a compromise, and in this Church we find also a very marked differentiation between ceremonial and workaday dress. The Established Church, and she alone it would seem, has been affected by that tendency of fashion which we have called

COLOUR PLATE I

Open-air Girl, 1759

COLOUR PLATE II

Open-air Girls and others, 1801

COLOUR PLATE III

Open-air Girl and children, 1845

COLOUR PLATE IV

Open-air Girl, 1975

PLATE 36

Archaism

Conspicuous Outrage. The fashion arose during the thirties of the last century and took the form of a more and more daring imitation of Roman vestments. Like every other fashion it caused scandal, and like every other it ended by becoming perfectly respectable.

The fashionability of Rome in Protestant countries is, of course, no mere matter of dress. In that it is an ancient cult, providing large opportunities for conspicuous consumption, the Roman Church has attracted the higher-income groups in Protestant countries ever since she ceased to be a political rival or an economic temptation. This has been particularly the case in those countries where the middle classes have established inexpensive and vulgar sects, and in which, therefore, the older ceremonies gain by contrast. The quality of fashionable outrage is intensified by the licence which the Roman Church, and in particular the Society of Jesus, is supposed to permit the individual in sexual and other modish indulgences. These manifest advantages seem to have been largely offset in countries such as the United States where Roman Catholicism was peculiarly the religion of the poor.

It is in the light of these subtler manifestations of conspicuous outrage, as also of more intellectual considerations, that we should judge the movement which shook Oxford and the Church in the last century.

The foregoing examples of archaism are all in a large measure the product of Vicarious Consumption; there is, however, another kind of archaism which is of quite different origin. At the very centre of the whirligig of fashion one may perceive a point which seems almost motionless.

The late Queen Mary, consort of George V, is still remembered for her hats, or rather her 'toques', which were decidedly fashionable around 1912, but which she persisted in wearing until the time of her death in 1953. She at least wore that which had been smart and was good of its kind, but what shall we say of that duke, the bearer of one of the most ancient titles of the realm, who, when he felt the need for a change of clothes, wandered into the fields until he could find what he needed upon one of his tenant farmer's scarecrows? What shall we say? We shall say that, since he really was a duke, it was perfectly all right.

There are people whose station is so very exalted, whose social claims are so obviously beyond all question, that they can remain largely, if not entirely, immune to the demands of fashion. To them the emulative process is scarcely applicable; they can, in consequence, be as completely lacking in sumptuosity as they please. To the millionaire or the crowned head all sins are forgiven. This clearly is one of those exceptions that prove the rule.

8
Recent History

> 'Where do these grand new winter sports beauty boxes come from? They are the Brainchild of Cyclax and contain a complete Romany Tan make-up protective Day Lotion, powder, rouge, lipstick and nail enamel, and a tube of Beauty Bronze. The outfit is made up in two sizes, for a two-week or a four-week trip at 25s. 6d. and 32s. 6d. And for your romantic, pink night make-up, Cyclax have nice coffrets of lipstick, rouge and nail enamel to match (14s. 6d. complete) for you to take abroad in your favourite shade.'
>
> *Vogue*,
> December 14, 1938

The argument which I have been trying to advance in the three foregoing chapters is that the history of fashionable dress is tied to the competition between classes, in the first place the emulation of the aristocracy by the bourgeoisie and then the more extended competition which results from the ability of the proletariat to compete with the middle classes. It is only when we take these facts into account that we can understand why fashion should be originally a European phenomenon developing in much the same way wherever the social situation allows of such development. It is for this reason that, while many political events leave fashion unaffected, those which alter the class structure do influence the course of fashion. If we can also admit the theory of Vicarious Consumption, the schism between masculine and feminine dress takes its place naturally as part of the same process, as does the persistence of certain archaic forms. Implicit in the whole is a system of sartorial morality dependent upon pecuniary standards of value.

There are, however, certain fairly recent events in the history of dress which cannot easily be reconciled with the kind of theoretical explanation that I have provided. I believe that these events, which are indeed of central importance in the history of twentieth-century costume, have done some harm to Veblen as a philosopher of clothes.

When, in the last years of the nineteenth century, *The Theory of the Leisure Class* was written, Veblen had no difficulty in finding contemporary examples to illustrate his meaning. Conspicuous Consumption and Conspicuous Leisure were carried to preposterous lengths in that gilded age of American Capitalism, and this was nowhere more evident than in women's clothes. It was a time of drastic tight lacing; skirts trailed; the hymenopterous appearance of women was emphasised by prodigious sleeves and capes (see Plate 37); a lady's neck was invisible by day, as indeed it had been ever since the 1870s, and her entire person was concealed from the chin downwards. Conspicuous Consumption was evident in the incredible elaboration of dress, the wild abundance of net and lace and ribbons and feathers and other trimmings. It must have been hard to walk, to eat or to breathe in the expensive carapace which fashionable women then wore.

But the development of women's dress in the years between 1906 and 1914 was in quite a different sense Veblenian. It was as though the American philosopher had brought mankind to its senses. Corsets, as we have already noticed, began to lose their hold, women could breathe again, and as they did so the bosom rose until the waist was nearly as high as it had been in 1800; there were indications that the waist itself was on its way out, the whole dress became a loosely fitted robe, something between a caftan and a himation, open – and it seemed to that age scandalously open – at the neck and revealing, in an even more scandalous fashion, a good deal of ankle. Hats which had been vast shrank to mere toques, hair which had burst out in opulent waves in the so-called pompadour style was abbreviated altogether; by 1914 there was a substantial liberation of women in so far as their clothes were concerned. And only one feature of the period could really be accounted a device of conspicuous leisure, viz. the 'hobble skirt'. This indeed, while it lasted, was as unpractical as any of the devices of the nineteenth century. It consisted of a kind of belt fastened around the legs about four inches below the knee. Sometimes it was a mere constriction of the skirt, but it did indeed hobble the wearer very effectually. It was very fashionable around 1911. At almost the same time Poiret introduced the 'harem skirt' which went to the opposite extreme, consisting simply of a pair of baggy trousers; but the world was not yet ready for such audacities. In an epoch of conspicuous outrage, and it was in this line that Poiret excelled, trousers for women was just a little too outrageous.

The influence of the Great War of 1914–18 – I am speaking now of the clothes which were worn during the actual period of hostilities – was very striking but very short-lived. In a sense the war seems to have produced a reaction against the fashions of the previous decade. Women have waists again in a more or less natural position, and the waists are diminished by the use of a rather bulky peplum ending at the hips; hats are rather larger than they were; the daytime neck-line plunges rather

Fashions for 1893

deeper. But the really striking thing about the fashion of that time is its erotic audacity. This is something which it is particularly hard for us to see. Satiated as we are with the spectacle of entire female legs, it is very hard to realise that the gift of an extra centimetre, the mere hint of a stocking, was enough to make our grandfathers quite breathless with emotion. As for the sensations produced by a feminine calf, the knee being in everyday life something beyond the dreams of concupiscence, they were of so wild and incontinent a nature as to beggar all description. Thus it was that when, in 1916, skirts rose some 9 or 10 inches from the floor, it must have seemed to contemporaries that they had a glimpse of paradise; for in fact this was, at that epoch, an all-time high for European fashion, and to the soldier on leave it may even have appeared that the war had its compensations.

For here I think we must allow that the fashion did result from the war. On the one hand war work of various kinds could be used as a justification for clothes which were at once more comfortable and more attractive than those of the immediate past, and even though the young ladies in Plate 39 look as though their contribution to the war effort would probably be confined to the important business of keeping officers happy, still the short skirt could be in a way excused on utilitarian grounds. On the other hand the war, by bringing death into every home and every family, served also to provide a licence for sexual indiscretions. Finally the war did up to a point slacken the demands of those social forces which tend to produce conspicuous waste and conspicuous leisure. The ethos of a nation in arms demands that class shall be forgotten, and for a time it was truly felt that all classes were united in the common effort to defeat the enemy. Here it does seem to me that an ideological explanation is perfectly justifiable.

The armistice brought a return to long skirts, a long loose line without any waist and a slight emphasis on the hips. In fact the fashions that prevail for about six years after the war are, roughly speaking, a highly simplified version of the fashions of the years before 1914. A little bit more leg is visible, but otherwise the apparent influence of the war is negligible. The fashion which we tend to think of as being characteristically 'post-war', and which consists of a kind of shapeless sack, ending just a little below the knees, adorned only with a string of beads and worn with very short hair, all secondary sexual characteristics being as far as possible minimised, hardly begins before 1924 and lasts for six or seven years. The very short skirt ended in about 1930 when the hemline descended abruptly in day dresses and in evening dresses reached the floor. This marks a permanent change in women's dress in that there is from now on a marked tendency for evening dress to be much longer than daytime

PLATE 38

Fashions for 1911

COSTUMES DE JERSEY

Modèles de Gabrielle Channel (*fig.* 257, 258 *et* 259)

Fashions for 1916

PLATE 40

Fashions for 1923

PLATE 41

Fashions for 1927

clothes. The fashion for flat chests and flat buttocks, which is very much a part of the mode of the late twenties, lasts longer than the short skirt; but the thirties sees a gradual return of the natural waist and a corresponding emphasis upon the hips, the bosom and the shoulders, these being enlarged or padded, as in the 1830s, to diminish the apparent size of the waist. (See Appendix B, pp. 231–7.)

Fashion seldom changes very rapidly and unless we are very alert we may not notice what is taking place. But supposing we could take someone from the year 1914, put her into cold storage for a generation and then show her what was being worn in 1939, might one not get a clearer idea of what had been happening in the interval? This is not simply a rhetorical question, for the thing has been done.

In 1914 Miss Monica Baldwin entered a religious house so strictly regulated that she had practically no idea of what was going on in the outside world. For twenty-eight years she wore the extraordinarily heavy and uncomfortable habit which in the fourteenth century had been designed for her order; her only knowledge of secular costume was derived from her girlhood memories before 1914, when she had been a rather well-dressed though not, I suspect, highly fashionable young lady. In 1941 she left the convent and found herself in an England which for three years had been at war and which was still, more or less, wearing the fashions which had prevailed in 1939. On the day of her release her sister brought her a bundle of clothes. Miss Baldwin looked with astonishment at the objects which it was now considered suitable that a middle-aged woman should wear. Her new underclothes seemed absurdly skimpy and diaphanous, impossibly so for a rather cold day. She was, as one might expect, horrified by the sight of such a short skirt and of stockings so transparent that they hardly seemed worth wearing. She protested that her legs would look naked, and her sister had to assure her that she would not look in the least conspicuous. But there was another innovation which she found even more shocking.

> An object was handed me which I can only describe as a very realistically modelled bust bodice. That its purpose was to emphasize *contours which, in my girlhood, were always decorously concealed* was but too evident.
>
> 'This,' said my sister cheerfully, 'is a brassiere. And it's no use looking so horrified, because fashions today go out of their way to stress that part of one's anatomy....'*

Miss Baldwin's astonishment was probably due in part to the fact that

---

* Monica Baldwin, *I Leap Over the Wall*, 1949, p. 11. (My italics.)

in Victorian and Edwardian dress the bosom, however prominently it might be displayed, appeared as a unified mass. The display of individual breasts is an innovation of the 1930s, or at least something that would hardly have been seen in European dress since the early years of the nineteenth century. Nevertheless, it is still a little strange that this should have been the most disturbing novelty for someone coming to the dress of 1939 from that of 1914. It may remind us how far the fashion had moved from the epicene 'boyish' mode of the late twenties, and also suggests that the concealment of feminine curves, which we think of as typically 'post-war', must already have been very much a part of the fashion in the years just before 1914.

Considering the period 1906–39 from a theoretical point of view, I think that one must treat the suggestion that there is some direct connection between the fashions of the late 1920s with the war of 1914–18 with very great reserve. The actual effect of the war upon dress is fairly evident and does seem to have produced a fashion which, in many respects, was radically different from that of the twenties, while the modes of the years after the war seem to have much more to do with those of the years which preceded the war than with the war itself. In fact if we consider the wartime fashions as a kind of deviation, then the general development from 1906 to 1926 seems regular, logical and the kind of thing that might have been anticipated. Certainly it is not necessary to introduce any theory about war and fashion in order to explain it.

The larger question is, why, after 1924, does fashion move away from the nineteenth-century pattern of conspicuous leisure and in the direction of something much more functional.

I suspect that one reason for this redirection of fashion is the growing emancipation of women, an emancipation which might, as in England, take a political form but which may be seen rather as that progressive decay of the purely patriarchal attitude of the nineteenth century, the gradual acceptance of an Anglo-Saxon rather than a Latin conception of the role of woman in society. The change would become important, so far as the history of dress is concerned, when woman is no longer regarded simply as an agent for vicarious consumption. In a sense of course women always had been consumers on their own account, but by the beginning of the twentieth century they were beginning to take their place beside their brothers as active participants in the business of social futility. Perhaps I can indicate my meaning by pointing out that whereas Frenchwomen had to wait much longer than Englishwomen before they had a vote, in both countries they were able to own and to drive motor cars long before 1914.

Men, it has been said, have for long practised various violent physical exercises of an uneconomic nature as a part of their social duties, and these have exerted a great influence on their entire wardrobe. Masculine dress, in so far as it has developed since the middle of the last century, has been changed almost entirely through the reflected influence of outdoor sports. This would not seem to be, as Veblen suggests, because of the particular merit attaching to personal prowess and the competitive spirit. It is not competition which makes a sport fashionable but expense, and indeed it is from sports which are not directly competitive that the majority of our masculine fashions are derived. The 'boater', the 'deer stalker', and the 'Norfolk jacket', to name a few of the articles of clothing which derive from sports, have been adopted because they are associated with expensive and purely wasteful pursuits. The directly competitive sports suffer in esteem because they tend to become professionalised and thus acquire a rational economic motive. Highly commercialised sports such as boxing and football have in fact come to be considered slightly vulgar and have set no fashions. Horse racing is of particular interest in that the spectators, who lose money, set many fashions; while the bookmakers, who make money, set none.

The view that the respectability of a sport depends mainly upon the opportunity which it provides for futile expenditure is strongly borne out by the fact that among the best considered sports of this century are those which involve not only an expensive outfit but an expensive journey in search of suitable conditions. Thus we find that an energetic but aimless expenditure of time and money on the slopes of the Alps or the mud banks of the Adriatic became almost a part of the routine of fashion in the 1930s.

It will be seen, therefore, that there is no pecuniary impropriety in the participation in active sports by women. The only objection thereto is that they may appear to be wasting money on their own account and not for the good repute of their owners. With the gradual improvement in the status of women this objection was weakened; the opportunity was eagerly taken, for it involved not only a futile expenditure of time but the provision of a more various wardrobe. The riding-habit had for long been a part of a gentlewoman's paraphernalia, but riding, like croquet, allowed a certain measure of repose. Late in the nineteenth century the attempt was made to conserve the fashions of leisure with the practice of more energetic sports. The effect was grotesque and was very similar to those earlier attempts of men to do likewise, as, for instance, to play cricket in top hats. Nevertheless, the effort to combine the incompatibles continues right up to and after the Great War; finally, and partly as a result of that war, it broke down, and in so doing combined neatly with the prevalent mode of Conspicuous Outrage, which consisted, not, as in previous ages, in a distortion of the waist, the buttocks and the bust, but in a flaunting of the legs. The two tendencies go hand in hand, and with them the contemporary ideal of the boyish (i.e. athletic) figure. At the height of the mode, woman was an athlete; she showed it in her dress just as seventeenth-century man showed that he was a soldier. It need hardly be said that in both cases there was much unjustifiable pretence. But the athlete in the ballroom was almost as grotesque as the professional beauty on the tennis court. The solution as we have seen was just the same as that arrived at at the time of the Industrial Revolution: one style, that of futile exercise, is used for day wear; another, that of futile repose, serves for the evening.

The manner in which women's clothes have been adapted not simply to sport but to the open-air is suggested by the colour plates. As the theatre of fashionable operations moves increasingly out of doors we find, not only a new kind of clothes, but a new kind of complexion.

Perhaps the most illustrative and remarkable feature of fashion after 1918 was the fashion in cosmetics. In the eighteenth century both paint and powder were favoured, but were, I suspect, to a large extent a part of the apparatus of the aristocracy in its defiance of the middle classes. At all events, with the triumph of the latter, cosmetics were not only abandoned but condemned, and their use, on honest women, was surreptitious and imitative. In our own time they have returned as a form of outrage comparable to short skirts and bad language and become so customary as to be respectable. Eventually it was scarcely thought decent for a young woman to attend an important function with her face unpainted. There is in consequence little artifice, little deceit, in the customary decoration of the face and finger-nails; the intention is clear and unequivocal.

A further innovation was the adoption of a new standard of beauty in pigmentation. Hitherto, the ideal had been one of shaded and unfreckled fairness; sunburn was felt to imply a healthy industrious open-air life, tolerable perhaps in a man but not in a lady. But in the twenties the woman who could prove that she was no city worker, but one of those able to bask in the sunlight of the Mediterranean, was esteemed for her tan just as her grandmother had been for her pallor. Thus we found the rare spectacle of women powdering themselves brown when unable to roast themselves to the same end. With the division of modes referred to above, it became necessary to exhibit two complexions, the sporting sunburn by day, the delicate pallor by night; the one indicative of Conspicuous Consumption, the other of Conspicuous Leisure. These 'unladylike' fashions belong to the history of the 1920s and, even more, of the 1930s; nevertheless at the end of the period, just before the outbreak of the Second World War, the general tendency of fashion in women's

PLATE 42

LAWN TENNIS

'Charlotte and Ethel, having accepted a Challenge to play against their Cousins, Tom and Harry, insist upon Handicapping them – as is only fair.'

PLATE 43

Fashions for 1948

clothes was towards more ladylike or at least more feminine silhouette. As we have seen, a new and very important emphasis was placed on the bosom and there was an attempt, even in the first year of the war, to revive tight lacing. To those theorists who connected the fashions of the late twenties with the influence of war it seemed clear that this tendency would be reversed. Post-war fashions would in all probability mark a return to boyish fashions; certainly there would be an end to corsets, hats would become very small and hair would be short. Prophecies such as these were freely made before 1948; but in that year Paris regained her position as a leader of fashion and, under the guidance of M. Dior, bosoms became more prominent, the waist remained in its natural position and so far from disappearing was constricted by artificial means, hats grew in size, hair was longer than ever. In fact the fashion did exactly what the theorists had said that it would not do.

Comparing the 'new look' with the fashions of 1939 it seems that, like the fashion that succeeded the First World War, it was a natural continuation of the pre-war style, the main difference being that skirts were a good deal longer in 1948 than they had been ten years earlier.

Were the theorists put out by this unaccountable reluctance of fashion to comply with their predictions? Not a bit of it. The 'new look' was but an incident; it had nothing to do with the war and if we only waited long enough the Zeitgeist would, so to speak, get up steam and the boyish fashions that had been so confidently predicted would make their appearance. After all it had taken six years for the 'post-war' fashions that followed the First World War to manifest themselves. Sure enough, after a mere ten years' delay, the prophecy *was* fulfilled and something, which if not exactly boyish was near enough for theoretical purposes to a 'post-war fashion', did emerge. For in time the new look lost its newness, the so-called 'A line' seemed likely to abolish the waist, and although this did not happen and hair remained long, we did at least witness a fashion in which skirts were very short indeed, much shorter in fact than they had ever been.

Whether in fact that vertiginous glimpse of girls' thighs which we called the mini skirt had anything to do with the carnage of 1939–45 may still be doubted; it cannot be disproved but it does make substantial demands on our powers of faith. As Mrs Langley Moore, one of our most brilliant writers on fashion, has said discussing the shortcomings of psychologists' theories, they are 'often inclined, like ill-made clothes, "to fit where they touch"'.

Having said so many disagreeable things about theories of fashion and made light of the prophets, it is rather awkward to have to admit that my own theory has led me to indulge in prophecy. In twenty years' time it may well be that the forecast that I am about to make may look as ridiculous as most attempts of the kind; nevertheless I shall commit myself to the view that fashion in clothes, as we know it, is coming to an end.

The situation in the past has been that a wealthy and powerful group of people set the fashion and that this elite was imitated, after a certain lapse of time, by less wealthy groups. Today it would appear that this process is being short-circuited. Clothes are exhibited at fashion shows in Paris, London or Rome, and although presumably a rich clientele does continue to buy clothes or have them designed by the great houses, the really important purchases will be made by representatives of those firms which can reproduce vast quantities of any given design at a price which can be afforded, not by the rich elite, but by the unmarried girl in a good job. It is she, if I understand the business correctly, who is now the best customer, for although as an individual she will not compete with the wives of the oil magnates, collectively her purchasing power is enormous. Between the moment when she starts to earn and the time when she begins to bear children, clothes will be her main item of expense. The power of her purse, that is to say the money she has to spend multiplied by many millions, for her name is legion, is what must determine the choice of models offered by the wholesalers. Such a clientele cannot be interested in workmanship and is probably more concerned that the goods should be pretty than that they should be durable. If it looks for leadership it will probably be from fashion magazines and from the world of entertainment. But I doubt whether it defers to any one authority: it will be, as Riesman puts it, 'other directed'; governed by the taste of groups, groups composed of people of roughly equal status, rather than by the 'duchess' who served as a reasonably effective symbol in the model of fashion that I constructed earlier.

The task of the producer must be extremely difficult, much more difficult than it would be in a socially acquiescent society in which he knew pretty exactly what the clientele was trying to look like. Now he has to try to gauge the public taste on the basis presumably of research but in an area where it is difficult to see how research can produce very positive answers. Under the circumstances the old pattern of class imitation must be considerably affected. This great youthful public is made more interesting but even less predictable by reason of an element which, though not of great economic importance, appears to be influential. I refer to the student body, a body which today is most strikingly adorned.

During the past twenty years we have seen a remarkable metamorphosis of the student. Students used to look very much like other people apart from the fact that they were, perforce, cheaply dressed and were usually content to identify themselves, except in those ancient universities where they were still compelled to wear some kind of academic dress, by the use of a scarf (usually a combination of strikingly ugly colours).

There was however one discipline of which this was not true; the art student has for a very long time been a non-conformist, in sartorial as in other matters. Thus in the studio of J. L. David there was a coterie – *les crasseux* – in which it was a point of honour to smoke at least three pipes a day (which at the time of the French Revolution was thought excessive), to change one's linen only when it had become totally unwearable, and never to wash except when one went for a swim. There were others, *les primitifs*, who imitated their neo-classical sisters and boldly stepped out upon the Boulevard in the robes, and the beards, of antiquity. Later in the nineteenth century there were always some students who were ready to astonish the world by what they wore and did not wear: the female art student, a creation of that century, while staying closer to fashion, was willing nevertheless to appear – as fashionable ladies contemptuously put it – 'arty'. Such eccentricities might persist in later life. The majority, no doubt, happily vanished into discreet bourgeois anonymity, but there were enough to provide some basis of fact for the more or less mythical stereotype of the artist: the bearded man in a smock with a lot of hair and a flowing tie, the inhabitant of an operatic Bohemia.

Both the artist and the art student are, as one may say, *déclassé*. The painter, and the sculptor, because they work with their hands, have seldom enjoyed the conspicuously leisurely character of the liberal artist, the poet or the philosopher. Already, amongst the ancients, the inferior status of even the most distinguished sculptor was a fact of social life, and the prejudice lives on almost into our own times. Readers of Tennyson will remember that when the Lord of Burleigh went courting he chose the humblest of social disguises:

> He is but a landscape-painter,
> And a village maiden she,

Social equals in fact. When, after marrying him, she discovered that he was really a gentleman the shock to her sense of social propriety was so great that she went into a decline and died.

On the other hand there were painters who achieved greatness. One might treat Popes and princes as his equals, another died in the arms of a King of France, a third entered the orders of chivalry and conducted the negotiations of a great power; more and more, as the years went by, they arrived at the gentility of a knighthood. The artist in fact was an incalculable piece on the social chess-board; usually he was the meanest of men but on the eighth square he might achieve royalty. In consequence he was hard to place and was by no means sure of his own position; he was apt to dress, not in order to establish his position within a recognisable social hierarchy, but rather to suggest that his genius was such as to place him above all social distinctions.

This digression is not so irrelevant as it seems. The point that I am attempting to establish is that, not being anchored to a firm social position, the artist and the art student tended to adopt an experimental attitude towards dress. In the nineteenth century when most artists came from the middle or lower middle classes, it was, quite logically, the characteristics of his own class which the artist tended to reject. The middle-class virtues of tidiness, cleanliness and inconspicuous decency had to be discarded by one who claimed to be above class; eccentricity which, in most social groups, was regarded as a fault was for the artist a cardinal virtue.

What has happened during the past twenty years is that the students of other subjects have begun to take the same sartorial liberties as art students, and have done so with a lunatic thoroughness which left their elders appalled but which has, I believe, had its effect beyond the groves of Academe. As far as my own observation goes one can tell fairly well what the young of all classes will be wearing a year hence by what is being worn on the campus now.

Certainly one reason for this development is that student ideology favours an intransigent attitude towards age and authority and what is believed to be non-conformity. As with the art student so with all modern students the desire to *épater les bourgeois* is important. Thus we have seen long hair, gaily blatant effeminacy, sheer dirtiness, the rejection both of fashion and of sumptuosity, the defiant display of battered jeans and ragged T shirts, the tendency to abolish distinctions, not only of sex but of class. Although such manifestations may involve an element of pretence and even of affectation, still they exemplify the passions and the ideology of a genuine revolt. And yet even here, an ideological explanation of dress, though certainly true up to a point, tends to be misleading.

The young woman who came draggle-haired, barefoot, in mended trousers and plebeian shirt to voice the doctrines of Chairman Mao at last Tuesday's tutorial, appears at Wednesday's seminar prim and pretty with flounces down to her ankles and her hair neatly bound in a knot. On the following Tuesday she is wearing a natty pair of trousers and a stiff-brimmed hat. On the campus anything goes. Fashions that seem to belong to the Edwardian epoch and that one had expected never to see again except on the screen are worn side by side with clothes which would be perfectly appropriate for a day's work on a building site. Young men appear with their hair half-way down their backs tied back with a ribbon; others are so cropped that they would pass the scrutiny of a major-general. Here at least it does seem that fashion, if by fashion we mean some generalised style worn by a class or a community, is being replaced by anarchy. It is my belief that this, the death of fashion in the universities, will presently lead to its destruction everywhere, that lacking the old pattern of imitation the old uniformity of dress will come to an end, first amongst the young, later in all ages and classes.

Here I must observe that this seems to me a wholly admirable state of affairs, that I already rejoice in the chaotic confusion of styles amongst my students, and that I should rejoice still more if it becomes general. Uniformity seems to me a cruel and unreasonable thing. I like to suppose that people may now cease to wear that which is worn simply because it is being worn by other people and may begin to dress themselves in that which suits them best. But having said that I would like this to happen, my reasoning becomes suspect, for it is only too easy to convince oneself that that which one would like to occur is in fact taking place.

Let me therefore admit that my view-point, that is to say my situation in a University which values eccentricity, may lead me to attach too much importance to the frolics of a minority. Let me also admit that there are probably more conformities and taboos within student groups than I am aware of. Indeed I am assured that this is the case and that there are student groups with very precise conformities and prohibitions. Groups of friends will dress alike and adopt a kind of uniform; certain garments and certain hair styles will for them be taboo. No doubt this is in a large measure true, although I must observe that some students seem so wildly various in their dress that it is hard to know what kind of regulations they can observe; but admitting that there are such peer groups and that they have their sartorial habits, still this is not the same thing as fashion, which is wider in its scope and imposes a much greater degree of uniformity.

Again it must be allowed that, despite the great variety of their dress, students usually try to look like students. In their different disguises they distinguish themselves from the rest of the community and it might be argued that ragged jeans and lettered T shirts do mark their wearers as the members of a distinct if not a leisured class.

Finally I must enter another caveat and admit that many writers on fashion, when they come to a consideration of their own time, tend to speak of 'anarchy' and to see diversity where a later generation is able to perceive unity.

Nevertheless I do believe that on a long view it can be seen that the old pattern of class emulation is already breaking down. In the 1950s Frederick Lewis Allen noticed that:

> A generation ago the great mail-order houses produced different clothes for the Western farmer's wife and for the city woman of the East [i.e. the East of the U.S.], today there is no such distinction, and a friend of mine whose train stopped recently at a small Oklahoma town remarked that the girls on the railroad platform were virtually indistinguishable in appearance from the girls on Madison Avenue or Michigan Boulevard. It could almost be said that the only visible mark of wealth which a woman can put on is a mink coat.
>
> At this point an explanatory word is in order. The trend that I am describing is not a trend toward uniformity. Among both men and women there is a great diversity in attire. The point I am making is that the diversity is more a matter of preference or of custom among the members of a local or vocational group, than of economic class.*

If one observes a longer period, the decay of fashion seems to me to become very perceptible. I have attempted to demonstrate this on Plate 44 which I hope gives a reasonably accurate notion of what has been happening. The examples numbered 1–6 are taken from fashion journals for the summer of 1904; those lettered A–F (also from fashion journals) are from the summer of 1974. In selecting the examples I have attempted to show how much variety was permissible within each period.

The examples for the year 1904 surely give an impression of considerable uniformity. The only large deviation from the norm is No. 5, which is a motoring coat, presumably worn over something like No. 3 or No. 4. There are but two neck-lines, a very high one and a very low one (for evening wear only). Waists are always in the same place, skirts are of the same shape and length, so are hair styles. We find the same type of sleeve in 2, 4 and 5. The dressmaker of this period had a clear sense of style; her art consisted in devising variations upon a well-defined theme. To invent a dress in 1904 was like writing a sonnet; you knew what you could do and what you couldn't do.

Now what generalisation can we make about the series A–F? Well, all the clothes are worn by women. Even this may be doubted, nevertheless Model D is in fact worn by a girl. What else can one say? There

---

* Allen, *Trend to Breakdown of Classlines in Clothes*, quoted by Roach and Eicher, *Dress, Adornment and the Social Order*, New York, 1965, p. 162.

is no general form of hat or hair style, neck-lines vary from the very high to the fairly low (with a larger sample it would have been possible to show models bare to the midriff), the waist – when there is a waist – is in its natural position. Clothes can be closely fitted or very loose, skirts may reach the knee or the floor, or any point between, or may be replaced by trousers. There is no quality common to all evening dresses or to all day dresses, as there would have been thirty years earlier; A and B are evening dresses, C, D, E and F are for day wear (the clear division between these types of dress which existed until very recently is no longer perceptible). It is perhaps worth noting that D and E would have been considered indecent in 1904; A, B, C and F merely odd. In short the series A–F is heterogeneous, so heterogeneous that it does seem to me difficult to speak of a fashion for the year 1974, even though there may be a common stylistic quality in all these very different designs.

Before leaving the subject of Plate 44, it may be useful to say something about the sources which I have used. It might well be supposed that it would be harder to collect information concerning the year 1904 than about 1974. But this was not altogether the case; in 1904 the makers of fashion magazines took a simple view of their task. *Figaro Modes*, on which I have relied for most of my examples, for it was already using photographs, attempts to give one a clear idea of what the duchesses and the actresses whom it portrays were wearing. It might sometimes have to touch up its pictures but the aim was a simple one, to give information. The modern fashion magazine will in the end provide information but you have to work for it. The photographer seems to avoid the simple, informative, accurately focused image or the complete picture. More significantly the editor seems to shy away from the subject of fashionable clothes and devotes a great deal of space to merely sumptuous dress, as for instance for the ballet, or fancy dress or various kinds of fantasy, while much of her space is devoted to articles on literature, science or philosophy. On the whole the advertisements seem to provide the most accurate picture of what is in fact actually being worn (A, E and F are taken from advertisements). One is reminded of the statement of Kurt and Gladys Lang:

> To the extent that one cannot readily distinguish the fashion worn by Mrs. Astor from that worn by the girl in the typing pool, novelty in dress has been de-emphasized. But fashions in hair styles, furnishings, music and art, houses, recreation and resorts, have become more important. Some of these are beyond the means of even the new middle class market. Therefore, the realm in which an individual feels subject to the dictates of

PLATE 44
1904
1
2
3
4
5
6

1974 PLATE 44

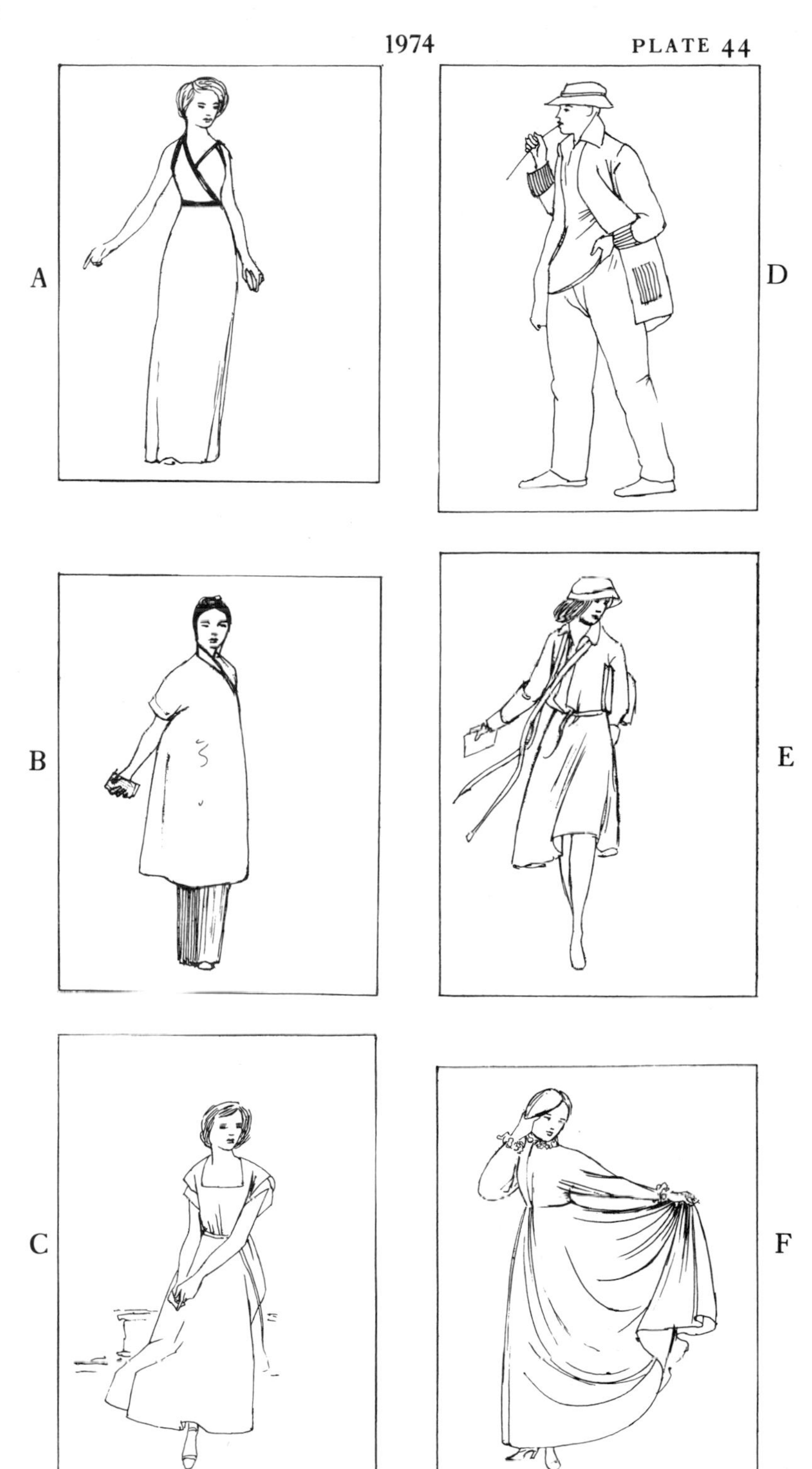

> fashion now seems a more meaningful hallmark of class in the mass society than do the externals of dress.*

What I am trying to suggest is that our fashion magazines, which certainly devote a lot of space to furnishings, music and modern painting, houses, recreations and, above all, resorts, seem to be aware that the old business of telling the world what is being or what will be worn is getting out of date. In 1974 there is no answer to that question. The old business of keeping up with the Jones's continues; but you can't do it by wearing the right hat.

This is no more than a tentative suggestion, but is it not possible that dress is ceasing to be a vehicle for the maintenance of status, that fashion is on its way out?

Let me conclude this part of my argument with a quotation from a source which, surely, represents the feelings of a youthful public.

> Fashion, in the sense of everyone doing much the same thing at the same time, whether it be mini-skirts or Oxford bags or wide brimmed hats or gangster stripes, seems completely out of place in the world we live in now.†

---

* Kurt Lang and Gladys Lang quote *Fashion Identification and Differentiation in the Mass Society*, quoted by Roach and Eicher, *op. cit.*, pp. 341–2.

† Karl Dallas in *Let It Rock*, No. 25, January 9, 1975, p. 55.

9

Deviations from Veblen

'Il n'y a de beau que les étoffes roulées sur le corps et drapées, dit Gamelin. Tout ce qui a été taillé et cousu est affreux.

Ces pensées, mieux placées dans un livre de Winckelman que dans la bouche d'un homme qui parle à des Parisiennes, furent rejeteés avec le mépris de l'indifférence.'

ANATOLE FRANCE

In this book I have made such extensive use of Veblen that it seems only fair that he should not be made responsible for all that I have written.

In this chapter I propose to consider two cardinal points of disagreement, and for this purpose have extracted quotations from *The Theory of the Leisure Class* which appear to me to contain untenable arguments. It must not be imagined that these extracts give a fair sample of Veblen's thought; they are indeed singularly unrepresentative, and have been selected simply with a view to bringing out fundamental disagreements. Veblen's theory can only be judged on a complete examination.

The value of Veblen as a philosopher of clothes lies in his economic approach to this subject, an approach which leads him directly to the formulation of those illuminating theories of social behaviour which he calls the Laws of Conspicuous Consumption, Vicarious Consumption, and Conspicuous Leisure. He fails, so it seems to me, to explain the history of dress when he relies upon notions which are not derived from economics, and when his attention has been too closely engaged by the conditions of his own time and country. Both these elements would appear to have moved him in the following explanation of the difference which then existed between the dress of men and that of women:

> At the stage of economic development at which the women were still in the full sense the property of the men, the performance of conspicuous leisure and consumption came to be part of the services required of them. The women being not their own masters, obvious expenditure and leisure on their part would redound to the credit of their master rather than to their own

> credit; and therefore the more expensive and the more obviously unproductive the women of the household are, the more creditable and the more effective for the purpose of the reputability of the household or its head will their life be. So much so that the women have been required not only to afford evidence of a life of leisure, but even to disable themselves for useful activity.
>
> It is at this point that the dress of men falls short of that of women, and for a sufficient reason. Conspicuous waste and conspicuous leisure are reputable because they are evidence of pecuniary strength; pecuniary strength is reputable or honorific because, in the last analysis, it argues success and superior force; therefore the evidence of waste and leisure put forth by any individual in his own behalf cannot consistently take such a form or be carried to such a pitch as to argue incapacity or marked discomfort on his part; as the exhibition would in that case show not superior force, but inferiority; and so defeat its own purpose. So, then, wherever wasteful expenditure and the show of abstention from effort is normally, or on an average, carried to the extent of showing obvious discomfort or voluntarily induced physical disability, there the immediate inference is that the individual in question does not perform this wasteful expenditure and undergo this disability for her own personal gain in pecuniary repute, but in behalf of someone else to whom she stands in a relation of economic dependence; a relation which in the last analysis must, in economic theory, reduce itself to a relation of servitude.
>
> To apply this generalisation to women's dress, and put the matter in concrete terms, the high heel, the skirt, the impracticable bonnet, the corset, and the general disregard of the wearer's comfort which is an obvious feature of all civilised women's apparel, are so many items of evidence to the effect that in the modern civilised scheme of life the woman is still, in theory, the economic dependent of the man, that, perhaps in a highly idealised sense, she is still the man's chattel.*

Historically, this is not tenable. Indeed where women are reduced entirely to the role of chattels and a man's wealth is counted by the number of his wives, it is he, rather than she, who displays wealth upon the person. The mere act of feeding and maintaining a seraglio is enough to ensure

---

* *The Theory of the Leisure Class*, pp. 180–2.

status in the world's eyes; the inmates are private property for private use. The demands of sartorial morality do, no doubt, impose a high degree of sumptuosity within the harem (just as they do in underclothes). But polygamous man is certainly not less, and is probably much more, ornate in his appearance than his monogamous fellow. It is when women begin to acquire status on their own that they begin to dress for the world; even so, in the earlier, the feudal stages, it is the men, not the women, who lead the fashion, and are the first to adopt a new style. Any survey of the history of fashion will show that the extremes of conspicuous leisure are common to both sexes; men have worn just those garments which Veblen considers particularly feminine; they are typical of feudal dress. Veblen's basic theory is, however, perfectly correct in that the noble, like the lady, was supposed to be incapable of manual labour. The difference, as we have seen, arises when a certain amount of work is no longer socially disreputable; it is then, and only then, that the corset and the high heel become effeminate.

The misconception would seem to arise from an attempt to apply certain essentially nineteenth-century characteristics of fashion to the history of dress as a whole. But there is another and deeper cause. Veblen is preoccupied with individuals, or families, rather than with classes; he is obsessed by the notion of personal prowess, which, I think, leads him astray in the field of sport, and he sees the main impulse as coming from the individual or head of a family who demonstrates his pecuniary strength through dress and thus maintains the 'good repute' of the household.

But the whole theory breaks down if we do not allow the claims of 'class solidarity' to be greater than those of individuals or families. For if the business of demonstrating pecuniary strength be regarded simply as a household parade before the world, there is nothing to prevent, and indeed much to encourage, each householder from adopting his own fashion; such eccentricity would have the supreme merit of avoiding the imputation of cheapness which must lie against all mass-produced goods. But in fact, although a certain degree of singularity is encouraged for this very reason (as for instance in the choice of women's hats), for another reason it is always subordinated to the standard of a class. Nothing is worse than too much originality in dress, and it will be found that individual prowess is severely held in bounds by the necessary uniformity of the mode. It may be safely asserted that the usual desire of the great majority of those who follow fashion is not so much to achieve personal distinction as to arrive at a happy mean and to emerge discreetly into a distinguished class. Sumptuous dress is of necessity a kind of class uniform which forbids prowess, and this is especially the case where, as in

Ancient Egypt, the social structure is of a rigid and unchanging kind. Here individual taste and fantasy are brought to a minimum; there is a universal sameness within each class which can hardly be altered, save by the introduction of a new class system.

What would appear to be an even more fundamental difficulty is revealed in Veblen's account of mutation:

> The standard of reputability requires that dress should show wasteful expenditure; but all wastefulness is offensive to native taste. The psychological law has already been pointed out that all men – and women perhaps even in a higher degree – abhor futility, whether of effort or of expenditure, much as Nature was once said to abhor a vacuum. But the principle of conspicuous waste requires an obviously futile expenditure; and the resulting conspicuous expensiveness of dress is therefore intrinsically ugly. . . . The ostensible usefulness of the fashionable details of dress, however, is always so transparent a make-believe, and their substantial futility presently forces itself so baldly upon our attention as to become unbearable, and then we take refuge in a new style. But the new style must conform to the requirements of reputable wastefulness and futility. Its futility presently becomes as odious as that of its predecessor; and the only remedy which the law of waste allows us is to seek relief in some new construction, equally futile and equally untenable. Hence the essential ugliness and unceasing change of fashionable attire.
>
> Having so explained the phenomenon of shifting fashions, the next thing is to make it tally with everyday facts. Among these everyday facts is the well-known liking which all men have for the styles that are in vogue at any given time. A new style comes into vogue and remains in favour for a season, and, at least so long as it is a novelty, people very generally find the new style attractive. The prevailing fashion *is felt to be beautiful.* This is due partly to the relief it affords in being different from what went before it, partly to its being reputable. As indicated in the last chapter, the canon of reputability to some extent shapes our tastes, so that under its guidance anything will be accepted as becoming until its novelty wears off, or until the warrant of reputability is transferred to a new and novel structure serving the same general purpose. That the alleged beauty, or 'loveliness', of the styles in vogue at any given time is transient and spurious only is attested by the fact that none of the many shift-

> ing fashions will bear the test of time. When seen in the perspective of half a dozen years or more, the best of our fashions strike us as grotesque, if not unsightly. Our transient attachment to whatever happens to be the latest rests on other than aesthetic grounds, and lasts only until our abiding aesthetic sense has had time to assert itself and reject this latest indigestible contrivance.*

This passage may serve to show how much this essay owes to Veblen and how far it deviates. Here again the actual history of fashion contradicts Veblen's explanation; this it does in two manners first in the mode of evolution, secondly in the history of the forms selected.

If we return to the example of mutation taken in Chapter Five we shall see that neither the crinoline nor the voluminous petticoats which it replaced had any ostensible usefulness, nor indeed does any full-length skirt. As Veblen says: 'It is expensive and it hampers the wearer at every turn and incapacitates her for all useful exertion.'† (This statement implies that nearly all European fashions for women contain a large element of futility and hence of ugliness.) Now the additional futility of the crinoline became apparent quite early in its history; as we have noticed, it forced itself 'baldly' upon the attention of the Empress of the French as early as 1860. The reply was, first to make it larger still, then gradually to gather it backwards into a train, which became a bustle. But the kind of change which we should expect, given Veblen's aesthetic laws, would be a rapid jump away from this species of futility to something quite different, the Directoire style perhaps.

Veblen's history is as unsatisfactory in explaining why the mode sometimes turns towards simplicity as it is in explaining why it usually moves in the opposite sense. On several occasions, as we have seen, the fashion has changed in the direction of austerity. In the French Revolution, the change was more or less transitory, in the Industrial Revolution it was almost permanent; no universal aesthetic sentiment can be applied to such seemingly inconsequential behaviour; a constant influence will surely produce a constant phenomenon, which fashion is not. Once again we are forced to admit the paramount importance of classes, in this instance class struggles, without which the history of fashion is inexplicable. It is only through a study of emulation, and of the effect of revolutionary crises upon the emulative process, that we can understand fashion in its stages of critical development.

---

* Veblen, *op. cit.*, pp. 176–8. My italics. It should, however, be added that in many other passages Veblen is far from rejecting the emulative process. The aesthetic theory here given would seem to be a kind of supererogatory theory.

† *Ibid.*, p. 171.

This quotation also brings us to a matter of even more fundamental importance. According to Veblen the prevailing mode is only 'felt to be beautiful'; in fact its beauty is 'spurious', as is the beauty of all fashions. Oscar Wilde took the same view when he said: 'After all, what is fashion? it is usually a form of ugliness so intolerable that we have to alter it every six months.'

Like Wilde and like Watts, Veblen is deeply affected by the discovery which we must all make in modern society of the odiousness of yesterday's fashions; therefore he turns naturally to an ideal of unchanging excellence. This ideal is perhaps hellenic, certainly it is what we should now call 'functional'. If the beauty of dress be measured against any such absolute standard, the pecuniary canons of taste will certainly be found wanting; all sumptuous, and therefore all fashionable dress must be condemned, and we are of necessity driven to admit the 'essential ugliness' of fashionable attire, and thence to the statement that its charm is spurious, 'it is only felt to be beautiful'.

But can we in truth say more of a beautiful object than that we feel it to be beautiful? Does not such a statement go as far as we can go in recommending a work of art? If we are to accept Veblen's evidence as it stands, perhaps we should rather say that only the prevailing fashion is beautiful. Either way we are forced back upon a position which is untenable in the light of general experience; in the presence of the fashion of the past six hundred years there are few who will condemn all as ugly, and it is only in the case of the immediate past and the immediate present that anything remotely resembling general agreement will be found, the former being frightful, the latter charming. Nor has there yet been a fashion which has not been judged in both manners; the crinoline was admired in its time, condemned in the age of bustles, and again admired after three-quarters of the century.

Veblen was not an aesthetician, neither am I; but I would suggest that the evidence of fashion must lead us to a conception of beauty which allows that quality to be composed of more than one element. Baudelaire I think, came near the truth when he claimed that there are two kinds of beauty, the one permanent, the other fugitive, the one eternal and invariable, the other relative and circumstantial. Certainly, if we wish to examine the nature and trace the complex operation of this second, fugitive element, Veblen will supply us with an abundance of illuminating material. Where he goes wrong, to my mind, is in his attempt to deny any validity to the kind of values that are represented by fashion and, still more, when he sets up as his eternal verity an ideal of functional beauty. With this in mind he is driven of necessity to condemn all fashions.

For him unpractical things are ugly; sumptuous dress is therefore ugly. Somewhere outside society there is, presumably, an aesthetically perfect form of dress, a platonic idea of dress so to speak, which in the nature of things cannot exist, for even the hellenic model is not purely practical. In fact, within Veblen's lifetime (he died in 1929) fashion did move in the direction of functional simplicity and yet, as we know very well, this relatively functional mode did not escape the censure of time. Like the highly unpractical modes of the beginning of the century it was, after all, only 'felt to be beautiful' and presently was just as severely condemned as any other fashion.

I think that any study of dress must lead us to accept a measure of aesthetic relativism,

> Past reason hunted; and no sooner had,
> Past reason hated ...

That is the history of any form of dress in a mobile society. The social forces that govern our tastes blow us hither and thither.

And yet a complete relativism seems equally unsatisfactory. It is true that in a socially stratified society we cannot but love that which is socially acceptable when we see it; but if we look at those fashions which have long ago ceased to be dowdy, the distorting glass of fashion no longer disturbs our vision and we seem able to exercise an independent judgment unaffected by social forces. At that distance of time we should most of us be ready to accept even the most unpractical fashions, for if, as Mr Laver has said, yesterday's frivolities are dowdy while those of ten years ago are hideous, in course of time the ridiculous will become 'amusing', then quaint, then charming, then romantic and finally beautiful, or at least, it becomes possible to think of them as beautiful, whereas when they are newly dead this is not possible. In other words, when a work of fashion has stood the test of time we can judge it dispassionately.

Even this is not quite true. There are 'fashions for fashions'; that is to say, some long-discarded mode may take the fancy of a later age and very likely inspire its couturiers. But even so a revived fashion is not so blindly accepted and certainly not so blindly rejected as one that is quite recent; certainly we become, as the centuries pass, more able to arrive at what we like to think is an objective valuation.

I am not equipped to take this argument any further. All that I wish to do is to suggest that it is an argument worth following. The mere fact that so purely social a consideration as the class structure of a society can to so great an extent determine our aesthetic feelings must give us pause and make us wonder how our value judgments are arrived at. For this is not simply a matter of human finery.

APPENDIX A

Fashion and the Fine Arts

I read Veblen for the first time in the late 1930s. At that time, like many people of my age, I had become very much interested in social theory and was attempting to square my new ideas about society with an interest in the visual arts, a subject on which I was rather better informed. Like so many others, I looked for answers in the works of Karl Marx and Friedrich Engels. I found a few and some, I think, have proved of permanent value; but it seemed to me then and seems to me now that marxists, in discussing art, made no real distinction between painting and literature. They were concerned with the message that the artist wished to convey and the circumstances which led to its formulation; they could then point, quite rightly, to the kind of society in which a certain kind of poetry occurs and to the kind of social impulses that it conveys. This, it seemed to me, was a perfectly legitimate proceeding and one that could, up to a point, be usefully undertaken; but in the case of the visual arts it was of necessity limited, for there are considerable differences between even the most poetical paintings and even the most graphic poetry; they are in fact commodities of perfectly different kinds.

There is indeed a sense in which a poem can hardly be described as a commodity. It is not, after all, very difficult to imagine a poem or a song passing from mouth to mouth, exported from land to land without any commercial transaction being involved or even being possible. But a work of art intended to appeal to the eye must have been made by hand or by machinery;* its construction must involve some actual expenditure of labour, and a part of its value must result, not from the message which it may or may not convey, but from the material of which it is made and the 'socially necessary labour time' – to use a marxist phrase – which is 'crystallised' within the object.

This indeed is something that we know very well. Imagine a Chien Lung vase, and endow it with all the symbolic value you like (it can carry a great deal). Such works have been exported from China to Europe since the sixteenth century; but if anyone supposes that the symbolism, the message, on the vase was exported along with the vase itself, they are

* This is not true of some twentieth-century works of art; but they, to my way of thinking, have only a poetical value.

greatly mistaken. The European market was greedy for such wares but that market certainly did not, and even today does not, value the symbolic meaning of such objects. In the same way a fine piece of Chinese calligraphy may be valued for its purely formal qualities by people who cannot understand a word of what it says. Even in the case of European paintings which speak to us through a much more comprehensible language it is by no means unheard of for scholars to attach radically different meanings to the same work of art.

Nevertheless, a work with a strong anecdotal or narrative element does offer much more opportunity to the theorist who is looking for ideologies and this, so it seemed to me, was what the marxists were doing. For this reason they tended to concentrate their attention on one particular form of art. There is, after all, a fairly clear affinity between a poem and a landscape or a narrative picture and a novel; but to me it seemed that an efficient theory should embrace not one kind of visual art but all kinds. It should be able to account not only for the landscape and the narrative picture but for bonnets and shoes.

To my marxist friends this seemed a very wrong-headed attitude. Bonnets and shoes, they told me, were not works of art; and when I answered that a fashion design by Pisanello or a salt cellar by Cellini obviously was a work of art, and that some of the humblest toys and trinkets from tombs or middens were works of art of the highest quality, they answered that these were exceptions and that what I wanted to do was to include the meanest objects from the sixpenny bazaar as works of art and further that these were contemptible works of no account. I had to admit that they were perfectly right but that a theory dealing with art should not be restricted to those works which we most admire. Indeed this was one of my chief grievances as against the theorists, that they decided which evidence suited them best and then constructed their theories accordingly. The point is one to which I shall return.

Now when one comes to a consideration of the minor arts, the trivial arts, and bad art, the marxists so it seemed to me were silent. Either they had nothing to say or, as I have already hinted, they look elsewhere. And yet it was here that any theory of art and society should start, for although we may dismiss the minor arts as being aesthetically unimportant, this is a point on which we may well change our minds, as we do whenever a value judgment is involved, whereas there could be no doubt at all that from a social point of view they were very important indeed. It was therefore with high enthusiasm that I read such statements as these:

> A fancy bonnet of this year's model unquestionably appeals to our sensibilities today much more forcibly than an equally fancy

> bonnet of the model of last year; although when viewed in the perspective of a quarter of a century, it would, I apprehend, be a matter of the utmost difficulty to award the palm for intrinsic beauty to the one rather than to the other of these structures. So, again, it may be remarked that, considered simply in their physical juxtaposition with the human form, the high gloss of a gentleman's hat or of a patent-leather shoe has no more of intrinsic beauty than a similarly high gloss on a threadbare sleeve; and yet there is no question but that all wellbred people (in the Occidental civilised communities) instinctively and unaffectedly cleave to the one as a phenomenon of great beauty, and eschew the other as offensive to every sense to which it can appeal.*

This went to the root of the matter, for here Veblen was looking at an aesthetic phenomenon within its social context.

Everyone except Veblen seemed to me to have begun the argument at the wrong end. Instead of discussing bonnets and patent leather shoes they discuss masterpieces. Masterpieces are certainly very important; but we are much more likely to understand their social causation when we know something about the kind of art that effects everyone. But there is a further difficulty about the discussion of masterpieces; not only are they, in a statistical sense, abnormal, the tip only of the aesthetic iceberg, but we are by no means in agreement as to what are and what are not masterpieces. Nor is this the end of the confusion. Judging simply on aesthetic quality I should call the landscapes of Claude Lorraine masterpieces, but I should use the same word to describe the Han bronzes. Socially these are two quite different things; the paintings of Claude are the work of one exceptionally gifted individual, the Han bronzes were produced by a community. We take it for granted that Claude's contemporaries will be lesser men; in the same way we take it for granted that any genuine Han bronze will reach very much the same aesthetic standard as any other Han bronze. The first thing that we have to discuss if we are going to talk about masterpieces is their incidence, the circumstances which produce great inequality of talent in some societies but not in others.

It is this concentration on the aesthetically exciting phenomenon that

---

* *Theory of the Leisure Class*, p. 131. It is true that Veblen goes on to confuse the issue by implying that he is not dealing with aesthetic emotions: 'it is extremely doubtful if anyone could be induced to wear such a contrivance as the high hat of civilised society, except for some urgent reason based on other than aesthetic grounds'.

leads the most persuasive of the marxist writers on art, G. V. Plekhanov, into impossible positions based simply on his own aesthetic predilections. Plekhanov does indeed come quite near to the fancy bonnet and the patent leather shoe, or at least to their primitive equivalents; there are passages in *Art and Social Life* in which one feels that if only he had pursued a very promising line of thought he would have arrived at something very close to a Veblenian theory. If he had done so perhaps we might have been spared those disastrous passages in which he believes that he has proved something when he declares that he likes Leonardo much better than he likes Monet and a great deal better than he likes Fernand Léger; passages in which he appears simply to be a tiresome old bore airing his prejudices about 'Modern Art' – if only he could have read Veblen.

And, one may add, if only Veblen could have read Plekhanov, for there is much in *The Theory of the Leisure Class* which might have been altered or amended by such a study.

Veblen's strength and also his weakness derives from the fact that he was not really very much interested in art; economics and sociology were his subjects, therefore it seemed natural to him to examine those humble phenomena which the aesthetician so woefully ignores. When he speaks of dress as satisfying a 'higher or spiritual need' he is not simply being ironical, although there is no doubt something of irony in his manner; he is making what seems to me to be a correct classification of popular emotions. For the aesthetic emotion is something 'higher or spiritual' in that it is not concerned with any direct economic advantage. It is not something that is governed by reason but one which is very deeply felt.

Let me give an example of the kind of thing that I am talking about. We all of us know the hard-headed, no nonsense citizen who tells us, almost with an air of complacency, that he knows nothing about art and even that he has no aesthetic emotions. He is the kind of fellow who enjoys his golf, his pint of bitter and a game with the kids. And yet with what earnest gravity I have heard him denounce a young man who allowed himself to be photographed wearing a B.A. gown but no tie. His disgust is aesthetic in that it is based on feeling even though that feeling is closely tied to questions of propriety. It was the same gentleman, or perhaps his brother, who, seated on the bench of a magistrate's court, condemned male witnesses who came into court wearing long hair, ladies in mini skirts, and more surprisingly, ladies whose skirts were too long.

Essentially these are judgments of decorum and are based on custom. We have only to remember how odd it would have seemed to the ancestors of these censors if in their day critics had complained that ladies wore long skirts or that gentlemen wore long hair to see that such moral indignation, sincere though it undoubtedly is, is based upon social usage and nothing else.

In the world of bonnets and shoes, then, it is fairly obvious that custom is everything and that that which we love today we may hate tomorrow. But it may be objected that in the more elevated sphere of aesthetic emotion the case is different, that rules which hold good for trivial artefacts will no longer hold good for major works of art. In consequence, it may be argued, Veblen's illuminations, although they may help us to see how society works at one level, will not reveal much at another.

That the aesthetic truths concerning costume cannot be applied indiscriminately to the history of art in general is true. Nevertheless there are facts in the history of art which lead us to suppose that the admirable can become the detestable and vice versa. The pattern is not the same but it is like enough to arrest our attention.

The splendours of mediaeval architecture and mediaeval painting were dismissed by a later generation with the ignominious epithet 'gothic'. The masters of the mid-sixteenth century were condemned as 'mannerists', the great painters of the seventeenth century received the opprobrious title 'baroque', their successors were dismissed as being rococo. Even Raphael has fallen from his high eminence, and it would be a great mistake to suppose that when Lord Elgin brought sculpture from the Parthenon to London it was universally admired by those whose taste for the antique had been nourished on Roman copies. Rome herself has fallen and there is no movement in art since the time of the Pre-Raphaelites which was not at first condemned. The opposite process is equally familiar; gothic, mannerist, baroque, are no longer words of abuse, and the nineteenth-century revolutionaries, once so repulsive, have become very fashionable indeed. As with clothes so with pictures and buildings; it is the more recent styles, those which are still dowdy, which we find it hardest to like.

These fashions in 'high art' which are so characteristic of our Western civilisation are much less characteristic of other cultures; the sartorial conservatism of Egypt, of pre-literate societies, and even of China extends in a large measure to all their arts.

In paintings, sculpture and architecture we find some, though not all, of the characteristics of sumptuous dress. It is perhaps natural that buildings which are a kind of outward covering for men should have some of the qualities of garments, that the functional nature of architecture should sometimes be obscured by frills and furbelows of marble and mosaic, that stone should be so drilled and chiselled into foliage, crockets, volutes and images as to present very much the appearance of expensive lace. I have, in another place, ventured to suggest that the architecture of the last century echoes the dress of the sexes, that the suspension bridges, warehouses, back-to-back tenements and gasometers were, as one may say, grim, grimy, dark, undecorated and *masculine*, while the English Decorated churches, the italianate club-houses, the chalets, kiosks and baroque city edifices were, in their exuberant and conspicuously wasteful decorativeness, the equivalent of the feminine dress of the period. Certainly a building can be an instrument of conspicuous consumption in much the same way as a dress.

We should also remember that of the great monuments which engage the attention of historians and the enthusiasm of critics many, perhaps most, were built for a purpose which Veblen would have described as futile. The great megaliths, ziggurats, pyramids, pagodas, mosques and cathedrals were not built to produce but to consume wealth. Mingled with the true religious fervour of the builders, may there not have been another kind of ambition?

> In 1163 Notre Dame de Paris began its record construction to result in a vault 114 ft. 8″ from the floor. Chartres surpassed Paris in 1194 eventually reaching 119 ft. 9″. In 1212 Rheims started to rise to 124 ft. 3″, and in 1221 Amiens reached 138 ft. 9″. This drive to break the record reached its climax in 1247 with the project to vault the choir of Beauvais 157 ft. 3″ above the floor – only to have the vault collapse in 1284.*

This passage in Gimpel's *Cathedral Builders* is quoted by Gombrich, who remarks that:

> There is a competitive element in art which aims at drawing attention to the artist or his patron.

Indeed Gimpel's account does very much remind one of the development of the crinoline or the bustle. And Gombrich continues by saying that the quotation reminds us that 'competition in art is not necessarily a bad thing'.

This is unquestionably true, but can one not go further and say that the comparatively static or non-competitive situation, that is to say the artistic situation of the savage, the Oriental or the Egyptian who experiences no rapid or dramatic development but produces generation after generation of artists each of which, presumably, satisfies its clientele, has also its virtues. But these are virtues of a different kind from those which we associate with the arts in a competitive situation. In the static situation

---

* Jean Gimpel, *The Cathedral Builders*, 1961, p. 44, quoted by Gombrich in *The Logic of Vanity Fair* in *The Philosophy of Karl Popper*, ed. Arthur Schlipp (*Library of Living Philosophers*, Vol. XIV, Bk ii), Vol. II, p. 929.

there is an equality of achievement unknown to us. Neither the genius nor the complete failure has any place in this scheme of things, and terms such as 'originality', 'self-expression', 'modernity', pastiche and plagiarism have no meaning. In a dynamic situation, the situation in Greece between 500 and 400 B.C. or in Italy after the beginning of the fifteenth century, all the foregoing expressions become relevant, gigantic individuals begin to emerge, individuals combine in movements, and the term 'modern' takes on a new meaning.

In a static situation a local centre, cut off from the metropolis of art, may be described as 'regional'; in a dynamic situation it becomes 'provincial'. In the same way, a society with its own regional dress exchanges, when it becomes competitive, a valid indigenous form for a desperate imitation of international modes.

If we could draw up an agreed list of the world's great masterpieces I think that we should find that the majority were the products of a dynamic situation. It is at all events arguable that mankind makes its most profoundly moving discoveries, not on a basis of long untroubled traditions, but under the stress and pain which come when an aesthetic is breaking or bending under the assault of innovators; that a genuinely savage work, howsoever impressive and assured, can never have quite the depth and resonance of Gauguin who is tormentedly trying to be savage. This at all events is arguable of painting, but it is not true of clothes. The art of the dressmaker, like the art of small children, may give us a lively pleasure; it may ravish the eye and exhibit a wonderfully pure taste, but it is too shallow a vessel to contain a masterpiece. I think that it may also be said that pictures and statues, although they may certainly be used for purposes of ostentation, are in their nature much further removed from the Veblenian concepts of excellence than architecture, moveables or dress. They appeal more to the intellect and are therefore less fitted to serve as instruments of conspicuous consumption. On the other hand, for that very reason, they exemplify, as clothes cannot, the principle of conspicuous outrage.

Conspicuous Outrage is the most sophisticated weapon of the fashionable person. It is a defiance of custom which serves to separate the outrageous person from the multitude, thus proving that he is a member of an elite. As we have seen, this has usually been effected in matters of dress by means of a blatant sexual provocation. A fairly recent example was the 'topless' fashion. You have to be, as our ancestors put it, 'uncommonly fast' to go about in public with bare breasts (also you have to have the right kind of breasts), but in a more intellectual form of art the possibilities are much more extensive. For in the world of ideas the 'in joke', that is to say the reference to a more or less esoteric fund of knowledge, is a device which can take an innumerable variety of forms and can be constantly changed.

Painting has often been used for this purpose but literature, an even more intellectual art form, provides the prime example of this kind of social one-up-manship. Indeed in many periods literature, in that it is addressed to a literate minority, was of its very nature an elitist art. This of course was one of the things that made it socially superior to the visual arts; it was left to the painter to undertake the socially degrading task of providing a 'Bible for the Poor'. Even in conditions of general literacy the writer can very easily demonstrate his social superiority by making use of learned language (the fruit of a conspicuously wasteful education), and to string together a series of more or less erudite quotations which will be understood only by an elitist audience is one of the commonest and most elegant devices of the modernist poet.

The painters have however responded bravely to the challenge of literature. Incomprehensible subject matter (incomprehensible that is to the vulgar) was already a device of the socially ambitious painter in the fifteenth century. In the following century the elegant rebus or recondite and allusive programme becomes enormously fashionable and no doubt kept the elite of that time, as it keeps the scholars of today, very happy.

But painting has always had this social disadvantage. The crowd might or might not understand the full meaning of a picture, but still there was a good deal that it could understand; the image was explicit, and the discoveries of the Renaissance tended to make it more recognisable and less dependent upon symbolic clues. After all, in the case of Giorgione's *Tempesta* the story, if it has a story, is unknown and none of us is any better off than the man in the street.

This mortifying state of affairs continued until about a hundred years ago when it was discovered that the image itself might be made so hard to understand that it would be recognisable only by the initiate.*

Here I must enter a caveat, which I am afraid may entail a rather long digression but seems unavoidable. There are occasions when an artist has observed something in nature which cannot be rendered except in a new, and for this reason an incomprehensible, way. The artist speaks in a strange tongue because it is only thus that he can tell us what he has seen; he would use the words of everyday speech if they were adequate for his purpose but they are not. It may well be that such an artist will be both detested and admired for being incomprehensible; detested because, as we have seen, any breach of custom is shocking, admired

---

* A part of this and the following argument has already been published by me in *Art and the Elite* in *Critical Enquiry*, Vol. I, No. i, Chicago, September 1974.

because an ability to understand a new kind of speech reflects favourably upon the critic. But when the language has ceased to be unfamiliar it will be generally understood and the artist's meaning will be made clear. When at the time of the First Post-Impressionist Exhibition critics complained of the blue lines drawn around objects in Cézanne's pictures, Roger Fry answered that they were no more unnatural and inexplicable than the conventional shading by means of parallel lines which we all understand and accept in a Raphael drawing, and he prophesied, correctly, that when the public had learnt to accept the pictorial language of Cézanne it would read his pictures without difficulty.

This kind of difficulty, a difficulty of vision which can be overcome by a new habit of looking so that, for instance, a spot of green paint on a man's cheek is seen as reflected colour and not as some kind of skin disease, differs from that which we confront when we try to understand a work of art with an obscure programme; for the difficulty of vision can be overcome simply by custom, by the acquisition of a new psychological set, whereas to understand the programme we need extrinsic knowledge, outside information. In short one needs to be educated.

It was a new and socially a most important step when artists began to depart altogether from the business of imitation. An observer who liked Watteau, when he had learned to accept a new idiom, might easily come to like Renoir. But to like a Mondrian or a Jackson Pollock is a social feat of greater difficulty, for to do so we have, or rather we had, to make a radical change in our ideas concerning pictures and what we are to expect of them.

I have called this act of appreciation a 'social feat', and in so doing have made assumptions which may very well be questioned. Let me at once say that a Jackson Pollock or a Mondrian or any other abstract painting may appeal to the spectator by reason of its formal qualities alone, or indeed by reason of some intellectual or emotional message which the observer may discover or possibly read into the picture. All that I am suggesting is that another motive may encourage the spectator to find those beauties of form and content and, in terms of the market, such reasons are important.

Pay a visit to Dives and there on his walls you will find a Pollock and a Mondrian, a Renoir and a Rembrandt, a Negro head, a Polynesian image, a Peruvian vase. What does Dives like about these things? Not their content, not the story that they tell; he, like us, is perfectly ignorant concerning the 'message' of the Negro, the Polynesian or the Peruvian. At best they are for him like men shouting in a foreign tongue; we may perhaps appreciate the urgency with which they speak but we do not know what they are saying. And yet, all these things are in fact eloquent, and they are all saying the same thing. It is being said also by Dives' carpet, his E-type Jaguar, his mistress, her diamonds and his shoes: 'we cost a hell of a lot of money'. The money is the message.

And notice this: if one of these things falls silent, if the Rembrandt turns out to be a fake, if the diamonds are found to be paste, they go into the box room and are seen no more.

This may sound like cynicism and pretty shallow cynicism at that. It seems as though I were saying that we admire works of art simply because they cost money. But really I am not.

If we set a bad reproduction beside an original, the reproduction may serve as a kind of a sieve which will retain nearly all the anecdotal, iconological or ideological qualities of the original while allowing nearly all its formal qualities to escape. Substitute for the bad reproduction a bald description of the picture and the separation is virtually complete. Conversely, if you set a picture upside down or stand fifty yards away from it, or put it behind a screen of reeded glass, most of the content will vanish while much of the form will survive. When we examine art in this manner, a manner in which the qualities dependent upon understanding and information are concealed, one may come near to seeing as an animal sees. As we have already observed, finery is not a purely human phenomenon; the animal kingdom is itself richly adorned and it responds readily to the decoration of plants. The fact that we, with our very different biological needs, can in some manner share the excitement of the mandrill or the stickleback would suggest that 'pure' form is a biological engine of considerable importance. Perhaps the word 'pure' is misleading in this context; but at least it seems unlikely that the perceptions of the brute creation have much to do with ideology or with Conspicuous Consumption.

Thus it is possible, when Dives looks at his Mondrian, that he experiences a sentiment as pure as that which draws a bee to a flower. But I must confess that I doubt it. In practice I believe that while he and I and the mandrill experience some kind of formal emotion, a pleasure in colour and in pattern, what we (Dives and I) usually receive is a whole complex of different feelings, connected with form, content and social decorum or the lack of it. It may be that we are ignorant of the 'message' of a painting and often we may misunderstand it, but I believe that we usually manage to invent some kind of content and read it into a picture; I believe also that howsoever pure our formal emotions they can never be quite the same when we discover that our Rembrandt is a Fabritius.

The importance of the social message is this: usually we are unable to see the formal beauty, the design or the sentiment of a work of art unless or until it is socially proper to do so. Someone or something is needed in order that we may be told where to look. Thus it was that paintings of the age before Raphael could not be appreciated by connoisseurs of the age which intervened between Raphael and Ruskin; thus in our own time we have learnt – but we had to be taught – to value the Negro and the Polynesian and it was thus that the Impressionists, after many years in the wilderness, became Dives' most expensive trophy and the Italian *tenebrists* were rescued from their long obscurity.

What I have called the 'social feat' is usually an unconscious exercise; but it is a feat none the less, and it is one which is of the highest importance in the social history of contemporary art. (Here my parenthesis ends.)

In the ten years before 1914 experimental art 'arrived', I mean it became smart. Poiret was one of the prime movers in the business of associating *avant garde* paintings with fashion. Before his time these two branches of the visual arts had for generations been almost completely separated in England and completely separated in France. Cézanne might take a fashion plate and copy it; but he had nothing to do with the making of fashions, nor I think had any of the French salon painters. The Pre-Raphaelites would have liked to have designed clothes but they did not get much opportunity to do so; a designer such as Worth had nothing to do with any art save his own. The emergence of a specifically modern style, *art nouveau*, did do something to awaken painters and to bring the two sides together; but Poiret had looked at the *Fauves*, he appreciated painters such as Derain, Segonzac, Picasso and Matisse and his designers, Lepape and Boussingault, were very much aware of the work of the *avant garde*. Perhaps even more influential than Poiret was Diaghilev, and with his aid the moderns certainly 'arrived'.

That arrival, like some of Poiret's more daring inventions, created scandal; but the scandal was not altogether a disadvantage. Modern art was certainly outrageous and at the same time capable, as Impressionism was not, of being used for decorative purposes. In consequence it could and indeed did become fashionable, and a taste for contemporary painting has become a part of the apparatus of fashionable living. Dives adds the abstract painters and more adventurous warriors of the *avant garde* to his Renoirs and his Rembrandts, and the modern artist, ceasing to be in any real sense a non-conformist, caters for a luxury market.

The feat of admiring abstract art has now been accomplished by a great many people, by so many in fact that its elitist character has in some degree been compromised. It has not been vulgarised as, say, the mini skirt was vulgarised, but it has become the art form of the establishment, of big business, of the Church and the municipalities; it no longer excites indignation or wonder, it can hardly be considered outrageous. Nor is this at all surprising for, when once we have accepted that a painting need have no mimetic function, the qualities of an abstract picture may be as pleasing and indeed as innocuous as those of any other work of art.

To obtain an outrageous and socially desirable effect something more startling is required. For this purpose something more incomprehensible and more obviously repugnant to common sense was sought and has indeed been found. An object which in common estimation is not a work of art and which is therefore safe from popular admiration, as for instance a snow shovel, a bottle rack, a urinal, a cheap advertisement, a frame from a comic strip, anything which is emphatically 'inartistic', is deemed to be a work of art and is offered for sale at a ludicrously high price. The pricing of the object is the essential part of the business; indeed it is often the artist's only contribution to the process, and it is the price, or rather the acceptance of the price by the market, which turns rubbish into art. The purchase of this kind of art is indeed a strikingly pure form of conspicuous consumption, in that the purchaser buys for large sums that which manifestly costs practically nothing. But the process has another and enormously important social advantage in that those who buy and those who sell are engaged in a transaction which to the great mass of the uninitiated must be virtually incomprehensible.*

A further and logical step in the same direction is to remove the object altogether. The purchaser buys not a thing but an idea, and the commercial act becomes a kind of religious ceremony.

The following report of a recent artistic event gives a very nice example of conspicuous consumption.

> Marioni's own earliest "sound piece" (which incidentally held an unseen time element since it involved drinking beer all afternoon beforehand) was the act of urinating into a galvanised bucket from the top of a ten foot ladder.†

In much the same way the painter Manzoni has sold, and a reverential public has bought, tins of the artist's shit.

Veblen talks of a higher or spiritual need, and here surely we have it; for these operations would not be only absurd but completely unprofitable to the artist if a religious or at least a mystical emotion were not at work. The value of the transaction lies in the ability of the performer (i.e. the salesman) to inspire faith in what in ordinary terms would be

---

* M. Yves Klein, who has sold wallpaper for large sums, also devised a scheme whereby the purchaser actually paid in bullion, a part of which was then thrown into the River Seine, a classic instance of Conspicuous Waste.

† *The Book of Pseuds*, 1973, p. 24.

an absurdity. It is his business to convince his congregation that something magical has happened, and indeed something magical does happen. The nonsensical act or the worthless rubbish becomes, by the mere laying on of hands, a valuable work of art. The exchange value of the thing, or rather its sudden appreciation, is the test of the artist's thaumaturgic powers, and the implication is that whatever can be sold as art *is* art. Thus in a society which has abandoned its belief in anything except money, art has become the religion of conspicuous consumption, in short the religion of money.

APPENDIX B

A Brief Survey of Fashion from the Fifteenth to the Twentieth Century

I call this a Survey in order to avoid the word History. A series of drawings and a few notes cannot be described as a history; moreover a history should be illustrated, either with very careful drawings, such as will show how clothes were constructed, or with contemporary images which, alone, can give the precise flavour of a period. Drawings such as I have made must carry something of the flavour of our own century; they will date. Nor does it matter at all if they do, so long as the reader is aware of the fact and allows for it – unless indeed he seeks historical accuracy. But accuracy is not my aim; this appendix is intended to serve as an *aide-mémoire* which should remind the reader of what kind of thing was being worn by fashionable people and of the manner in which fashion follows fashion throughout the centuries. It is what you might call 'instant history' and, like 'instant coffee', provides something which, when good, may be serviceable but is not for that reason to be compared with the real thing.

The reader then must not look for exact information concerning the detail and structure of clothes. Pattern and surface quality are, at the most, suggested. There are some very familiar quotations from the old masters and, if you are at all acquainted with the literature of fashion, you will recognise some old friends of both sexes who appear and reappear in all the books, simply, I suppose, because nothing more informative can be found. This reliance upon the commonplace is part of a deliberate policy; for this as I have said is an *aide-mémoire*, and it is my hope that, being reminded of a well-known image, the inward eye will at once recall those details which I must omit.

The Fifteenth Century

I had intended to start with the Fourteenth century, but the fashions of that age are a mess and a muddle, and the more one studies them the more messy and the more muddling they appear. The trouble arises in part from the fact that local fashions are still very strong; clothes are divided as much by geography as by chronology. This state of affairs persists to a large extent in the Fifteenth century. Thus, in the picture on the opposite page, 'a', 'b', 'c', 'd' and 'e' are from Northern Europe and may be described as gothic (that is to say, they will be so described by some writers though how much they have to do with the architecture of the period I am not sure). But certainly they are richly fantastic. I do not think that I have overstated the exuberance of even such a wild confection as that worn by the Dutch gentleman at the top of the page ('b'). It must be admitted that 'd' is not a completely fair example for he is a herald and therefore, one may suppose, professionally ornate; but in fact it is difficult to exaggerate the fantasy of the dress of this age. This 'gothic' style had its influence south of the Alps, but by the end of the century something more restrained and something which seems more specifically 'renaissance' prevails in Italy.

a. mid-fifteenth century (Roman de la Violette)

b. Dutch, first half of the fifteenth century

c. Early fifteenth century

d. *c.* 1415 (Pol de Limbourg)

e. Dutch, first half of the fifteenth century

f. 1470 (Ferrarese School)

g. 1474 (Mantegna)

h. *c.* 1490 (Ghirlandaio)

a
b
c
d
e
f
g
h

The Sixteenth Century

For all its slashings, jewels, furs and gold chains, this is an age which, when compared with the fifteenth century, seems comparatively sober. Also it is an age in which people are, to an increasing extent, hidden away, packed into their clothes, therefore increasingly modest. In this matter the sexes run, as one may say, neck and neck. Observe the German gentleman 'c'; he has what you might call a low neck and a loose gown, in fact he could swap clothes with a lady of the early 1920s and you would hardly know the difference. At the beginning of the century décolleté chaps such as he were common enough, particularly on the continent. But the future lay with the collar; it develops from the comparatively modest affair worn by that familiar figure in the top centre 'b' and grows into a ruff, a continually expanding adornment, which is still expanding at the end of the century. In the same way the ample display of bosom offered by 'a' is covered up by 'f'. These portraits are of the same year. A generation later we find that very grand and dignified but not very seductive style which flourished all over Europe, but particularly in Spain, 'e'. Women never completely accepted this style in all its splendid chastity; here and there a neck may be discovered, but the general tendency at the end of the century was certainly towards a high degree of decorative concealment.

a. 1535 English (Holbein)

b. 1539 English (Holbein)

c. 1504 Germany (Claus Stalburg)

d. 1565 French (Clouet)

e. 1571 Spanish (Sanchez Coello)

f. 1535 Italian? (Titian)

a
b
c
f
d
e

The Seventeenth Century (first half)

'Woorser and woorser' cried the indignant Stubbes in 1583, and there was still worse to come, for Stubbes was protesting against the ruff.

> There is no amendment in anything that I can see, neither in one thing nor in other, but every day woorse and worser, for they not only continue their great ruffes still, but also use them bigger than ever they did. And whereas before they were too bad, now they are past all shame and honestie, yea most abhominable and detestable, and such as the divell himselfe would be ashamed to weare the like.

Poor Stubbes, he died in 1593 and ruffs were still growing. The typical big ruff of the early seventeenth century is shown in 'a' but there were a great many different ways of dealing with it; 'b', 'c' and 'd' show three of the many solutions that were adopted at the beginning of the century. It was about 1630 that the ruff began to collapse, it lost its starch, it fell in a floppy way upon the shoulders, it became a lace collar, and with this change came a general relaxation of costume; easier, more natural, more comfortable-looking fashions, usually of French origin, coexist with the old stiff beruffed dress of Spain. Victory lay with the simpler style; 'g' is taken from Rembrandt's *Staalmeesters of* 1661; it shows the plain white collar which had replaced the ruff and is worn by all six members of the group. In the Anatomy Lesson of Professor Tulp of thirty years earlier, all the eight men, save for Tulp himself, wear ruffs, for the most part like those worn by 'b' but with plainer clothes than his.

a. 1625 Italian (Van Dyck)

b. 1625 English

c. 1605–10 English (Van Somer)

d. 1616 English (Oliver)

e. 1633 French (Abraham Bosse)

f. 1633 French (Abraham Bosse)

g. 1661–2 Dutch (Rembrandt)

b
c
d
a
e
f
g

Late Seventeenth, early Eighteenth Centuries

One would have expected Versailles in the days of its greatest glory to have produced something rather more superb and impressive than the fussy inconclusive costumes of the late seventeenth century. Perhaps Louis commanded so much real power and had so regulated behaviour at his court that dress became a matter of secondary importance. However this may be, to my mind at all events the Bourbons do not succeed so well as the Hapsburgs, or even the Stuarts, in dressing for an aristocratic role. The 'fontanges', a fan-shaped headdress worn by ladies, and the masculine periwig, certainly aspire and give the wearer additional height; but there is no unbroken ascending line; everything seems abrupt and inconclusive. It is one of the least memorable periods in the history of fashion. With the Peace and the Regency (1715) a new grace and a new fluency (at which Watteau had already hinted) seem to enter into the design of dress; clothes grow simpler. I have no doubt over-emphasised this simplicity by taking 'a' and 'b' from Versailles, 'c' and 'd' from English provincial sources, nevertheless the simplicity was real enough; the lines are more decisive and more harmonious, and they are those on which dress will be designed for the next seventy years or so.

a. 1695 French (Bonnart)

b. 1700 French (Bonnart)

c. 1720 English

d. 1737 English

a
b
c
d

The Mid-Eighteenth Century

It is impossible here to examine the many subtle changes of style which enable the expert to find his way through the history of dress in the eighteenth century. Nor shall I look at the aberrations of fashion, the grotesque 'macaroni' style of the seventies which led young men to wear vast buttons and enormous wigs. It is interesting in itself, but runs counter to the general tendency of the century which, so far as men were concerned, was towards greater and greater simplicity. Compare 'f' with 'b' and notice how his wig is shrunk, how plain his coat has grown; no embroidery is left at all, the colours are dark or drab; very smart and tasteful no doubt but not gorgeous. The ladies on the other hand were set upon a diametrically opposite course; the simple cap or hood of the beginning of the century, or the relatively simple flat hat tied under the chin à la Dolly Varden, is replaced by the most prodigious structures, elaborate affairs of false hair, flowers, ribbons and millinery which were not easily erected or easily removed and which proved, so it is said, a perfect breeding ground for lice. The seventies is the epoch of the great wig; the great hat follows, as will appear on the next page.

a. 1740–50 English

b. 1740 English

c. 1778 French

d. 1776 French

e. 1777 French

f. 1788 English (Reynolds)

a
b
c
d
e
f

The Late Eighteenth Century

The old regime takes its congé with a stupendous display of millinery. Never had the inherent lunacy of all hatters been more dramatically displayed. It has even been suggested that those who could run to such extravagance in the matter of headgear were bound, before long, to lose their heads along with their hats. Let us then remember that we are looking not only at the clothes which Parisians wore while they awaited the great tempest of the revolution but, also, those with which it proceeded from the National Assembly to the Legislative Assembly to the Convention and the Republic and the Committee of Public Safety. The great hats sailed under new colours: *coiffure à la nation*, *coiffure aux charmes de la liberté*, etc. Probably, under Robespierre, they were out of sight much of the time, and contemporary drawings suggest that those hats which were worn were higher in the crown but much narrower in the brim. At the *Fête de l'être Suprême* and the execution of Marie Antoinette a simple form of mob cap was generally worn by the woman.

Notice the tailor-made look, not only of the gentlemen but of the ladies.

a. 1785 English (Gainsborough)

b. 1785 English (Gainsborough)

c. 1788 French

d. 1788 French

e. 1786 English

f. 1786 English

e
f
a
b
c
d

The Early Nineteenth Century

The stark classical purity of 'a' (who is a Dutch lady called Mrs Schimmelpenninck, see Colour Plate II) is about as far as everyday fashionable dress went in the direction of simplicity. The neo-classical style kept waists a few inches below the arm-pits, fabrics very plain, and the general outline more or less columnar for about a quarter of a century; but almost from the first the strictly neo-classical element in women's dress was modified. Even Mme Schimmelpenninck has unclassical sleeves and shoes. 'c' wears sleeves which are, from an antiquarian point of view, even more incorrect, and there is a fitted tailored look about her dress which would not have pleased a disciple of David. As for 'e', look at her head-dress. In fact, from the beginning, the Directoire style is evolving very slowly but very surely towards the tight-waisted full-skirted fashion of the 1830s.

The gentlemen have completely sobered down. Observe that 'b' wears a kind of proto-trousers. We have gone so far that the fine clothes of previous centuries are a cause of embarrassment.

> ... and I am to be Count Cassel, and am to come in first with a blue dress, and a pink satin cloak, and afterwards am to have another fine fancy suit by way of a shooting dress. – I do not know how I shall like it.

Thus Mr Rushworth in *Mansfield Park*, and the horrible thing is that he speaks not only for his own foolish self but for his own and many subsequent generations.

Note below that 'e', a fashion plate, was published in London. It may actually come from Paris; it is hard to tell. From now on I cease to give the country of origin of my examples. For our purposes they mean little; broadly speaking fashions come either from Paris or from London.

a. 1801 French (Prud'hon)

b. 1801 French (Prud'hon)

c. 1810 French?

d. 1810 French?

e. 1819 published in London

a
b
c
d
e

The Eighteen-Thirties

The sartorial division of the sexes is now almost complete, but not quite; the gentleman in this picture does faintly echo feminine modes with his tight waist and his sloping shoulders. This is because he is a young man of fashion; an older or a shabbier man would be less effeminate. And no man can have been as uncomfortable as were most women of the romantic epoch. The constriction of the waist, after an interval of about forty years of comparative freedom, must have become increasingly cruel during the years 1820 to 1830, after which it had diminished to a point at which nature could not tolerate further decrease; the small waist was made smaller, in appearance, by the addition of voluminous sleeves and wider skirts, the latter enlarged by the addition of more and more petticoats, also on occasion by a deliberate juggling with scale, as for instance a very large buckle or belt to suggest a very narrow waist. It is from about this time that we hear stories of eighteen- or even seventeen-inch waists, stories which, if we may trust Mrs Langley Moore, and I think we may, are largely untrue. 'e' shows a day dress with a surprisingly low neck. Many years were to pass before so much of a lady's neck and shoulders were again to become visible before dinner time.

a. 1834 mantle

b. 1828 seaside riding dress

c. 1829 dinner dress

d. 1834 gentleman's morning dress

e. 1830–6 day dress

e
a
b
d
c

The Eighteen-Forties and -Fifties

The constant demand for wider and wider skirts led to the supply of a substructure, the crinoline. Various mechanical contrivances such as hoops, panniers and bustles had been in use for a very long time, but the true crinoline, a light metal frame, was introduced in 1856 and marks a tremendous improvement upon all previous devices. With the aid of the crinoline a prodigious aggrandisement became possible; the gentleman (wearing the 'lank' hair style) cuts a rather insignificant figure amongst these grandly voluminous females. I think that one may fairly suppose that the crinoline must have been very good for morale. So vast a circumference, so much elegant bulk must surely have engendered a feeling of dignified importance. Whether this compensated for the manifest inconvenience of getting in and out of railway carriages, moving amidst brambles, wet paint, dogs and so on, one cannot tell. Despite sermons, pleasantries and more serious protests, the enormous skirt, although somewhat modified in shape (it tailed away behind), survived until about 1869.

a. 1841

b. 1850 afternoon dress

c. 1857 theatre dress

d. 1859 walking dress

e. 1857 theatre dress

a
b
c
d
e

The Eighteen-Seventies

The crinoline was so monstrous a thing that it was widely criticised on aesthetic grounds. A certain number of ladies, influenced by the Pre-Raphaelites or G. F. Watts, refused to wear it. But when, in the late sixties, it folded and was gathered back into a bustle, one may wonder whether the critics were pleased. This first bustle – for the bustle went into two editions – was once described in my hearing as the ugliest of all Victorian fashions; it belonged to a time, said the speaker, who was an art critic, when women were upholstered; it was appalling. I agreed, partly because I respected the critic (who was Mr Raymond Mortimer), partly because we were then living in the 1920s and admired swift functional athletic designs and found in all this tight padding and profuse decoration something ugly, awkward and unhygienic. I wonder if Mr Mortimer has changed his mind? I have changed mine. The bustle was of course an absurdity, but all human finery is somewhat absurd, and in the profusion of bows, flowers, flounces and frills there does now seem to be a reckless gusto which is at once naive and formidable.

Notice how swiftly and easily the demands of conspicuous leisure are met, first by excessive bulk, which forbids locomotion, then by a fussy constriction which serves the same end.

a. 1875 walking dress

b. 1878 frock coat

c. 1877 walking dress

d. 1875 walking costume

e. and f. 1875 evening dress

a
b
c
d
e
f

The Eighteen-Eighties

The bustle of the seventies is ornate, that of the second edition is almost severe. It depends more upon perfection of cut and less upon lavish decoration and may in consequence be regarded as a finer and subtler form. On the other hand the deformation of the figure is more complete. The earlier bustle could be regarded as no more than a gathering up and tying back of superfluous drapery; the second edition (see 'd') involves a patently artificial rump tied on behind. Perhaps it is the dehumanisation of this kind of dress which brings 'artistic costume' off the drawing board and into the drawing room. 'Aesthetic' or 'artistic' dress becomes in a sense fashionable, and the aesthetic joke now occupies a considerable amount of space in *Punch*. *Patience* had its premiere in 1881, and for years the 'Cimabue Browns' and their cultured friends provided Du Maurier with a laughing stock. Reformed dress, although usually a protest against current fashions, is usually very much influenced by fashion. The forms that it takes reflect the mode of the moment; like fashion it dies, or at least is transformed, and the aesthetic dress of the eighties did not survive into the twentieth century. But then the bustle was quite dead by 1895.

a. 1880 day dress

b. 1888 'aesthetic' dress

c. 1885 ball dress

d. 1885 outdoor costume

e. 1888 Inverness cape

c
a
b
d

Fin-de-Siècle

The Victorian age, the great age of conspicuous leisure in women's dress, enters its final phase, and the twentieth century bursts in swiftly and dangerously riding a bicycle. It was not in order to make that sentence that I have broken my own tacit rule in accordance with which I have shown neither military nor ecclesiastical dress, nor the uniforms of venery. I have done so because the baggy-legged 'bloomer' (the name derives from an earlier and less successful attempt at women's liberation) must have seemed, and indeed was, a portent. To modern eyes the 'rationals' of the cyclist are neither shocking nor seductive. In a fussy rather incoherent epoch, an epoch in which women borrowed some of men's uglier haberdashery, this rather awkward attempt at masculinity in feminine dress strikes a somewhat dismal note. Nevertheless, the bicycle, which became enormously popular, was an instrument of social liberation, something on which the young could ride away to freedom. It was to be followed by that more deadly and even more disruptive device, the internal combustion engine. In other ways women seem as hampered, as muffled, as constricted as ever. But the bicycle promised freedom.

a. 1900 ball dress

b. 1901 chiffon dress

c. 'rationals' 1895

d. 1899 cycling dress (irrational)

e. 1895 promenade dress

b
c
d
e
a

Circa Nineteen Twelve

A survivor of this period has told me with what amazement and delight she learnt from a reliable informant in Paris that waists were to be allowed to return, after nearly half a century of fierce compression, to their normal proportions. This was about 1908. Thus, in its first decade, the first decisive step was taken which was to give the fashions of our century their predominant character. Clothes rapidly became much more comfortable; they may have been, indeed they must have been, difficult to get about in, but they were no longer actively painful. Nor was this the only innovation. Examples 'a' and 'b' are taken from elegant, but in a sense conservative, originals; one feels that the designers, knowing their business very well, did not look beyond the world of *haute couture* to the world of the *avant garde*; but 'c' is a much bolder and a much more theatrical design. In fact this very odd contrivance, the 'lampshade' tunic, was originally designed by Poiret for a fancy-dress party, but it was readily adapted for the everyday needs of what was, clearly, an aesthetically adventurous public.

a. 1910 dress for Longchamps

b. 1913 evening dress

c. 1912 evening dress

a
b
c

War and Post-War 1915–23 (I)

There is a certain irregularity about the history of fashion at this time. The war brings a kind of reaction. Waists reappear, although I do not think that they were artificially induced, and in many ways the fashions of the post-war period, long and loose, obliterating the figure, seem a natural development from the fashions of the period immediately preceding the war. But the surprising, and the contemporary observers 'outrageous', feature of the fashions for 1915 and 1916 was the short skirt. The fashions of 1914 had afforded glimpses of ankles, which are hardly visible in documents of the time but which did give rise to protests; the revelations of the war years seemed much more audacious. After the war the hem line went down again so that the wartime fashions must have seemed almost like a momentary aberration; but in fact there seems to have been a good deal of uncertainty as to just where it should be. I suspect that, having once lifted it to what then seemed dizzy heights, designers must have kept this possibility in mind although it was not until about 1924 that they began thoroughly to explore the possibilities that had been suggested.

a. 1915 day dress

b. 1920 travelling costume

c. 1923 day dress

d. 1923 evening dress

a
b
c
d

The Late Twenties

When people talk about the '1920s' or the 'post-war period' this, I think, is the kind of thing that they usually have in mind; very short hair, very small hats, very short skirts, nothing to tell one whether the dress was being worn by a boy or a girl, and that kind of dreary art-deco ornamentation which, at the time, we hated so much but which is now so perversely esteemed. Actually, the only persistent feature of women's dress between 1920 and 1930 is the flat-chested look. The very short skirts were worn for about five years.

At times, and particularly in evening dress, there seems to have been a certain lack of conviction on the part of the designers; they seem to have been half dissatisfied with the short skirt and, by means of an uneven hemline, or a vast bow such as that worn by 'e', to have been reaching for the floor; as in the period before 1925 they seem to have been preparing to lift the skirt so, in the succeeding period, they appear to have been planning to lower it again.

a. 1926/27 evening dress

b. 1928 day dress

c. 1928 day dress

d. 1927 cloche hat

e. 1928 evening dress

a
b
c
d
e

The Early Thirties

I think that it was in 1930 that I met a girl at a party who had a discernible waist and skirts which fell to the floor; I cannot be sure of the date but I do remember very clearly how much I admired that dress. It was a casual meeting and I had no particular reason for admiring the wearer. My enthusiasm may have been the result of natural conservatism for, after all, fashion was reverting to what is, by and large, the normal historical shape of European women. It could also mean that a change of fashion was badly needed by a generation which had grown up amidst long legs and sexless trunks. At all events, during those years skirts fell almost as rapidly as share prices, and for a time it seemed that the transformation would be complete. In fact it was not. Throughout the decade the hemline gradually rose again in the daytime; it was only in evening dress that the short skirt was abolished. But the waist did not disappear and in fact became more and more important. One oddity of this period and indeed of the 1920s was that the neck-line, which was rather high in front, fell drastically at the back.

Men's clothes suffered no radical change in the first third of the twentieth century; but there was a steady tendency towards greater and greater informality. The dress of leisure and of sport slowly replaced the dress of ceremony, and the 'plus fours' which became popular in the twenties were certainly not confined to the golf links.

a. 1928 plus fours

b. 1931 walking dress

c. 1935 evening dress and cloak

d. 1935 evening dress

e. 1933 evening dress

f. 1935 dress for the races

a
b
c
d
e
f

War and Post-War (II)

The decade ends with skirts that are short by day and long by night. The waist was increasingly emphasised and, as in the 1830s, its apparent size was diminished by adding to the bulk of the shoulders. There was some talk of tight lacing but certainly it was not general. Nine years later the 'New Look' brought much longer skirts, a more resolute restriction of the waist and sloping shoulders; it now seems, in many ways, to be a continuation of pre-war fashion. Attempts were made to prohibit or at least to discourage so wasteful a style at a moment when austerity still seemed very necessary; but this, like all other such attempts, failed.

The interregnum, that is to say the war, brought fashion in England to a standstill, and certain modes, like the very high turbans worn in France, never reached us. Everywhere it was a time of very slight development. One sign of the times was the great increase in feminine trousers, a convenience which has never been relinquished. Western woman's long struggle to be recognised as a biped began in the nineteenth century and achieved some success, as we have seen, in the 1880s. This was not a wartime innovation; women had for a very long time slept in pyjamas and had worn some kind of bifurcated dress on beaches and mountains and in moments of leisure. But it was in 1939 that the victory was decisively won. In Latin countries, this is still regarded as an achievement of some importance so that amongst Italian women of the wealthier classes skirts are now a rarity.

a. 1939 'afternoon outfit'

b. 1943 'utility dress'

c. 1947 New Look

a
b
c

The Last Twenty Years

A very tentative offering. We are too near to this period to see it clearly. One may however suggest that two opposing tendencies have been at work, the one romantic and ladylike, the other epicene and jocose. The former tendency is more characteristic of the fifties, the latter of the sixties; the former consisting of variations on the New Look, the latter more vigorous, more youthful and at times deliberately inelegant, tending to abolish the distinction between the sexes. I have given 'c' glasses which she (I had almost said, 'it') did not have in the photograph that I have used; but insect-like black spectacles were very much a feature of the period. The tendency would, from my illustration, appear to be in the direction of epicene unisexual fashions, but this is to some extent misleading; in fact the heterogeneous situation, in which fashion itself is called in question, is already developing. It would have been perfectly possible to have found some trousered big-booted examples of the earlier period and some fragile romantic examples from more recent years.

For the seventies, *see* Plate 44.

a. 1954 'late day' dress

b. 1958 evening dress

c. 1966

d. 1965

a
b
c
d

The Flowers of Academe

Glancing through a window which gave upon one of the main highways of a new university, my work has been continually interrupted during the past eight years by sartorial phenomena of a kind which could not easily be disregarded. I am sadly conscious that my pencil and my memory have done but scant justice to the extraordinary procession of improbable-looking people whom it has been my privilege to observe. Of course there has been a majority of blue jeans, of T shirts, lank, long hair and so on; but these student conformities are frequently enriched by hair styles of splendid eccentricity, by robes and ruffles and garden-party dresses which really do strike an original note. Somehow, when I try to recall the actual details of the more extravagant creations, they escape me. Let this therefore stand as no more than a feeble hint, a pale recollection of eccentricities which I remember, but cannot exactly recall, with gratitude.

By the same author

THE SCHOOLS OF DESIGN 1963
RUSKIN 1963
VICTORIAN ARTISTS 1967
BLOOMSBURY 1968
VIRGINIA WOOLF, A BIOGRAPHY 1972